Totally Bound Publishing books by Aurelia T. Evans

Single Books
Red Queen
Intervention

Arcanium
Fortune
Carousel
Aerial
Ringmaster
Contortion
Spider
Funhouse
Haunted
Skeletons
Silk

Collections
Frostbite: Gravedigger

Arcanium

SILK

AURELIA T. EVANS

Silk
ISBN # 978-1-83943-952-0

Interior text design by Claire Siemaszkiewicz
Totally Bound Publishing

Published in 2021 by Totally Bound Publishing, United Kingdom.

Totally Bound Publishing is an imprint of Totally Entwined Group Limited.

SILK

Chapter One

When Sera emerged from the woods, the cacophony from the circus assaulted her. So did the light. Squinting didn't help, but still she stepped out into the sun, half afraid that she'd start smoking.

An iron fence lined the circus's borders. Arcanium was now secure enough in its own offerings that it no longer had to attach itself to another event or park. Rumors continued to flit about that Bell had lost his nerve, that the empathic, empathetic, pathetic self-styled leader of Arcanium had finally tasted humble pie—humility that edged awfully close to mortality. But the gradual return of Arcanium to its former glory suggested that if Bell had been spooked by the demonic theft, he had since regained confidence.

Sera could scale the fence, but there were too many people who might see her doing it, and climbing it physically in a more innocuous way would hurt her hands.

She followed the fence to the entrance, an iconic, elaborate iron gate more theater than security. A place like Arcanium didn't need iron for security.

She hesitated to enter. Too many people were coming and going, and they all stared at her, but she forced herself to press forward. She didn't have time to waste fearing the stares or letting them bother her. She could suffer self-consciousness and question her decision later, when she was safe.

If necessary, Sera could have fooled the ticket-takers into letting her in free of charge, but the golems took one look at her and assumed she was just another member of Arcanium. That the soulless automatons of Arcanium used their limited deductive skills to conclude she was an oddity ached in her chest, but she passed the ticket booths with the fool's gold coins in her purse untouched.

As she strode through Arcanium, some of the adults she maneuvered around turned to admonish her as they would any child in a brightly-colored, multi-layered chiffon skirt and faerie wings. The sight of her face drew their sharp words up short, and her determination ensured that she didn't have to see their shock for too long. Like the ticket-takers, once people got a good look, they assumed she belonged there.

She knew exactly where she wanted to go but not exactly where it was, because Bell changed the arrangement of the circus at every location, more to suit his ever-changing whims than to disorient. Her gait was resolute, her footsteps quick. The uneven ground couldn't unsettle someone accustomed to soil, stone and bark rather than slats of wood or concrete. A few of the glances intended for her face or her dress dipped down to her heels—sturdy heels, yes, but her people liked to give themselves a little height for special occasions, like weddings or going out among the ungainly people who had taken over the wild places and made them barren for their less steady feet to walk. It took more than a stray stone or clump of grass to slip her to the ground.

Urgency finally rose in her chest when she'd searched the entire circus with no trace of the tent she was looking for. She'd found many tents, from those in Oddity Row to the big top, but not the tent she was trying to find. Fear—bright, unkind and rare as lightning splitting a tree—quickened her heart and her step.

If she had been there for sightseeing, oh, the sights she might have seen. She might have even enjoyed herself. Arcanium wasn't the average carnival or circus, although those had sometimes been pleasant, too, on the occasions her kind hadn't been forcefully kept out. Magic made for far more convincing illusions, and none of the Arcanium oddities were disappointments, enhanced and enchanted and *real* as they were. But Sera couldn't dwell on them, even when they noticed her and tried to stop her—perhaps simply to talk or make sure she was all right. She avoided their attempts, brushed by them without a word. She couldn't afford to stop looking.

After the third circuit through Arcanium, tears like seawater slipping down her cheek, she understood. She couldn't find the fortune teller tent because he didn't want it to be found. Bell had let her into Arcanium, but he had no intention of letting her stay, no intention of giving her a chance to stand in front of him to make her case. He'd let her in so she could see what she was not allowed to have, to torment her with her last bit of failed hope.

Sera swiped at her eye and ducked behind a midway booth, leaning back against the wood. The structure was flimsy, intended for transport and easy assemblage, but, like most temporary structures, it would stand most stress short of a tornado, even without magic. It shifted a little when she leaned against it, but she had no concern that it would topple, any more than the tents would fly away in a powerful breeze. The flimsiness here was as much an illusion as the cheap material.

She closed her eye to surround herself in far more comforting darkness. "I'm here in peace."

The purr of his voice arose in the darkness she had given herself. *"You do not bring peace with you."*

She opened her eye, expecting him in front of her. But there was only her. "I need your help."

Contempt surrounded her like incense smoke. *"And why should I help you?"*

"I didn't hurt your circus."

"You watched and did nothing. I'm not accepting new recruits, darling. Go back home."

"I can't go back there. Please..." Just saying the word was like swallowing needles. "Help me."

Silence followed her plea. But the contempt, too, dissipated, and she still sensed his presence around her, inside her. Had he been a demon, such presence would have been unbearably intrusive. But jinn, though hot as fever, were not the danger that those who called themselves demons could be.

When he said nothing more, Sera took a deep breath and rounded the booth again to search, desperately, for the fortune-teller tent once more.

This time, it was next to the entrance of the big top. It hadn't been there before—or rather, Bell had kept it from her and only her, based on the number of people standing in line outside the closed tent flap.

It went against her training—and her principles, even for those who showed her people less consideration—but she couldn't afford to wait. She superseded the line, billowing the closed flap open. Any protests from the people waiting died as soon as they saw her more clearly.

When the people to whom Bell was giving a reading took in the sight of her—with her opalescent dress, faerie wings, pink braids and half her face smashed into nothing—the couple stepped out. Maybe they thought, based on her grim half-expression, that she had come to tell Bell some kind of terrible news—a fire in the big top tent, an injured member of the cast, a fight among guests or perhaps that someone in his family was hurt or dying or dead.

Sera spared them a moment's gratitude. Then she gave the whole of her attention to the man slouched in the parlor chair. He didn't try to stop the couple from leaving nor did he demand that she leave, intended for paying customers only.

He said nothing, stroking his lip as he took in the sight of her. His posture remained deliberately casual—his legs spread, chest bare, spine curved—as though he couldn't destroy her in less than a second if she tried anything against him.

Unlike the guests and his cast, she didn't startle him—no recoil, no automatic disgust, no double-take. He considered her as any arrogant ass might consider a woman for his bed, although if he thought he'd have her in his in return for any favor, he would learn better quickly.

"I seek sanctuary," she said.

"Does this look like a sanctuary to you?"

"Yes." Sera crossed her arms, her face heating with his regard, with the prodding of his magic. It was nothing like the magic she was used to among her own. That was kindling sparks in comparison with the forest blaze of him, though he appeared as innocuous as any delicate human being, his human disguise more seamless than any other she had seen. He would be confused for human by even the keenest demon or god if he held his magic secret, rather than the way he made it known to her.

Sera lowered her eyes. It would be a mistake to believe that she could stand against him if he intended to make her kneel. But she didn't kneel. Not yet. "If I wish myself in, what would you do to me?"

Bell didn't move and blinked only once, more like a feline in derision than a sign of weakness or weakening. "I told you I'm not accepting recruits. As much of a headache as the humans have been, I am *not* taking in a stray faerie, especially not a member of the royal family—not when that same royal family availed itself of Locke's Arcanium all too often. I know every single instance one of your brothers or cousins—and even your father—reveled in the downfall of my circus. In fact, I have one of your brothers here with me now."

The lid to a chest next to the display sideboard swung open. Bell conjured a cluster of spirit quartz onto the parlor table. It gleamed against the dark velvet, shone different rainbow colors from different angles as she slowly approached the prison of her brother Falconell. He had been given up for dead, like all of the demons, monsters and immortals from the night Bell had taken back Arcanium. Sera reached for the crystal but Bell clicked his tongue, gathering the spirit quartz in both hands to rest on his lap.

"He's mine now. He isn't suffering. He isn't anything. But when I release him from this prison, it will not be to save him. It will be to make my people stronger, not to give your people closure. All of you should know better than to step foot in Arcanium."

"That's why I came. They'd never think to look here first." The fear that had cracked her chest had since warmed and melted away, leaving mere wariness in its wake. He had given her a chance to find his tent, to argue her case, and he hadn't spirited her away into her own spirit quartz prison. That was something. "*Look* at me."

Bell straightened, shifting his entire demeanor. Just like that, he became a coiled predator, his golden eyes gleaming, although she doubted the humans in his employ had ever seen them like this. They might have interpreted his change in posture as attention and concern, but Sera knew better. He had been at his most dangerous when most casual, but that didn't mean showing her his claws meant she was safe—only that he respected her enough to cast off the mask and present his cards in anticipation of her own.

"I see you." He held out a hand like a king to his subject.

After a beat, she allowed him to pull her in, close enough for him to take her chin and lift it.

He traced his gaze over unfamiliar territory, then turned her head to consider the undamaged flesh. "I'm sorry this happened to you, princess. But I don't need your family's attention on Arcanium again."

"I can't live in the human world on a good day, much less like this. But I can live in yours, and they'll barely bat an eye. You take in strays of all sorts. Everyone knows that. That's what I am today, Bell Madoc, forged from fire."

When Bell tried to turn her head back around, she wouldn't budge. All she let him see was her unharmed side, the smooth, china-doll skin and painted features of her face—beautiful to lure, lines soft and cheekbones like knives, deceptive danger in all her miniature glory.

She was young, the youngest of the royal line. The *last* of the royal line, although with immortals, such lineage wasn't needed to carry on a family name, and there was a reason they limited the number of children a king and queen could produce—enough children for diplomacy's sake and no more. As a young woman, Bell could use her, even if she had to be a doll on a shelf.

"I need your help." She met his gaze without flinching, without blinking, although he would know that she trembled. "You are, at best, amoral, but you are known for the fierce protection you offer those who are yours. Please don't make me go back to them. If I wish myself in, will you protect me? Or will you take your revenge for the actions of my father and brothers and cousins on a sheltered child?"

"You are young, princess, but you are no child, neither by human standards nor those of your kind."

"It was not so long ago." If he hadn't already known, her wedding gown would mark her youth, for her parents had waited until she was just of age to marry. For diplomacy's sake, a king did not leave his children unwed for long. "You wouldn't throw me back to them, not like they would do to me."

"And it only took them doing to you what has been done to far more vulnerable beings for you to rebel against it. You have my sympathy for the marring you suffered, but do not ask mercy of me."

"Don't speak of my people's cruelties, jinni. You are not so removed from demons that you are spared from association. Locke's earthly torment was legendary, but everyone knows that you harbor the Ringmaster. Keeping a demon such as he suggests that you have a certain tolerance for cruelty. Keeping the humans, however, suggests that you have a weakness for the vulnerable as well. They will be coming for me. If I could not control them when they were frequenting the brothel—despite my disapproval of such retribution upon humanity for their callous disregard—I will certainly not be able to control them once they return me to my betrothed, from whom I will not be able to sneak away again. If I wish myself in, *will you protect me*?"

Bell released her chin. He stood with a heavy sigh, the movement of his body in the close tent air unsettling the scent of the incense that he burned to conceal what came from his own skin.

His body was his temple, and though she had never known a man's body before, the way he moved, the shift and play of muscle under deceptive flesh, made her crave such worship. She recognized his manipulation, involuntary though it might have been, and resented that he might use her inexperience to create that craving in her—and that it would strike her so strongly.

Fifty-three years was a long time to preserve one's chastity. Her mother had enforced such patience in all of her daughters, most stringently in the last. The last daughter was the last of the king's line to the throne and had little royal value as a match but for that preservation and the intensity of magic it fostered.

Guards had stood outside her room and her bedroom window at all hours. Guards had been assigned to her schoolrooms. There had even been guards for her guards.

She was not innocent—to keep whispers, gossip and idle chatter from virgin ears was impossible, especially now that the rings had brought in Wi-Fi. But the guards had sheltered her as much as possible, monitoring her, standing over her shoulder, drowning out voices, shuffling crude word and deed from earshot and sight.

Though she was no longer sheltered and though it had been a long time since she was innocent, Sera was still pure. Magic welled in her with sudden, unwanted heat of desire, wildfire in wind swept by the incubus and succubus magic.

His sex demons were as infamous as his Ringmaster. She shifted uncomfortably, tried to brush the magic aside, but it fondled her like the fronds of ferns when she ran through the woods.

Bell paused in his pacing to face her. "The rules of my Arcanium are stricter for those with power, Sera, than for the human beings in my care. I don't judge you by your size. I know what you and your kind are capable of, and I do not underestimate you. I hope you do not underestimate me."

Sera crossed her arms, her wings fluttering and unsettling her skirt. "I knew what I was getting into when I came here, of all places. I won't hurt your children. I won't try to take over. You made it clear to everyone that Arcanium was not for the taking. Why would I even want it?"

"If I take you in, I certainly won't punish you for the sins of your blood. You yourself have done nothing to my circus. But I won't heal you." He traced his fingers where the left side of her face should have been. "You're far more interesting to me like this than whole. If you wish yourself in, that's the price. That you know your price is more than I offer most. Then again, most don't know what Arcanium is when they wish themselves in."

Sera had dared to hope that entering Arcanium and offering herself to him would earn her enough good will to fix her face—perhaps just to spite the man who had done it and those who wouldn't punish him for doing so. But she had also known better than to *expect* such magnanimity—not from a jinni who kept freaks for his amusement.

If she went back home, her betrothed would eventually kill her. Of that, she had no doubt. Here, at least, she might survive, for the price of the dignity that had already been stripped from her.

"They will come after me. They'll want me back," she reiterated.

"That's why I'd rather not do this at all. But if you wish yourself in, I'll have little choice—and neither will you. You haven't put yourself in my hands yet, princess. I can't do anything to you or for you without a wish, except force you to leave."

Of course he could do any number of things to or for her without a wish. There were so many spells tied into the magic of Arcanium that Bell could do almost anything he liked within its boundaries, as a king could within his ring. Sera couldn't tell whether Bell was being falsely modest or whether he wanted her to believe that he wasn't as powerful as he was—just a humble fortune teller with a little magic in his fingers, nothing more.

Or whether he meant it just for her, someone whose only threat to the circus was who would come after her.

There was no honor in her name, no glory or power in her title. She had a little magic—which *was* false modesty on her part, because her chastity over the years had earned her exceptionally intense magic. After what had happened, though, she'd learned how little her magic could actually help, that she'd had to retreat to Arcanium.

That she was putting his Arcanium in danger from her parents' army, they both understood. Yet here she still was. He hadn't brushed her away, discarded her back into the wild. He was giving her a chance to sign herself over to him like common chattel in exchange for the protection she needed.

"I wish myself into the service of Arcanium," Sera said, "however you see fit to use me."

It was dangerous to give the jinn carte blanche on how to execute a wish, but she would risk more by trying to steer him. As much as jinn manipulated, they hated any attempt to manipulate them in turn. Wishmasters found loopholes out of spite. Given the state of the subjects of his circus, Bell was no different. In his capriciousness, he would be unable to resist.

It would be better for her to make this transition easier on him. Perhaps he wouldn't make her face worse than it already was.

"Your wish is my command, princess." His bow was ironic, but the kiss to her hand was not. His gaze burned into her. She had heard tales of his revenge, yes, but also of his tenderness.

However, she saw the warning in his eyes, fervent and sincere as the color of a poison dart frog. It was not an aggressive warning, as it was not with the frogs. They didn't go looking for trouble, but they could guarantee that anyone who caught one in their mouths would have it in spades.

"If they come for you, they cannot take you. Welcome to Arcanium."

Chapter Two

Bell led Sera from the tent, effortlessly transforming his solemn intensity to the animation of every carnie barker in the world, with twice the charm.

"Sorry, folks. Just a little circus drama. Hard to imagine, don't you think?" he said to the crowd with a wink, to the guests' amusement. "I'll be back in less than fifteen minutes. Everyone in line gets a five-dollar discount for the inconvenience. Don't worry, Dana. You won't lose your place if you use the ladies' room."

Bell clasped the grateful woman's hand. To Sera, she looked old, clumsy, inelegant and sloppy, but most human beings looked like that in comparison to the people she knew better. Sera was incapable of seeing humans the way they saw each other, at least after about twenty-three years old. Age meant something different to the fae. She would look very much the same in fifty years and in five hundred years. Her light pink hair would silver after two hundred, but the fae had caught on to the trend of hair dye and taken off with it. She would never grow taller than her four-and-a-half feet. To the giant people of the world, it made her seem like a child at first glance, although no one would confuse her with one by the second.

Bell grazed his lips over Dana's cheek. The woman fairly swooned like a Victorian aristocrat, her breath shallow, cheeks flushed, pupils dilating—everything that indicated without guile or concealment how easily Bell had manipulated her.

"Horace will keep your place, won't he?" He slapped an old man's shoulder with good nature. The old man laughed and nodded, shaking Bell's hand in greeting. They'd met before, and Bell must have made a good impression, given that most people who entered a fortune teller's tent were single females or young couples in love.

The old man's face was a chiseled treasure map of age that Sera simply would never understand. From the perspective of an immortal, it was like decaying alive. Bell had chosen to affect some elements of age, but his physique had the same carved, dense quality of most demigods and their immortal progeny. It was mortality that made flesh sag, muscle lose its tone, hair and eyes and skin dull. Bell might have chosen some age, but Sera doubted he would ever take a less pleasing shape. He was charming to men and women alike, exactly what they needed from him—a flirt, a lover, a confidant, a pal, a poker buddy, one of the guys, one of the girls.

Shapeshifters, especially when they could change into multiple visages, were sometimes difficult to pin down. It made him an excellent host but a suspicious master.

Sera suspected Bell lingered a little longer than necessary to force her to endure their stares after they'd finished with him. She would consider such lingering malicious, except she had volunteered to join Arcanium, not just take sanctuary within it. She would be expected to endure far more stares than the ones upon her now—their pity, their curiosity, their abhorrence of how her face had changed.

She had never been abhorred before.

Bell drew Sera's hand into the crook of his elbow, treating her like a lady, if not a princess. He elevated her among all those curious stares, challenging any insulting assumption.

Arcanium is better. She told herself that in a steady mantra, trying to ignore the stares and determined non-stares, trying to ignore the fever of Bell's skin under her hand as he led her to a caravan of vehicles, most of which looked as though they'd shake apart if they hit a pothole too hard. Then again, her kind had always viewed vehicular transportation with wary contempt, even when they deigned to use it.

Bell gestured to an RV the size of one of the midway booths. "You won't be accustomed to such spare, small quarters, but it'll be a place to sleep and have some privacy, and there's no reason you can't use the rest of Arcanium as your home. Some of our cast, like the Spider and the Creature, sleep under the stars rather than be contained by metal and linoleum, but you'll get used to spartan accommodations."

Sera arched an eyebrow, an automatic reaction.

Bell gestured to the RV more grandly, the quirk of irony returning to his otherwise sober expression. "It has to fit onto the road, love, and you need a castle no longer. If I expect Miss Delilah and Ciarán to live in Winnebagos—with roommates, no less—tiny little you can live in one of these alone."

"What about clothes? Shoes? There's barely enough room for a bed in there, and I know how elaborate

Arcanium's costumes are." Elaborate enough that her own wardrobe would have fit right in.

"Kitty takes care of that. She's allowed some magical space for the costumes she keeps for the circus, and I'm sure she'd be thrilled to have a sewing partner. Sasha does leatherwork, of course, but Kitty can't work across from her very well. I'm sure you understand."

"Kitty…the Ringmaster's consort."

There had been speculation about Kitty in the midst of all the other whispers about Arcanium—inevitable, given the company she kept. A mortal woman who looked like something a jinni would create as a pet, she'd been given unusual favor by Bell but more peculiarly by the Ringmaster, who kept her as a different kind of pet than one would have ever expected from a hellborn demon. As friendly as she was purported to be, she remained something of an enigma, even more so than Bell, because no one could figure out why she looked the way she did or how someone who looked that way could have earned the favor she carried.

Bell opened the RV door without touching it. The quirk of irony disappeared, and with it any illusion that Bell was human, even if he kept the guise. "She's hypertrichotic. It's not a magical mystery, just a singularly unique genetic mutation that they don't have a name for yet. I know you've heard all the whispers, my dear, but don't carry their disdain into the circus. It doesn't suit you."

"That was not my intention. I was merely curious."

"And my people will be curious about you. Will you still bristle?" Bell said.

Sera didn't answer, because they both knew she would.

She stared up into the dark cabin of the RV. It looked peaceful. At the very least, the sun wouldn't burn her nocturnal retinas. But since birth, she'd never been confined. The royal estate had enough room for each of the king's seventy-five children in addition to guest wings. This was smaller than her formal closet.

Bell gently guided her head toward him again and traced down the center of her face, the edge of the damage. "If there had been any lingering pain, I would have taken it. But it's completely healed over, isn't it? It just healed over the damage without reconstruction."

Sera lowered her eyes. "There's no more pain. It seems like there should be, but except for not being able to see through my left eye because it's not there anymore, I wouldn't even know anything was wrong—not until I touch it…or people look at me."

"If you wake up with phantom pain because you think you should have it, I can take that away, too," Bell said. "You're here voluntarily. There's no reason for you to be in pain, even psychosomatic. You may keep your title, princess, but remember that it means little to the people of Arcanium, even those who know your world. I suggest you get your feet dirty and your nails chipped, my dear, because now that you're in, it will be a long time before I let you out again."

"I know how to get dirty."

"Do you?" Another quirk of irony, but this time in genuine humor, before she understood the inadvertent joke she had made.

She was comfortable with grit and stone and earthworms under her feet. Some of the fae, especially those of noble or royal lines, had separated themselves from the earth, surrounding themselves only in the spoils from it. But Sera was the baby of the family, with fewer responsibilities, fewer expectations to affect luxury, and her bedroom had opened out into a garden all her own.

That was all she'd meant. That Bell could make her blush embarrassed her on its own. That the trail of his fingertip made her wonder about the bed she had sworn she wouldn't warm shamed her further. But she turned her head away, because she shouldn't have his bed, and she couldn't have anyone else's. Not anymore.

He kissed the shell of her ear gently, where the damage ended. "I wouldn't be so sure about that, love," he murmured.

Perhaps he felt how hard her heart hurt at tenderness, as though he were mocking her precisely as he didn't want her mocking his people. She didn't think he was, but her heart couldn't tell the difference, and she was still suspicious, especially now that she was part of his Arcanium. She had his protection, yes, but that and humiliation had been his promise to her. This could easily be part of that humiliation, even if she didn't want to believe it of him.

She'd been burned before by the inclination to believe better of those who owned her.

Bell nodded again toward the RV. She reluctantly stepped up and through the doorway.

He braced his hands on either side of the door frame. She could have ducked underneath, but he was a faceless shadow blocking the way, and she stepped farther into the vehicle instead.

"I recommend you stay here until after the circus closes. It'll be dark then, easier on your eye. Have a drink, take a rest, change into something more comfortable than a wedding dress. I know you won't be inclined to sleep after the guests all go home, although you'd benefit from developing more diurnal habits. I'll provide darkened contacts—or whimsical sunglasses if you prefer—because you'll walk the circus during the day like the rest of us going forward. Meet me tonight in the big top tent. Feel free to stop by the food booths for a snack before then, if you have the stomach for it."

He started to close the door. Sera's throat tightened, as though shutting out the light also shut away the air. She wouldn't die, but she still needed to breathe, and it was suddenly harder to do just that.

"Mourn if you must." She still couldn't see his face, the backlight too bright to make him anything but darkness, but his voice was as buttery and warm as his skin. "However, I think you'll find Arcanium much more to your tastes than you thought."

* * * *

The previous night…

Her mother stood behind Sera, who fidgeted with her skirt and shifted from one foot to the other. If anyone else had been waiting outside the audience chamber with them, Vinia might have told Sera to stop such juvenile behavior, but there was no one there but them.

Sera's mother wore the mantle of a matron queen. It took a lot to wear down the fae, but seventy-five children had taken its toll, and it would take another century or two before she appeared more like she had before her tenth child. Vinia was a matriarch, her hair half silver, unlike her husband's, which had turned all the way. She walked with some effort, pain low in her body between her hips that no amount of ginger and turmeric could alleviate. It would go away on its own, but there was no telling when. However, though her gait lacked the grace of youth, she had taught each of her daughters the grace she had sacrificed for them.

Vinia rested a heavily ringed hand on Sera's shoulder. "I've been where you are. I wore my engagement gown before I'd even met your father, nervous about what to expect during the wedding ceremony…and after. I had to learn from your father—and from the other wives in secret once I had been bound to him. I promised each of my children I would not be so circumspect, even to preserve innocence. But just because you know what might come, you cannot anticipate everything. I've only given you what I know. Your husband will have his own knowledge to impart."

Sera trembled under her mother's hands. When she'd imagined wedding nights to the dawn with faceless spouses, those prospects had been unknowns, people who didn't exist and would always work in her favor—and if they didn't, she could always end the fantasy. She knew from all seventy-four brothers and sisters before her that matches made from royal families were not always ideal, that the husband or wife chosen might be unpleasant, boring, disinterested, engaged in affairs with others or worse. A few dozen of her siblings had come to develop affection, at least, with their partners. Love, even for immortal pairings, was more luxurious than gold. Only three of her siblings could boast love in their union. At best, one hoped to tolerate their spouse or live somewhere where they had separate quarters and could go their own way for all but formal occasions.

The queen had forbidden Sera from the assessment of her match, which had been shared among the queen, the king and their respective viziers, although Sera had contributed to marriage assessments for almost all of her siblings after she'd turned fifteen. Her mother had always valued her input, her considered calculations, her almost unwavering practicality. When Sera's siblings had asked to marry for love, Sera had always been the one who Vinia would come to, to advise if such a match was advantageous for the kingdom. Sera was not inclined to be cold or deny her siblings a good future, but that wasn't what her mother had asked of her.

And now she didn't know what such cold calculations had decided for her.

"The important thing is that this is for your family and for your ring," Vinia said. "You must not turn away from your duty, nor must you break your father's and my promise to the family we have sworn you to."

"I am prepared to accept the betrothed you have chosen, Mother."

I just hope he will be kind.

Since the solicitation for her hand had begun, Sera had hoped that the relatively low stakes of her marriage, as the last and least valuable to trade, would afford her more consideration in terms of her betrothed's temperament. She could not imagine her mother or her father agreeing to foist her off to someone callous or cruel, but they had done so before with her sisters and brothers. To assume that just because her mother favored her advice that she would also favor her youngest daughter would be foolish. Sera had inherited not only her father's idealism but also her mother's brutal pragmatism—qualities that often warred within her. She wondered how her mother and father did not battle more in their more private moments.

The door to the audience chamber opened. The king stepped through the narrow gap. Sera curtsied, her chin to her chest and her knees bringing her almost all the way to the ground.

The king brushed his fingertips under her chin to lift her back to her feet. "Seraphina, my darling girl. I long thought of when this day would come, but it still feels impossible that you are this woman, that you will be a wife."

When he glanced over Sera's shoulder to the queen, his demeanor changed so quickly that Sera knew the queen must have had a particularly long-suffering expression at his sentiment. "The contract has been signed," he said. "Go on in and meet your future husband. His family will be in the great hall for the betrothal feast. We will join you and your betrothed there."

He kissed Sera's forehead, as he had since she was no higher than his knee. Then the queen locked her arm around his and led her husband down the corridor before the mist in his eyes could solidify and Sera's betrothed perhaps hear his weakness.

They would not even give her a clue before she went in, nothing that would brace her for the impact of meeting the man she would spend the rest of her immortal life with.

Romantic though it seemed with a love match, Sera had never believed such life pairings practical for the fae, when their lives extended into the infinite if someone didn't kill them. It encouraged far too many immortals to kill their spouses just to escape them. Marriage became purgatorial, something to be endured indefinitely, even among those who married for love.

Unlike some societies in the human world, there were few legitimate grounds for the fae to divorce. To part was too much of an insult to both families and sometimes whole kingdoms, spawning worse feuds than if one of the spouses killed the other. Magistrates often ruled on the side of accidental death, even when it was plain that the death was no accident, because it was more politically safe to rule in favor of peace among families and rings rather than encourage vengeance on one or both sides.

Sera took a shaky breath to convince herself to be the steady, practical woman her mother had raised instead of the dizzy schoolgirl her father would have preferred her to remain.

Then she entered the audience chamber.

The man standing with his back to the door was human-sized, almost two feet taller than her. Such size disparity among immortal matches was not uncommon. It rarely impeded the couple's ability to produce children. That her mind immediately went in that direction brought a rush of blood to her cheeks she hoped would disappear by the time he saw her.

He was bare to the waist, a kilt of roughly tanned hide around his lower half, reaching to the ground to cover his legs and most of his boots. He'd pulled his long, gray-brown hair back into a tail, with bits of bone sewn and knotted into strands. At first glance, he looked like a human man from the wilds of another time, but when he turned around, the scarification of constellations over his chest marked him as one of the Ursal sleuths from the north—a Bearskin.

One of her sisters had married into a werewolf pack to forge an alliance for foot soldiers and sentries in exchange for providing the wolves safe forests where humans could not shoot them when they ran. It seemed Sera had been chosen for a similar arrangement, although Bearskins couldn't impart their magic to her as the werewolves had done to her sister Cora.

That did little to diminish her trepidation as she approached her future husband.

He looked her up and down—mostly down, from his height—his expression impassive but for a lift to his lip that was not humor. "So you're Seraphina."

"I'm sorry I disappoint you."

"What makes you think you disappoint me?"

"It's not often someone looks at me like a stain on their shoe. You haven't even met me properly."

"I don't need to meet you. I would have been fine seeing you for the first time at our wedding." The Bearskin turned away again.

Beauty was so common among the fae that it was hardly worth a mention—except to those who were not fae. She *should* have been remarkable. Since she had grown into her adulthood, her beauty was the very thing the king and queen had fought against with every guard who had watched over her all that time—eunuchs who couldn't take advantage of her and mercenaries who could be paid well enough to slake their interest elsewhere, each to keep a wary eye on the other. Upon entering the court a woman, no one had called her inadequate. Yet as the Bearskin vaulted over the table away from her—the signed marriage document curled between them, inks still drying—she felt unseen.

Sera touched her face. She was not as strikingly beautiful as some of her sisters and brothers, but she had never considered herself undesirable before. Such a self-conscious thought wouldn't have entered her mind. With a whiff of disgust and gesture of dismissal, he had made her a toad.

She had already been vulnerable, sensitive, scared to leave the world she knew—surrounded by guards and by her family, the same estate in which she had been born and raised, to be then passed over to someone in the name of alliance. That was the reason she'd been born, the reason kings and queens had children—leverage. Nothing bound a magical knot better than blood, and no blood bonds were greater than that of family.

Sera pulled her fraying edges back in, tucked them out of sight then straightened, smoothing her hands over her red gown. Just because she had resigned herself to her fate did not mean that the Bearskin had as well. The Bearskins operated under another hierarchy, one of chieftains rather than kings and queens. Unlike the fae, they were often loners, in small family groups at most except when gathered together as one for legal disputes and feasts.

She imagined the quiet, oppressive emptiness of a forest populated by trees alone—not even dryads or nymphs to laugh or whisper—and this carved stone man in the fur of kills or brethren wrapped about him, facing away from her, nothing but a frigid north wind between them, until ice froze them in that tableau forever.

When she shivered, part of it was from cold. Her skill was not in seeing the future, but if she thought something too hard, she could almost make it real. When she'd been younger, magic had sometimes seeped from her, out of control, and those things almost real to her now had manifested. Her power had since grown, but so had her control.

Perhaps the Bearskin sensed it, because he glanced up, disdain giving way to a calculation Sera almost recognized from the mirror—and from the visage of her mother, which was a kind of mirror, too.

Sera approached the table and sat on the bench across from him. The bench and the table had been made for the fae of her family's ring. It fit her, and she didn't feel too diminutive, but he seemed a giant.

"I'm not seeking a happy marriage, sir," Sera said. "Happiness would have been a fortunate end, but if you seek something else, can we not at least attempt to tolerate each other? What did you need from my family that will come from my hand?"

"The Bearskins are dying out. Like our furskinned brothers who cannot become man, we are threatened by human encroachment, pushed farther and farther north. Our bearskins can tolerate that much cold, but only if we hibernate. Our manskins cannot. It forces us out of commission for months, forces us to produce bears instead of our own children. Though that aids the crisis facing our furskinned brothers, it does not help ours. The alliance is in exchange for a ring—our own wilderness that cannot be encroached upon—so that we may replenish our numbers. The marriage itself is for whatever Bearskin children you can produce. Our women age out of childbearing, albeit slowly, while you can produce many. The faeries you make, you can keep. The Bearskins will be mine."

"Last I checked, both are coming from my womb," Sera said dryly.

"And both will come from my seed. But we don't need more fae in the world. We need more Bearskins. Even half-breeds will do. As long as they transform, they belong with us, to diversify our line."

"I haven't agreed to that."

"The king has." The Bearskin gestured to the contract.

Sera furrowed her brow and pulled the contract to her to read the elaborate calligraphy scrolled by the court scribe and signed in her father's fine hand with the blood pen. With his own blood, the king would never have signed away blood of his line, nor would he had ripped a child away from her.

"I am not without compassion, Seraphina. I will not tear them from your arms while they are still connected to you by cord. You may raise them until they are weaned. At that point, they would be better served by someone who knows how to teach them to be bear as well as manskin. They will be of no use to you, just as the fae children you produce will be of no use to me."

Sera scanned the lines of the contract as she had marriage contracts past. It was all standard, no unconventional addendums, all the way down to her father's signature, under which the Bearskin had signed his own—Ursalem of the Saskatchewan Ursal sleuth, son of Ursadam and Ursilvia.

She hadn't even known his name until she'd read through the entire contract.

That she was bound to a contract she hadn't even read until after it was signed struck her full force with the injustice, but it was legally binding—blood-binding—whether she believed in it or not.

"There is nothing in here about division of assets, much less division of children," Sera said.

"Your father signed you to *me*. The undersigned agreement codifies the construction of a ring within the next hundred years to hold dozens of sleuths and for us to produce children to repopulate the Ursal bloodlines. There is nothing that stipulates any kind of choices on your part. I don't need you to like me. I don't even need you to tolerate me. I just need you to obey me. If you do what I need you to do, I don't see any reason we should have to spend more time than necessary with each other."

Sera pushed the contract back to the center of the table. "It's true that the contract doesn't codify my choice, but neither does it codify taking my choice away. I'm more than willing to give you and your people the children that they need. What I object to is being told that if they can shapeshift into bearskin, I have no claim to them whatsoever, and that any fae children mean nothing to you. Just because they cannot shift to another shape does not mean that they won't carry your line—if not in their own magic, then in the magic of their children, or their children's children. If you must look at it with such an unfeeling eye, they can still be useful to you."

When Salem stood, the planes of his body and the folds of the furs conjured the shadows of the room. "I ask very little of you, Seraphina."

"Sera. There's no need to swallow a mouthful every time you say my name—for the sake of efficiency, which you seem to value." Her wings fluttered in agitation, threatening to flutter her right off the bench. Salem wouldn't be the first to stand before the fae to try to intimidate them, but the fae had far more tools than size to intimidate. "And I ask so little of you. If it is your preference that we maintain separate lives, that gives me freedom as much as you. But don't shut me out from my own children just because they won't be like me."

"I believe we've had some kind of misunderstanding."

Salem stepped onto the bench, then the table, his leathered boots crushing the scroll of the contract with an eggshell rustle. Then he stepped onto her bench and onto the ground.

Sera scrambled to her feet on her own bench so that he could not look down upon her, but he grabbed her arm in a flexing hand. He shoved her to the ground, and she struggled not to kneel before him just to get away from the pain, but he did not release her.

"I own you, Seraphina. The wedding is a spectacle. The formality is finished there on the table. After the wedding, you will be my wife in name only, as you are a princess. You have no position from which to argue, no leverage to sway this situation in the direction you want. The only way I was going to sign that contract was underneath the king's name to ensure a transfer of ownership, and that was what he agreed to. I've built you a cabin, your own little palace in the woods. You'll never have to leave, and how you raise the fae children means nothing to me. But there you will stay, and you'll stay out of my way. I don't even want to see or hear them when I return, and I don't want to see or hear you unless I come to your bed after you've recovered from the last pregnancy. You'll recover quickly. All the fae do."

His grip still bruising her arm, he reached with his other hand and gently stroked the frame of her face with false tenderness. "It's your hardiness and the diversity of your bloodline that I came here for...and the ring for my people. I don't want or need a mate—I take what I want in the wilderness—but you'll do, and you know you'll do. That's all we will be, Seraphina. You don't need to speak for that."

Then Salem shouted, jerking his hand away from her. His sizzling palm blackened and smoked from the fire that Sera had set against his skin where it had touched hers.

"Until we formally wed, that contract can be voided by at least one undersigned party without loss of good faith," she said, barely reining in her fury. "My mother and father gained a great deal from the arrangement you made, but I can think of at least three other proposals surely sent to them that would be better matches *and* make better use of my talents. You don't even want me. You can barely *look* at me."

Sera's iridescent dragonfly wings—ostensibly too small and delicate to hold her—fluttered until they were almost invisible to lift her from the ground. Electricity sparked from her fingertips and toes and the ends of her hair.

"Call us vain, but that's what we're for. In addition to all of our different magics, we're supposed to be pretty baubles for the arms of kingdoms all over the world, brought out for special occasions, worn as a sign of wealth and prestige or kept safe under enchanted glass from any who would steal us. It is a badge of glory for any race to bind into the bloodlines of the fae. But you're just going to hide me away and treat me like a broodmare. Even if Mother is as calculating as I, she will understand what a waste it is not to use me. Gold is little to my parents' ring in comparison to influence, which you have admitted you will refuse."

"Where do you think you're going?" Salem's hand was already scarring over. Their healing was more inelegant than that of the fae, and they were easier to kill, but they were still immortal and healed almost as well.

"This marriage is not going to happen. I don't know why they gave me to you when there are better prospects, unless you lied to them about what you wanted with me. How do you think the king and queen will react when they find out your true intentions?"

Fear, sharp and deadly violent as a knife, flashed in his eyes when Salem darted after her as she flew toward the double doors of the audience chamber, confirming Sera's suspicions that he'd either lied or not been completely forthcoming with her parents before they'd signed the contract.

She got to the doors first, yanking them open and flitting out into the corridor toward the great hall, where her family and the Bearskin's family would be waiting.

All her life spent with her chastity enforced to enhance her magic, and he just wanted to put her to dam. He wasn't even interested in what her magic would bring to their children, only that it would heal her from each pregnancy—although if he kept her pregnant as often as he suggested, she would wear down like her mother...and much more quickly. How many children would she have to produce before Salem decided there were enough new Bearskins to diversify the species without overwhelming it? Two hundred? Three hundred?

A fae pregnancy lasted five months. How long would a half-breed pregnancy last? And how big would some of the children be, if they took after their father in size instead of their mother?

Sera sped through the halls until she reached the courtyard, where she had to fly lower to the ground to avoid the massive trees with their overlapping branches overhead and their gnarled roots lifting from the earth. Sera could have gone above the trees, but she wanted to reach the door on the other side of the courtyard without having to dive down through the branches.

A bellow rumbled through the corridor behind her and through the courtyard like thunder.

The massive grizzly barreled into the courtyard, trembling the earth with the collision of its paws. Sera flew fast, but the bear ran much faster, despite its clumsy size.

Sera screamed when claws found her leg and hooked into her back. Then a paw the size of the world slammed into the left side of her head.

* * * *

Sera groaned, pain still burning in the left side of her face as her magic continued its healing. But something was wrong, and not just that she was still in pain at all.

Morning light glowed blue through a bedroom window, indirect, rising on the opposite side of the castle. Not her bedroom—one she'd never seen and lacking personality, which told her that it was one of the many guest rooms. But she couldn't see as much of it as she should have been able to. There was more darkness in the room, a whole half of it settled in shadow more total than night.

She was groggy enough that it took her a while to realize she couldn't open her left eye.

Sera sat up, trying to reorient herself.

She was still in the engagement gown. Blood had soaked her left side, darkening the already red fabric. On the bed, instead of resting her wounded head on a pillow, she'd been lying on a rock. The places where its jagged edges had placed pressure against her face now throbbed.

Salem sat, spread-legged, in an armchair made for a smaller frame. His blue eyes were emptier than glass, his expression as impassive as a carving. "You really should be more careful, losing control of your flight and dashing your head against a rock like that."

"What happened?" Even moving her mouth felt strange. It wasn't as wide as it should have been. Something was missing.

Teeth. Teeth were missing from the left side.

Sera's hands flew to her face. Her fingers met smooth, scarred skin, a healing cave where the left side of her face had been. She searched the depressed, unfamiliar terrain, like a collapsed melon under her palm. She'd either lost the teeth, swallowed them or they'd been crushed in the blow. Her nose was still there, but her eye was not. Scar tissue hadn't covered her eye. It had covered the places where her eye had been.

"I don't understand." Her healing should have pushed the broken skull back out again, like fixing the dent of a car. The teeth and eye and the bits of scalp that had been removed should have regenerated.

But the hair had grown back patchy, and scar tissue had formed and smoothed over the cavity that the Bearskin paw had created, almost a seamless transition from the unaffected side. The skin was still tender, though, like the whole side of her face was a bruise.

When she tried to get out of bed, the room tilted and she tilted with it, staggering to the side before slipping on the wooden floor.

"I brought you in here." His tone remained even, unaffected. "Then I pressed your face into the rock as your magic healed you, so that it wouldn't rebuild your face."

"W-Why would you do that?" Sera crawled across the floor, digging her nails into the wood as though that would ground her and keep the room from turning her over again. She cried out as one of her nails tore, but that wasn't as important as reaching the dresser and pulling herself up to see herself in the silver-backed mirror.

The woman in the mirror was a stranger. She looked unfinished, deflated, as bruised as she felt. Open-mouthed in horror, Sera choked on a sob, almost clawing her face with her broken nail, trying to find the rest of it.

"Why would you do this?" Sera kept blinking, hoping that this time her left eye would open and everything would flicker back into the image she remembered. She moved her head, as though a mere blind spot hid the rest of her face from her, but the reflection still didn't change.

"You said that people wanted the fae for their beauty. It would have made the marriage bed a little easier, yes, but it's nothing that I need, as long as the rest of you is intact." Salem met her eye in the mirror. "Of the prospects you believed available to you before, which of them do you think will marry you now?"

Sera stumbled to the door and out into the corridor.

The shocked gasps from two servants walking through answered his question.

* * * *

The reflection in the closet mirrors showed Sera wrapped in the opalescent white of the wedding dress into which her mother had bound her. There were floor-to-ceiling mirrors all over the closet, reflecting light from the lanterns until the room was aglow like a firefly and displaying her disfigurement from every angle.

The ripped nail had been clipped and filed. The claw marks on her leg were gone. The crater of what had been her face seemed like it had been there for decades. No longer tender to the touch or discolored with bruises, the nerves there had completely regenerated, and in an hour or two, it would look as though it had been there since birth.

If she had done this to Salem, he would have died or the brain damage would have rendered him incapacitated. Her brain was already adjusting to its rearrangement. There were still moments of vertigo. Speech was also still difficult, and not just because a whole part of her mouth had been crushed into nonexistence. Those problems would fade soon enough.

He hadn't utterly destroyed her, and she certainly wasn't dead. She just might as well have been both.

Her mother stroked Sera's hair on the good side. "What he deserves in retaliation is immaterial. He's right. Your father signed you over to him, which means that any retaliation would have to come from him or his family, and they will do nothing. You already know that we cannot find you a more suitable match who can offer as much or more than the Bearskins offered for your hand. There's no choice here, Sera. We would need an alternative if we were to break contract with them, and he eliminated all alternatives in one fell blow."

"Yes, he did. He lied to you and Father, ensured that he owned me, then made sure no one else would want me. And you're just going to let him manipulate his way into doing whatever he likes with me, with no recourse?"

Sera's practical side understood her mother's position. Her idealistic side didn't understand why that overcame how Sera was their daughter, nor why they were willingly letting her go into the arms of someone who would permanently damage their daughter. And for what? Mere gold?

As though Sera couldn't earn them just as much by refusing to marry and continuing to build her magic, helping her mother and father in matters of state. There were options just as lucrative to her family that would also have protected her. The queen should have known that, as Sera did.

"Marriage is not always ideal, my love," her mother said. "By his own admission, your husband will leave you to your own devices for much of your time with him. Many unhappy wives cannot claim that kind of autonomy."

"It's not autonomy. I'll be a prisoner in a cabin in the middle of nowhere. My fae children will be prisoners with me while the Bearskin children will be taken. Your own grandchildren, of our ring's lineage and magic, will be hidden away like their broken mother, discarded like trash."

Her mother gathered her daughter's hair up from her neck, her fingers quivering where the scalp had been pulled away and the rock had prevented regrowth. "Perhaps when the time comes, he will permit them to return to their grandparents' ring," she said mildly.

Sera recoiled, jerking from her mother's touch. The queen had spoken with complete certainty, not speculation. "Did he promise that at the time of the contract? Or did he promise that before you came here to fit me in my wedding dress? Is that the payoff, Mother, that you get your fae grandchildren? Will you discard the Bearskins the way Salem will discard the fae?"

"He'll take care of his own. And you will be taken care of. You'll be almost a Queen of the North. No last princess could ever claim such an honor."

"A queen who can never show her face."

"You wouldn't be the first mad wife hidden away, dear." The queen stepped away, inspecting her handiwork, though she winced when she glanced above Sera's gemstone collar necklace.

"I am not a mad wife."

"You will be."

"How can you let him get away with this? How can you be so cold?" Sera's wrists strained under the weight of the golden bracelets, as though shackled.

"I'll never understand how someone so calculating can be so naïve." The queen shook her head, smiling sadly. "Circumstances will change, Sera. Perhaps he will recognize the treasure you could be for him. Perhaps you will find a way to have your own life separate from your husband, freer than you believe you will be."

"No one will be able to look at me! Not even *you* can look at me. How can I find a way if no one even wants to see that I'm there, when they'd rather forget I exist?"

"Some of your sisters were sure that their lives were over, too. Some of my sisters as well. But they are all still alive. Many of them would kill for their husbands to want nothing to do with them. Count your blessings, Sera, because he still wants to marry you and give you children. The contract is still valid. You marry after the fall of twilight. You have no choice."

The queen left Sera alone with her infinite reflections.

Sera still couldn't stand to look at herself, kept seeing the void in her face as some kind of selective blindness. The rest of her was as it had been, diminutive but as beautiful as ever, but who cared that the rest of her was immaculate if her face was shattered? She was just the kind of broken china doll her parents would throw away from her collection. That they *had* thrown away.

It didn't even matter to her mother that Sera might have died, as long as the family could keep the gold and would eventually have some of the children of the union back within their ring. The fae collected new magic the way they collected gold coins. That was at least part of the reason they had agreed to the marriage. The royal family had seventy-five children but only one alliance with the Bearskins.

Sera was their daughter, but all of their children were means to ends. The quality of their life was secondary to what the king and queen of the ring could gain. She wasn't a party in the contract. She was a commodity.

She didn't have a lot of time. The sun was still up. That didn't mean that everyone would be asleep, but most of them would be. There were day servants, and her family would be preparing for the wedding, but they wouldn't be watching her too closely.

After all, where was an ugly faerie going to run?

Chapter Three

Present day

By the time someone knocked on the RV door, Sera had changed out of the wedding dress.

She wasn't accustomed to casual wear, but it was far more comfortable than anything in either her formal or her semiformal closets, coarser though the fabric was. They even fit her, the hooded sweatshirt just the right amount of oversized without drowning her, the pants tailored to her unique frame that would usually require children's clothes in the human world, though children's clothing wasn't made for a woman's frame.

Bell had arranged the condensed wardrobe and the space just for her. It was smaller than anything she was used to, and thus, by its nature, confining, but everything was proportioned low so that she didn't have to find a stool just to use the toilet, and she didn't have to climb up onto the bed or the small sofa in the living room-kitchenette. All the clothes fit someone of her stature, and the books were just the sort she had on her own bookshelves at home—a mix of old and new, fae and human, because of the many things human beings lacked, imagination was not one of them.

But though she had assumed a human wardrobe and had drawn the hood over her head to hide her face in shadow, the layers and layers of skirt on her wedding dress still took up most of the living room, reclined on the sofa like the ghost of her former self.

The woman on the other side of the door eyed it with unmistakable envy, and no wonder, since she was the one who sewed costumes for the circus.

"You must be Kitty," Sera said. "If you want it, you can have it."

"I don't know if it would fit anyone else."

"You can salvage whatever pieces you want. I have no emotional attachment to it. It was nothing but gift-wrapping."

"If you say so," Kitty replied. Sera couldn't tell what Kitty had been told, but a woman with ginger fur all over her body had likely learned something about tact. "May I take it with us?"

Sera nodded, gathering the dress over her arm to pass it to Kitty. "Bell didn't need to send an escort. I would have come myself."

"He just wanted to let you know he was ready for you to come out now."

Everything inside the RV was proportioned to Sera, but the step down to the ground from the stairs was still a little high. Her wings would usually steady her, but the hoodie tamped them down.

Kitty offered a hand. Sera considered whether she wanted help or her pride more, then decided that falling to the ground would do nothing for her pride. She placed her hand in Kitty's, and Kitty helped her down.

"What has Bell said about me?" Sera asked as she and Kitty left the caravan.

"Very little. Unless you need a warning label, Bell doesn't tell us much without a more personal flourish. I assume that's what this is about." Kitty was tall for a woman—and curvy. Next to her, Sera felt like a child—just another reason fae didn't like to walk among humans. But Kitty had let go of her as soon as Sera had both bare feet on the ground, and she gave Sera enough space that her fanciful skirt never brushed Sera's legs as they walked together.

"You mean I'm going to meet everybody at once?"

"Everyone who's curious and isn't otherwise distracted. Enough of us will be there. We don't often get to see an audition." Kitty went suddenly silent. A line formed between her eyebrows—slightly denser areas of hair on her face. At least she had all of her face.

"What?"

"You wished yourself in of your own volition, yes?"

"What?" Sera repeated, concern lifting the tone of her voice.

"Nothing. It's just that the last audition, as such, didn't go well." Kitty shook her head. "Don't worry about it. She wished in by accident, and Bell was feeling particularly whimsical with his good fortune."

"Do you not believe that he has received good fortune with me?" Sera asked.

Kitty glanced at her, her worry line still prominent.

"I'm not seeking validation or fishing for compliments," Sera said dryly. "If I fished for compliments now, I'd starve."

"I don't know you well enough to know whether you're a good addition to Arcanium. Our last add was a pain in the ass. She still is, to be honest, but at least those impulses appear to have been more constructively directed. What do you do?"

"What do you mean?"

"I mean, what's Bell's plan for you? What will you do for the circus?"

"Aside from looking like this?" Sera stopped under the beam of one of the lights leading to the big top tent, mindful of the limitations of human vision.

Kitty didn't even blink. Sera hadn't been trying to shock her so much as prove a point, but given what the woman saw in the mirror every day, Sera guessed very little in the realm of physical deformity would shock her. And given the person she woke up with in bed, Sera guessed very little else shocked her either.

Her own quiet admiration surprised her. Few human beings who weren't artists or authors earned it.

She didn't look down on humans the way many of her brethren did, but she'd avoided them until now. They were simply not of her kind, and when compared with those who were, there was often no comparison. Humans were what they were—lords of creation, hardy, short-lived mortals with rich and varied dreams to make up for the magic most of them couldn't touch. Clumsy, confused, often easily manipulated—creatures of flesh and splinters of bone, passionate because they didn't have time for patience and dangerous for the same reason.

But though Kitty had much in common with her own kind, the hair that covered her—mixed with an aesthetic that wouldn't be out of place in a faerie ball—meant she wasn't quite part of her own kind either. Not really. The Ringmaster, as well as Bell, must have sensed that quality.

Sera had not earned her parents' confidence in matters of the court without the ability to assess people at a glance. In that moment when she didn't blink, Kitty earned respect as well.

Kitty touched Sera's shoulder, turning her toward the big top to start them walking again. "You'll find that's not as much of an issue here. Most of us have more than one thing that we do in Arcanium. At the very least, you're expected to know how to juggle. Plain rubber balls are fine. You don't have to take on flaming chainsaws the first time."

"I know how to juggle."

"Good. You'll do just fine here."

Sera sighed. "I don't think Arcanium is going to be content if the 'Girl with Half a Face' only juggles. I can't see that earning much in my tip jar."

"You wished into Arcanium voluntarily." Kitty's glances had shifted slightly from concern to curiosity. "We probably share similar reasons. But you *know* what Arcanium is, don't you?"

"Everyone knows Arcanium." Sera wrapped her arms around herself, the fleecy inside of the hoodie doing its best to comfort her. "If they didn't before, they do now."

"You're referring to the—"

"To the abduction, yes. Beings have tried to take Arcanium. They are footnotes in the appendix of its history. No one ever succeeded before. People will remember that."

"And that Bell took it back. And that everyone who was there when he took it back was imprisoned and sentenced to a terrible death. They're remembering those very important parts of the story, too, right?" By all accounts, Kitty hadn't been available to anyone but the Ringmaster in Locke's Arcanium, but fear tightened her words, such that Sera wondered what had happened to her during those months that Locke had run Arcanium. Or what had happened to people she'd known.

"Yes. They remember those parts." Sera stared down at her feet. "I'm counting on it."

Sera didn't elaborate and Kitty didn't ask, but the conversation dissipated into tense silence from both of them.

As they reached the big top tent, Sera's anxiety interwove with the tension. All the lights were on in the tent, and there were more people in there than she would have thought were part of Arcanium. With the crowds gone, they couldn't hide among them or in whatever dark corner they were usually kept. They'd gathered on the bleachers around the circus ring, where spotlights rendered the sawdust blinding.

Sera stopped and turned her head away, exposing the damaged side, just so that her good eye could have the shadow.

"Are you okay?" Kitty asked.

"It's very bright."

Kitty raised her hand and urged whoever managed the set from above the ring to lower the intensity of the light. Whether the crewman was golem or sentient, they obeyed and the spotlights dimmed. It was still the intensity of the sun, but more like indirect summer sunlight now.

"Thank you."

"You're welcome. Are you sure you're okay? Not just with the brightness of the lights. It's been a while since Bell let in someone who wasn't human with any kind of fanfare. They usually just…show up and start scaring the shit out of people. Since they're monsters and demons, that's what they wanted to do all along. But you're not a monster or a demon. Nor are you human. The physiology is wrong, somehow. And I'm not talking about the damage."

"Did Bell tell you what I am?" Sera peered through the big top, the people on the bleachers clearer in the dimmer light. Candlelight would have been kinder to her, but that would have made it more difficult for the humans to see, and human beings were the majority in the tent, at least from what she could tell. With the alterations that Bell had made, there were some from whom she couldn't determine origin—people who felt like demons but looked human, people who felt human but looked like demons and those who straddled those worlds in the most disorienting way.

"I didn't spend much time out and about in Locke's Arcanium to get a good view of all the different kinds of beings out there." Kitty hovered her hand behind Sera's back to urge her forward toward the ring. "I only know what we've had here, and I've never seen your kind. But I've worn faerie wings enough to guess. We've never had fae in Arcanium before. Not as long as I've been here, and Bell's never spoken of it. This has always been a demonic circus."

"Well, the fae wouldn't generally find themselves in a freak show. If that offends you, I apologize." And Sera was sincere, because she'd decided that she liked Kitty. The woman had a matter-of-fact way of speaking that didn't leave room for judgment.

"Are there not outliers, even among faeries?" Kitty asked.

"No. If we suffer, it's usually our minds, not our bodies. This…" Sera tucked herself farther back in her hood, although lights from every angle meant there was nowhere to hide. "This was unique—a deliberate attack intended to disfigure a body that resists disfigurement."

"I'm sorry to hear that. I can relate with being one of a kind. I can't relate with it being deliberate. Most of the freaks here are either an accident of birth or created by Bell. He'll feel compassion for your suffering, but was he really the one you wanted to come to for that compassion, since he's given others the need for that compassion as well?"

"From human to demon, is Arcanium anyone's first choice? Or is it the place you come when you have nowhere else to turn?"

Sera wished she could turtle herself in the hoodie as more and more people on the bleachers stopped conversing to consider the newcomer in their midst. Arcanium had several giants, but she was noticeably smaller than the rest, barring the dwarfed demon and a man with no legs. Even the petite humans among them were taller than she. Swallowed by an oversized hooded sweatshirt seemed to only emphasize her size.

She would usually be surrounded by people of her own kind. She hated how uncomfortable she felt in her own skin, that she had been put in a position where she wanted to crawl out of herself the way a butterfly emerged from a cocoon. Except she was trapped like this—safe but distorted, the monster Salem had made of her.

That she was surrounded by other monsters aplenty—human and otherwise—did nothing to assuage that discomfort, only enhanced it.

Bell stepped over the edge of ring, the spotlight catching his sunglow skin and making him shimmer, as though he'd painted his body in gold dust. He met Kitty at the partition, kissing her cheek. Something seemed unresolved between them—with tightness in Kitty's shoulders and care in the gentleness of his fingers on her cheek—but she leaned into the kiss, and Bell lingered his fingertips over the grain of fur.

"How are we getting along?" he asked.

"She seems stressed. Uncertain about her position here, maybe?" Kitty checked back with Sera. "What have you two discussed?"

"She was brought in during circus hours. I've waited longer to give assignments to my cast." Bell gestured for Sera to approach.

She'd held back from the spotlights, every new member's attention adding to the burning sensation under her skin, although the wound had healed and looked entirely natural now.

"I told you, Sera, that if you suffer any pain, I can take it away." Bell gestured again. "Come closer. I can take care of that."

"It's not real," she said.

"Just because it's in your head doesn't mean it isn't real. You'll grow accustomed to attention. It is usually well-meant."

Bell nudged the hood back. Sera winced, but she let him hover his palm over the cavity, sending a burst of cold into the flesh to dispel the burning—which wasn't aided by the sudden swell of murmurs at the sight, even among the other freaks.

Immortal and mortal. Demon, human and monster. Freak and normal. Oddity and talent. Tall and short. Skeletally thin and monstrously large. Women, men and everything between and other. And Sera wasn't the only one with scars.

One of the small, skeletal women—who sat with other women as bony as she—had gashes in her body that looked like fresh wounds, except for the teeth that emerged from the healthy red gums.

A woman in elaborate black-and-white body paint and costume that marked her as a variant of a mime had her mouth sewn shut with thick black thread. A stocky, muscled man and a slender demon flanked her, in the same costumes but without the thread.

A human woman with a sex demon on either side of her had been slashed and sewn back together, leaving thick, dark scars all over her exposed body, and she wore a bejeweled eyepatch over the same eye that Sera had lost, although the scar tissue on the woman hadn't healed nearly as well as Sera's. But in spite of the scars' gnarled appearance and livid skin, Sera was struck by how lushly beautiful she still was.

The sex demons both had their hands on her, and the woman's one good eye had dilated as deep and dark as that of fae. Like a handful of Arcanium cast, Neve—now also called the Patchwork Pirate—had a vast and whispered reputation that had spread all the more voraciously as the new Arcanium had gained ground. When someone like Locke or Bell acquired a human pet, people noticed and craved the prize that the powerful had taken for their own. Everyone who heard stories about Arcanium knew Neve like they knew Kitty and Maya, although Maya no longer worked in Arcanium and had since vanished. Bell had sworn no vengeance for her disappearance, so everyone assumed she was still under Bell's protection—or under someone else's with Bell's blessing.

Human women. By accounts, Maya had looked normal, but Kitty certainly didn't, and Neve had taken on the scars of the violence she had suffered—or scars of the violence she *hadn't* suffered, depending on who was telling the story. They were desirable enigmas, along with the Spider and a few whispers about the lead singer of the Skeleton Band. Human women could be damaged and still earn the affection and lust of the powerful, even of the fae.

What did they have that she couldn't? How could her brothers and uncles and father desire the humans of Arcanium then cast her out to forget the sight of her, because someone had sought to make her undesirable and succeeded?

"Well, there's no accounting for taste, is there?" When Bell finished soothing the phantom pain in her face, he took her hand and drew her toward him. She had to work harder to climb over the ring partition, but Bell was patient, tightening his hold to give her something to brace against. "I am no fool, and I suffer few fools in my circus. Trash and treasure, love."

"Stop trying to make me feel better." Sera tried to retain some dignity after clambering over the partition like a child scrambling over a log. Living in a world made for bigger people would take some getting used to. Given some of the costumes and even self-consciousness among those looking down at her, Sera suspected that dignity was in short supply in a circus like this.

"Oh yes. We'll have to rid you of that, won't we?" Bell led her to the center of the ring. "I believe you're going to need those wings, love, for whatever you're going to do for us. I can have Kitty retrieve a cover for you if you need it. The Spider has her own additional limbs she has to contend with, so we have a wealth of halters to choose from."

In building chastity magic, keeping herself covered and less accessible was part and partial to the effort. Modesty had a different meaning in faerie rings—a means to an end rather than a deterrence of behavior. Once the fae decided to cease their magical growth, or if they decided to amass power in other ways, modesty no longer constricted them. Some women preferred jewelry alone to set off their wings and avoid having to tailor clothing around them.

Sera had never availed herself of nudity before, but she didn't have the same squeamishness about it as perhaps some of the humans in Arcanium. Even so, she couldn't deny trepidation as she brought the hooded sweatshirt over her head, leaving herself only in the fitted jeans.

Wolf whistles erupted from a cluster of demons, one of whom looked like a rumpled rock god, deceptively human, the other two a giant and dwarf pair—black-eyed, sharp-toothed and undeniably demonic. The humanlike one laughed as though he would fall off the bench at any moment, but he whistled again when he noticed her looking at him. She couldn't tell whether he and the short demon were mocking her, and the wink he gave didn't clear up the question. She wasn't quite psychic, not like Bell. Her natural and developed skills lay elsewhere.

Sera still wore the jeweled collar, because it was a traditional wedding necklace that couldn't be removed by her own hands. The gemstones glittered in the sharp light, but at least her wrists were lighter without the golden bangles.

She handed the hoodie to Bell, who accepted it then stepped backward to perch on the partition.

Sera spread her dragonfly wings, now free of confinement. Only two members of the cast could boast wings of their own—a man with dove-gray angel wings who sat alone and a gargoyle-like monster who sat with the Spider. But they weren't close to faerie wings, colorful as stained glass and as seemingly delicate as spun sugar, wings with magic running through the etched veins, magic that trailed light in their movements.

The rock god still chuckled to himself, but the wolf whistles quieted, and so did the rest of the crowd. That silence was not completely awe. Jaws clenched all around the bleachers as she turned in the center—and she clenched in sympathy, that those of her blood were responsible for the jolt of fear that her still-beautiful wings inspired. There was some awe, however, which she took from them gladly. Bell lifted his chin, the gold in his amber eyes glittering in appreciation.

"Why am I here?" Sera asked. "I don't know any kind of circus craft."

"You can juggle."

Psychics thought they were so clever, referencing conversations and thoughts they shouldn't have heard. It seemed such self-amusement spanned species.

"I don't need my wings for juggling." Sera hid her fists by placing them on her hips, as though that had been the only reason she'd made them. She couldn't shake the idea that Bell, like the demon in the bleachers, was somehow laughing at her.

"You won't wear such casual clothing when the circus is open. All our different kinds of bodies are on full display, whether for the guests out there or in here. I didn't need to see your wings so much as free your body."

"For what?"

"That's up to you, love."

"I don't understand."

"Seraphina of the far-less-menacing-than-it-sounds Devil's Circle, you are a woman of many talents. You were prepared for marriage to all kinds of partners, and so you are accomplished in many things."

"Sera, no longer of the Devil's Circle, thanks you." The contract had signed her over, so not only was she no longer technically a princess, she was also a faerie with no ring. Or rather, she was a fae of the Saskatchewan Ursal sleuth, which didn't have the same dramatic quality.

"Of your many talents, I'm sure several can find a home here. We have a veritable playground for anyone to perform."

Bell gestured to the crew above the ring. With a series of mechanical whirs, all manner of objects rattled down into the ring, and three golems entered through the red velvet curtain from backstage, carrying something that looked like a liability lawyer's dream of a jungle gym, all soldered metal and hard surfaces, designed for some kind of swinging and climbing act. It complemented the trapeze swings, the white ring, the orb chandelier, the dangling lengths of silk and—to Sera's private mortification—a pole lowered down dead center.

Pole dancing was different in the human world, generously called exotic but often viewed as a low art, despite the skill involved. In fae society, it was considered a higher art, but one entirely reserved for the bedroom. The queen had taught pole dancing to each of her daughters and a few of her sons. In fae tradition, it was done on a smooth wooden pole, easy to add to the bedroom of any venue, whether rustic or ostentatious. Among the wealthier families or royalty, they were sometimes embedded with tumbled crystal or adorned with precious metal.

"If you'd like, I can bring out an upright piano for you, saloon-style. But I don't think that's the skill you want to bring to Arcanium, is it, Sera?" Bell draped the hoodie on the partition next to him to free his hands and open his stance. He wasn't hard—at least not that she could see, and loose cotton trousers did just as little to conceal such things as the tight leather trousers of many of the other cast members. But his position was sexual, all the clearer to her because she knew what she'd never had, what she'd sometimes wanted more than anything and which made her magic rise and bloom and reach and stretch and strengthen with all the creativity she denied.

"You're a real bastard, Bell." Now Sera wanted to cover her nakedness, but only because she felt touched as well as seen, and her nipples were gradually hardening, though the temperature in the big top was innocuously comfortable.

Bell crossed his arms with a smile, as though he could wait for hours. "I know no one likes a telepath, but precogs aren't exactly the most charming party guests either. You could always work with me, except a true psychic learns the art of when to tell customers what they want to hear and when to give them what they need—and how to do it without getting a knee to the balls—and you haven't quite mastered that art. I think someone as glittery and colorful as you belongs in *my* ring."

Sera finally gave in to the impulse to cover herself, which somehow worsened the embarrassment, because it told everyone in the bleachers that she thought there was something to be embarrassed about. "I don't know what you want from me."

"I'm prone to throwing newly inducted cast into deep, shark-infested waters on the first day in, barring complications. I'm not treating you with any special sort of sadism, if that makes you feel any better."

Music, heavy on strings and with a sharp, strong, deep bass beat, swelled to fill the bleachers. Without a full audience, the sound had almost an echoing quality, despite absorption from the canvas—as though she and Bell were alone in the big top tent. Sera couldn't pretend that she was, but she could silently ask Bell to dim the lights in the bleachers to add to the illusion.

To her private surprise, he did.

"You don't have to use the pole, love. There's plenty here to choose from that doesn't depend on skills you learned for your husband's bedroom—although the husband chosen for you would never have appreciated such skills, so perhaps you would prefer to put them to more appreciated use."

"I am not meant for such things." If he could stop treating her like she was, she could go through her private grief so much more easily.

She didn't want him to treat her like anyone else. She wanted someone to acknowledge the damnable tragedy that had happened. She wanted someone to point and laugh at the very idea that Bell wanted her to display bedroom arts at all, as though anyone would want to see them from her. She wanted the disgust and shock on other people's faces that she felt for herself.

She wanted the truth of things, not the ideal that had already been shattered with the now-misshapen structure of her skull.

She didn't want Kitty to tell her that everything was going to be okay, that no one in Arcanium cared about what had happened to her because it was barely a blip among the other deformities that made up Bell's famed collection of oddities. She didn't want anyone to say that nothing was wrong with her when her face had been whole just a day ago. She'd been beautiful and now she wasn't. She needed them to acknowledge that loss, rather than pretend it didn't or shouldn't matter.

"I told you to take time to mourn, but I won't lie to align our reality to your feelings. You don't have to rush into those

intimate explorations, though. It is not a requirement of Arcanium—more of an inevitability. Participating in the guests' entertainment is *a requirement for your stay, however."* Bell nodded to the various circus tools for her to select her medium of choice. *"I could pick one for you, but I'm not partial to one or another, which gives you plenty of room to choose."*

"I don't know how to do anything in a circus." Sera glanced from one trapeze swing to the other, considered the jungle gym.

"Then don't do it in a circus way."

She hadn't choreographed anything to this music. She wouldn't know where the crescendos and fortissimos would hit, so she didn't know what to build up to. But the music was four-four time, and she knew routines to that count.

Her mother had taught her the importance of improvisation on a pole, whether that pole was horizontal or vertical, though Sera wasn't the most adaptable dancer, not like one of her eldest sisters, Victoriana. Being seen making those mistakes before she'd had a chance to even rehearse and by strangers who judged her for the ugliness of her face, for her race, for the fact she'd come in willingly while some of them had not... It was enough to keep her from moving at all.

Bell flicked his fingers on his trousers as though brushing away lint. Sera felt it as a sharp switch-sting against her ass.

"They will not judge you as harshly as you believe. They just want a good show. Please them, errors and all, and you will please me."

With the dimmer light on the other side of the ring, she couldn't see anyone anymore but Bell. She had no reason to like or dislike Bell, only to be wary, but she felt more comfortable with him, a creature from her world, than with Kitty, although Bell was the one who could crush her under his boot. He was familiar. He was jinn. She knew how to handle jinn. Though unpredictable, one could predict that they were unpredictable and plan accordingly. She knew enough about him to tentatively trust that he wasn't seeking to humiliate her, that only she could humiliate herself and it probably wouldn't be anything she would do here in this ring, even if she fell.

Sera inhaled sharply as she gathered her courage then peeled off her jeans.

Now she wore only the undergarments that she'd donned for the wedding dress, because she felt more comfortable in her own underwear than what Bell had provided. They were closer to bloomers or shorts than the common mode among modern women, and perhaps they seemed strange to the rest of the people in the room, but Bell didn't so much as smirk at her as she ran to the jungle gym.

Her wings gave her lift and balance as she leaped from one bar to the next, running all the way to the top with her feet alone. Instead of mounting the pole, which would have been too intimate for her, she jumped with all of her running momentum to the aerial silk that dangled from the ceiling.

Sera hooked her arm and leg around the fabric and spun around, her right leg stretched out and toe pointed to create a line away from her body.

The aerial silk swayed outward as the track turned on and sent it on a path to circle the ring, with her still spinning, until the tension of the twisted rope absorbed all of her momentum and she swung her leg back to spin the other way, this time with the releasing tension of the silk to speed her up.

She hadn't done dance-craft in years, but it all came back to her, even if silks hadn't been her implement of choice. The hardest part wasn't remembering the positions but in finding the strength she needed to hold them. She had flexibility for days, as evidenced by her present position with one foot behind her head and the other pointing at the ground. Then she demonstrated even more as she swung her downward-pointed leg forward up almost to her head, her legs at eleven and one on a clock as she clung to the silk.

To the beat of the drums, she spun and swung, toes pointed and arms and thighs tight as she wrapped the silk around to bind herself into each position. Dancing in the air was like dancing through bedroom sheets—still seductive but more coy than a pole, even playful, with silk both strong and sensuous over her skin, hiding and revealing her in turns. She stayed careful, however, not to let the silk bind her wings for too long.

Near the end of her routine, Sera unraveled herself down the length of the silk before flipping back upright just short of the ground and taking flight. The buzz of her wings vibrated through her, their shimmer like the streaming tail of a comet from beating so fast. With silk wrapped around her leg, she moved as though floating in water rather than air.

If her parents' ring hadn't wanted to hunt her down for escaping, they'd want to do so for using her wings in the human world for everyone to see. But no one would believe what they were seeing. The ignorant masses would think she wore some sort of new-technology, clear-wire harness. She could do something like this on a technicality if Bell wanted it of her. There was always something in Arcanium, something impossible that revealed it as the magical circus that it was to those precious few who recognized real magic, and as something extraordinary to those who believed it was illusion.

The music reached its conclusion. The buzz of her wings was all the more obvious in the silence.

As she lowered herself to the ground, a slow clap startled her. She dropped the last few feet, falling into a crouch.

Bell clapped from the edge of the ring. Then the rest of the cast joined in—piecemeal and inconsistent, not the proper swell of a full audience. More wolf whistles and howls signaled a different appreciation.

"You have the right idea." Bell stood from the partition and helped her upright again. He didn't bring the hooded sweatshirt with him. "You're more of a credit to your mother than she gave you credit for."

"Please, let me wear a mask," she muttered, hoping the others wouldn't hear. "My face… It will only distract."

"My dear child, that would only allow everyone—including you—to miss the point entirely."

* * * *

A man whose legs ended in scarless stumps approached her outside the big top, walking effortlessly on his hands. "So how much of that was you and how much of that was Bell? It's sometimes hard to tell around here."

"Bell's manipulations would have fit the music better." Sera had pulled the sweatshirt back on in the ring. Binding her wings down, while self-conscious, made her feel forced to the ground, especially when confronted by someone new.

"I don't know much of anything about faeries. They never confided in me. Are the circus arts common or is running off to join the circus just as much of a rebellion in your world as in ours?" The man matched her pace away from the big top, flexing like a gorilla for each step. He wasn't bloated with muscle, but his arms had strengthened from all the carrying and maneuvering he must have been accustomed to, and he kept the rest of himself fit as well. The sweep of his heavily styled, dark brown hair suggested a predilection toward vanity, as did his wide grin, the kind that developed from certainty that what people saw of him was attractive. But it didn't devolve into narcissism, at least not in her early impressions—otherwise, she wouldn't have impressed him. And a faerie could hardly criticize vanity as a vice.

"We don't learn to dance to entertain a crowd—not these kinds of dances anyway." Sera shifted away from him a little, taken aback by his immediate familiarity, his arm brushing her leg as they walked. She hadn't put the skinny jeans back on, so her legs were still bare. The tickle of the thick hairs from his arm against her sent goosebumps up her leg to the nape of her neck because it was unexpected, and though nudity was fairly common among the fae, skin contact was more significant. The fact she'd done a bedroom dance while under the influence of incubus magic only made that significance keener. "Running off to a circus isn't a common rebellion, nor did I come here to rebel."

"Did your family always want you to become a doctor, like your parents before you and their parents before that, but you've always had this secret dream to dance that just will not be denied?"

"Okay, we do have your movies and television. How many inspirational dramas have you been watching?" Sera tried not to smile. She didn't want to smile, not with a human, not so soon after entering Arcanium, wary of its cast and they wary of her.

The man's grin broadened. "I have no idea what you're talking about. But if you want to tell me that you beat all the odds to achieve your dreams, all while saving a puppy and learning valuable lessons along the way, I won't stop you."

A trio of white-skinned, white-haired, pale-eyed women, unrelated but similar enough to be confused for it, walked past her and the man. One of them touched Sera's shoulder—fortunately over her sweatshirt, because the hand lingered and Sera's magic surfaced for a connection, like reaching out into darkness to find the edge of a table. Through the thick fabric, it couldn't find anything to grasp. Bell had held himself back from her, considerately, and all other contact had been too brief for that connection to be forged—including the blow of a grizzly paw to her face.

Her magic wasn't a burden. She'd worked all her life to build it. Precognition was a gift. But it could be exhausting, and knowing what had happened to Arcanium, she wasn't eager to glimpse what they'd seen. She didn't know which of the cast members had been there for the abduction and which had been brought in after. It was simply better to be careful until she knew who to avoid.

"The Albino Triplets," the man explained as the three women went their separate way. "Kari, Sin and Marina. They're showing acrobatic solidarity. Used to work a number of acrobatic dance shows in the vein of Cirque du Soleil. Here, they do ground routines and trapeze."

"Are you showing acrobatic solidarity?" Sera asked.

"During the day, I tumble and climb on whatever I can find, but I'll use the jungle gym now and then in the ring. Do the wings help with your balance? They don't look like they could hold a cat, much less you, unless you're hollow-boned like a bird."

"They're stronger than they look, and yes, they help with balance, although I have exceptional balance without them. I'm also not hollow-boned, but I am lighter than you might think."

"People say that about me, too," the man said cheerfully.

But as they stepped under one of the circus lights, she noticed wear at the edge of his smile, the forced lift of his cheekbones crinkling the corners of his eyes more like a grimace. It wasn't insincere, necessarily, just that he had to work harder than he once had, given his smile lines.

He paused in his walk, swinging slightly on his hands as he tilted his head, looking up at her. "What?"

"You were part of the circus when it was taken. That's why you've met fae before."

The smile disappeared a lot more easily than it had stayed. "Word really does get around, doesn't it?"

"Valid warnings should, to forestall retribution," she replied. "I didn't intend to resurrect bad memories. You've been pleasant, but please don't feel like you have to be polite on my account."

"Okay, then. Politeness aside, you don't look familiar to us, but if we're going to work in close proximity together, we have to know. Did you ever visit Locke's Arcanium?"

"They thought you would be the least threatening to me." Sera didn't blame them, sending the one human in the lot shorter than she was. Sending the short demon wouldn't have had nearly the same disarming affect.

"Oh, I can be threatening. But I'm not being all 'You killed my father. Prepare to die' about it. Bell let you in. I don't think he would have done that if you'd been there. But I want to hear it from you."

"If I say I never came to Arcanium, before or after Locke, would you believe me? Humans aren't known for trusting the fae, and fae aren't really known for being trustworthy with humans, if we're being honest."

"Why is that? You're not demons. At least I think you're not."

"You people are the explorers, treasure hunters and conquerors. You tell me."

The man gave a slight nod in acknowledgment. "You were never in Locke's Arcanium, then."

"I'd only ever heard of Arcanium, both when it was Bell's and when it was Locke's. At neither time was it a place I wanted to attend. I had no use for a circus, and I certainly had no use for a dungeon. I find them distasteful, cruel, demonic playgrounds, not intended for our kind."

Speaking plainly to a man, to a human being, was a new and slightly thrilling experience. She'd spoken to humans before, but always in the practice of deception. In Bell's Arcanium, jinn, demons, monsters and humans interacted freely without needing to hide what they were. Why not the fae as well?

"Not intended for your kind?" The man settled onto the stumps of his legs, balancing himself quite well, considering they weren't flat.

"Dungeons were created by jinn for jinn alone, for those forged from fire. But the jinn open their dungeons to the enjoyment of the fae because we have gold and favors to sell, because we often do not like those imprisoned within them and because we are immortal—honorary jinn, in their eyes. Don't look at me like that." Sera crossed her arms over her chest. "Are you telling me that if demons opened their dungeons to humans, your people wouldn't avail themselves just as enthusiastically? Demons aren't the only purveyors of horror, my dear sir."

"Fair enough. But humans never trafficked me before. Only a demon." The man didn't appear aggressive in his response, but the defined, developed muscles from shoulder to neck had tensed almost into stone.

"I'm not defending my brethren. When they were stolen away after Bell regained Arcanium, I can't say we looked too hard for them."

This time the clench in his jaw was more evident. "Did you know them?"

"Some of them." If she was going to be honest, she also had to be honest about what painted her in a less flattering light, even if that light was simply a familial connection.

"Is that why you're here? To free them?"

Sera blinked. The spirit quartz had glimmered in Bell's hands, but it hadn't occurred to her to even try to free her brother. Only the greatest of fools—or the most powerful—would consider such a flagrant maneuver in Bell's own house. "I wouldn't dream of it. We didn't look for them, just as no one will think to look for me."

"What about when word gets around that there's a faerie in the cast?"

"That's where Bell comes in," she replied. "He's sworn to protect those in his circus, including me."

"He's failed before."

"You obviously trust him to protect you now, or you would have run with the rest while you had a chance."

"Can't run as fast as you might think." But he lifted himself back up on his hands. "You pass muster, for now. Sorry for the interrogation. As long as there are those of us still here from Locke's Arcanium, we'll continue to worry. The newbies worry, too. I don't think any of us will fully trust Bell the way we used to until we're a few 'generations' removed from what happened."

Sera wrinkled her nose. "You call that an interrogation? I didn't see so much as a single thumbscrew."

"More like an introduction, really. I'm Carlo." He balanced on one hand to hold out his fist to her. It took her a moment to realize he wanted her to fist-bump it. Learning her human social niceties from screens didn't give her everything, at least in immediate context. "I'd shake hands, but I know exactly where my hands have been. I wouldn't say this is the last interrogation-slash-introduction you're going to have, but you seem…well, normal to me. I don't know if that's offensive to a faerie or not."

She had to fight a little harder against a smile as she gave him the fist-bump he offered. "Normal is relative."

"I've lived in Arcanium for eight years and a few other freak shows for five years before that. You don't have to tell me." Carlo adjusted back onto two hands. "Mom and Dad wanted *me* to go into law. *I* was the one who ran away to join the circus. I am my own inspirational drama. Though my interrogation skills probably show I wouldn't have done so hot on the law circuit."

"You can learn almost anything. You were steady, even with someone you believed might be a terrible person. I might still be a terrible person, good sir, but I am not *that* kind of terrible person."

"'*Good sir.*'" His own smile returned, with a little less wear. "I don't get called that often, even when we're at a Renaissance faire. I like it. Well, good night." He started toward the caravan.

"Aren't you going to ask?"

Carlo paused. "Ask you what? There are a few questions percolating up in here, but I don't want to put my hand in something I shouldn't."

"Why I came to Arcanium? What happened to me?"

He shrugged. "I wasn't planning on asking. Most of us voluntaries were already freaks well before we walked in. There's not much of a story there."

"I wasn't born like this."

She'd tried to keep her tone even, but there must have been an offended quality in her voice because Carlo explained, "I knew someone born with half a face. It looked a lot like yours. I've seen cleft lips, random holes, hair growth, almost every weirdness the human body can produce. *I* was born like this. Did Bell make something awful look...smoother?"

"You knew someone born with half a face?"

"Yeah. Some warehouse-line angels got to be fans of Picasso. They come up with some weird shit to pop out of a uterus." He rocked on his hands, kicking where his legs would have been. "But it doesn't make *them* weird, you know? It didn't make me weird. And it doesn't make you weird. We look strange, but we're actually not—not me, anyway. I don't know about you yet."

"Except for how I look, I'm not strange in my world. I can't speak for yours."

"Do you *want* me to ask what happened?" This time, curiosity rocked him as he turned back to face her. "It wasn't Bell, was it?"

Sera shook her head. "No, Bell didn't do this to me, but not fixing it was part of the agreement before I wished in. And no, I don't want you to ask about it. I just expected that you would."

"Fair enough. People still might. Guests definitely will. If I had a dollar for every time someone asked what happened to my legs, I wouldn't need Arcanium to live free and wild." Carlo started again in the direction of the caravan. "Honestly, after eight years, I should come up with a more interesting answer. Being born with it isn't nearly as exciting as gangrene or a vengeful pirate or some Jigsaw-type scenario."

She didn't quite join him, but she was walking in the same direction, so he slowed down to walk with her again.

"What should I tell people who ask?"

"Frankly, anything you like. I don't recommend telling them nothing, unless you want to go the vow-of-silence route like Caroline. Still don't know why that was a condition of her return, but whatever gets her through the day. With the guests, if you don't want a long, involved lie—or the truth—you can just say what I say, that you were born with it. No one questions whether it's true or not. Arcanium is expected to be interactive, but it's up to you what you want to share—a lie, a truth or nothing at all. That's your prerogative."

His analysis hit all the major salient points, thorough enough to please her. Some fae thought humans unintelligent because they couldn't see what was deliberately hidden from them, which had always seemed unfair to her. Another reason was their lack of foresight, even if they were told what to expect. In that respect, Sera believed mortality worked against them. But humans had their own aptitudes that immortals lacked—and their own kind of intelligence. She enjoyed the fruits of analysis, no matter whose branches they came from.

"I don't even know if I need a story. It seems Bell wants me in the big top performances," Sera said.

"Oh, you'll be walking around the circus with the rest of us when you're not in the big top. It involves a lot of taking pictures and being charming. I hope you know how to do charming."

"Of course, good sir."

"Oh, yeah, I forgot about '*good sir*' already. The heart doth swell. You'll do swimmingly."

They reached the strings of bauble lights strung between vehicles in the caravan. The golden light was a complement to his form—already darker-skinned than she was, a combination of genetics and time in the sun. His briefs cut off right above the place where his legs hadn't grown, the leather ties bound tight over the front. He was lightly haired, graining his chest and arms in black, which she wasn't used to among her own kind, although Salem had had hair aplenty. The fae were generally smooth-skinned, smooth-pored. The differences, imperfections and alterations to Carlo's skin—apart from the obvious, which she was already beginning to accept as his normal—were impossible to ignore in comparison.

Scars roped around his shoulders where his arms began, almost invisible except when the light hit them just right. Four more slashed just above the shoulder blades. It was impossible to tell what they were from or how old they were. If recent, Bell could have easily healed the damage, but Sera would have thought he'd render it completely invisible rather than partially.

Carlo also boasted a few tattoos—a laughing, flaming skull at his hip, Roman numerals and Cyrillic on his arm, a sunflower over his left ribs—and a nipple piercing that gleamed in the light. The fae weren't strangers to body paint and permanent jewelry, but the way he wore them was quintessentially human.

She didn't think she had ever been this close to a human man when she was alone rather than part of a crowd where she could get lost. Even with his attempt at an interrogation, he seemed nice enough. Before the circus's abduction, he'd probably been a delight. A tad simple, but Arcanium didn't lend itself to much in the way of variation, which seemed ironic from a certain angle. Still, the circus was only a few booths, a few tents and a collection of the same oddities visiting the same kinds of places, so that the only difference between New Mexico and Alabama was the humidity and whether or not there were cacti.

He'd said himself that circus life was all he'd known for thirteen years. A person had to be intentional with variance in a place like this. She'd spent the last half-century immersed in all the knowledge and experiences that wealth and nobility afforded her—not that her wealth of knowledge had much use now, and not that the privilege had ended well for her or many of her siblings.

"See something green?"

"I beg your pardon." Sera blinked, startling out of her reverie.

"You were staring."

She shook her head. "Lost in thought. I wasn't seeing."

"You were staring really hard. Don't get me wrong. I'm not complaining if a gorgeous woman wants to stare at me for a few hours."

If he was flirting with her, he probably flirted with anyone, but it pinched Sera's still-raw nerve. "Come now, sir. Surely you aren't that desperate."

Carlo's thick, sculpted brows drew in. "I don't see what that has to do with anyth—"

He stopped at the thud of a large pair of boots grinding into the dry dirt on the other side of her RV. He pitched forward on his hands, balancing himself parallel to the ground and bringing himself low to peek under her RV. There was less of him to balance, but it still impressed her.

"Sorry. Just checking it wasn't the Ringmaster." Carlo popped back up. "It's only the—"

The first thing Sera saw was the massive hoof crushing the grass as he stepped around her RV. First or an ignorant glance might have confused him for a satyr, because his hooves were cloven and his lower half was furred up to his waist. During the day, she assumed the thick white fur at his groin would be enough to cover his cock for human modesty's sake, but he'd reverted to his more natural state, mostly covered but visibly male.

On hooves, he stood as high as a tall human man, almost a head taller than Bell in bare feet, but the antlers gave the impression that he was larger. They emerged proudly from behind his pointed ears, his hair wild beneath them, as though the branches had tousled the hair as they had grown out. Stubs of antlers dotted his shoulders and the blades behind as well, with two more on his forehead, like the costume of a demon.

But this wasn't a demon or an earthborn satyr or faun. Like a white stag, he wasn't made to hide in the forest. Unlike a white stag, he had nothing to fear from hounds or the rifles of man. He stood steady and still as birch, his pale skin dove-gray and white-irised eyes unblinking.

Tattoos spanned over his chest and abdomen, thin symbolic lines interspersed with ancient runes. Ink was atypical, as was the thick silver piercing through his septum like that of a bull. To see him at all shocked her on its own. To see him altered so, and of his own volition, shocked her more.

Carlo looked between her and the being with more than a little confusion. There was the familiarity of recognition, but he showed no sign that he understood what he was seeing.

Sera could only react as was the newcomer's due. Though she no longer wore a gown, Sera curtsied to the ground, lowering her head in respect. Her hair swung in on both sides to cover her face. It shamed her more that he would see her like this than any of the humans among the cast or guests.

She finally raised her head after proper respect had been shown for several minutes. She would have genuflected even longer in her father's court.

She leaned back, startled and stunned, at the sight of the glorious being bowing to *her*, bent at the waist until his antlers traced patterns in the ground.

The cloud of his hair brushed thick and soft against her fingertips.

He looked up from the unsettling of his hair. She'd only wanted his attention so that she could urge him upright again, because she didn't deserve his respect and no longer had a title that would earn a fraction of it from him in the best of times.

The being raised himself until his face was level with hers. He touched her tentative hand, fingertip to fingertip, deliberate contact.

The vision plunged her into darkness, but it wasn't frightening. Though he ran through that darkness, his body a ghost in the forest, what he ran from couldn't hurt him. There was only the overwhelming urge to move, to get away, to avoid that which violently creeped in on the worlds that he had once called his own.

They crept in with machines now, with steel and concrete instead of swords and lances. He was not a creature of machines nor partial to loud, angry voices, accusing fingers pointing at him as though he were the strange thing, as though he were the intruder. Ever since they had come after him with stone and wood, they had always thought him strange, unwelcome, even though he was the thing that made his world more welcome to them.

Never mind… There were other worlds in which he could roam. Gods didn't need to linger where they were not wanted.

He had a mouth but did not speak, patient as she rode the vision. With those she knew, her magic gradually became accustomed and no longer pulled pieces of the past to the present every time they made skin contact. But strangers triggered her magic like fish to bait.

The being parted their fingers and straightened. Ribbons of magic curled around her arms and legs to pull her to her feet as well. He no more wanted her genuflecting to him than she wanted him genuflecting to her.

He touched the cavity where her left cheek had been, a dull scraping of fingernail that wasn't painful or stinging—as though he searched for an illusion, only to find there was none.

For a moment, she flashed not to his past but hers—the massive bear paw slamming into her face, the Bearskin's dispassionate expression as he watched her wake into a world irreparably altered by his own hand, for his own ends.

Sera jerked away from the dent of a fingernail in the new skin.

The being's face was also dispassionate but not cold or inaccessible, not when those wide white eyes stared so intently down into hers with terrible, wonderful madness—the kind that arose from time and darkness and sadness and torment. Madness, yes, but it was not unkind.

He lowered his head in a brief, less formal bow then backed away, rounding her RV again and disappearing from sight. The clomp of his heavy hooves could be heard for a dozen more yards.

"Well, that's something you don't see every day." Carlo hadn't moved from where he'd settled next to her RV door. In fact, Sera suspected he'd barely breathed with the other being there, because she couldn't remember seeing him at all while the being had stood before her.

Even though Carlo didn't seem to understand, she knew what the being was, what he was supposed to be. She knew how small he had made himself, for whatever reason gods made themselves small—which seemed to happen in Arcanium. Did its humans comprehend what had been sacrificed for them, or did they assume that what approached equality within the circus was simply their due?

"Do you know what he is?" Sera asked.

"You clearly do, which suggests I clearly don't." Carlo gathered himself back up to his hands. "As far as I know, that's the Horned God."

Sera tilted her head to figure out whether he was just being sardonic or ironic, but nothing in his face or tone indicated that he meant anything other than what he'd said.

"And what is the Horned God to you?" she asked.

"He's not very forthcoming, as you've discovered. Like the Gentleman, he's a mystery that Bell has no interest in illuminating for us. Most of us figure he's some kind of faun, although Kitty says she's seen a satyr and the Horned God is no satyr. I voted for a wendigo who got tired of touching people into cannibals, so maybe I need to back away slowly now..."

"You call him exactly what he is." Sera opened her RV door to sit on the first step. Her legs were strong but suddenly unsteady.

Carlo searched her face, his own expression transparent in comparison to the Horned God's. He was earthly and grounded and as rough as an amateur carving. That wasn't a bad thing. If she touched the hewn planes, it wouldn't splinter into her skin.

"You're not joking," he said. "You're telling me he's *the* Horned God. An actual deity."

"He is *a* Horned God. There are a handful of them, but only a handful. It shouldn't surprise you. Jinn are demigods in their own right, demons of the Ringmaster's ilk princes of hell. Arcanium is a circus of gods and monsters before Bell even brings in the freaks. Did you not know this?"

"We all know Bell is more than he appears. We saw it when he took Arcanium back. But Arcanium wouldn't be as effective if people weren't inclined to be easily fooled." Carlo shrugged. "Perception is imperfect. You stick some latex and fake blood on my legs, and I've had a few people call nine-one-one because they thought I'd really been sawed in half. If Bell and the Horned God want to fool us, is it any wonder they succeed?"

Sera smiled, this time simply unable to hold it back, though she was ashamed of how her broken half might show such a smile. She liked Carlo. She liked what was underneath the surface, because it wasn't what she'd expected either.

"Am I supposed to bow to him, too?" He glanced in the direction of wherever the Horned God laid his head in the evenings.

The thought of him cooped up in an RV seemed cruel to her—far more likely that he was one of the cast members who slept in open air. It was tempting to do the same. She would have to get used to a diurnal schedule eventually but not tonight. She didn't expect that she'd be able to sleep at all.

"If he hasn't required it, then no," she said. "It's our courtesy, not yours. He came here of his own free will, knowing what I knew as well."

"Which is what?"

"That we were trading honor for safety."

Carlo considered her reply, his eyes all the darker against the memory of white. Warmer. Sweet. Sane. "Is that why people like you come to Arcanium? Because it's safe?"

"It's why I came."

"It's been unsafe before."

"They're still here, aren't they? And here I am."

Carlo laughed a little. "You know, that actually makes me feel better. Good night, tiny dancer."

"Good night, weird acrobat." All at once, it wasn't so difficult to infuse her words with affection. Even in the midst of the interrogation, he'd been nothing but kind, when he could have distrusted her completely from the beginning. After all, he had earned far more wariness of her kind from direct experience than she had his kind from mere tales told by others.

Chapter Four

She spent the night reading on the picnic tables, alone but for the chatter of other nocturnal creatures and the odd sounds around her that she recognized as an attempt at sex in privacy. With her faerie hearing, it simply wouldn't be as private as they'd like.

It wasn't very private in the fae world either for the same reason, no matter how well they insulated the rooms, so hearing such things wasn't unusual, per se, but she couldn't remember the noises unsettling her so.

She was uncomfortable, restless, desirous, from resisting for so long. She'd had bad days—bad weeks, really—but she'd grown accustomed to the discomfort when it surfaced, resilient until it subsided on its own.

When everyone else settled, so did she, and she was able to go to sleep after dawn, although the circus opened only a few hours later, before which Bell knocked on her door.

"You'll want this." He held out his hand, a darkened contact lens in the center of his palm. "Your sight will be no different than that of our humans, so you'll still squint when it's bright, but it won't be such a knife in your eye. Look up and carefully place…just like that."

She'd worn contacts before for masquerades. Like hair dye, the fae had grown fond of character contacts when their own uniqueness wasn't enough for the more elaborate of their feasts or more innocuous contacts to obscure their strangeness when moving among humans.

"There's no need to change," he continued. "You won't be performing yet. Your improvised dance was inspired, of course, but we'll want a tighter routine choreographed to music you choose. Were you wished in against your will, I would give you everything you need, and I will boost your proficiency, but you already have many of the skills, and I think you'll enjoy discovering what you want to do yourself. Most of my acrobats and dancers go that route. It fills the time and gives them more of a sense of accomplishment. Some of the humans in my circus don't quite understand time. You do, don't you, love?"

Humans thought they lived so long, that a lifetime was forever. But elephants sometimes outlived them. Tortoises could live to well over a hundred years. Immortals didn't understand time in terms of life, because forever was all too possible. Their experience of time was so much slower. In their immortality, the fae believed in patience and savoring, but there was also the risk of numbness, becoming jaded when new experiences were in short supply.

Arcanium was a small world and, as she'd already noted, barely variant. Anything that whiled the hours and stimulated her brain would be welcomed. She doubted the aerial silks would be the only skill she would take on while under Bell's reign, not if she stayed as long as she thought he would have her.

When Sera pulled the hood of her sweatshirt over her head again, Bell did nothing to stop her, simply gave her a hand down to the ground and allowed her to adjust to the brightness. The darkened contact helped, but it still took a moment.

"Today, you don't have to be one of my oddities. You were so busy searching for me yesterday that I don't believe you really saw Arcanium. You'll have plenty of time to do so, of course, but when you join my oddities, either on the Row or walking the grounds, I want you to have an idea of how you'll comport yourself."

"I wasn't planning on demanding that people kneel."

"Well, you can if you want to. With the right accessories, such as that crystal diadem you came in with and a lovely white riding crop, you might be able to convince people to play along. Perhaps even with some sincerity, if you ask it of the right people." The creak of his black leather pants—like Carlo's but clinging to his legs down to his ankles—punctuated the unnuanced innuendo. "It won't be for the reason you're used to, but you can still enjoy a man on his knees if it pleases you. Valorie would lead John on a leash all through the circus, but she once managed to talk five other men into crawling behind them for over an hour."

"I doubt they'll be falling over themselves to fall to their knees for me, Bell. I understand that you're teasing, but I'm just not in the humor for it."

Bell stopped them halfway to the circus. A line was already forming on the other side of the gate, waiting for the wrought iron to open and welcome them in.

"I understand your self-pity," he said. "It's not unwarranted, and I don't intend to diminish it. Being a freak is not the exploitative entertainment among the fae as it can be among humans, so rarely does it happen. But when I respond to the lies that your heart tells you, it's not to make you feel better, merely to correct what you assume to be true."

Sera shifted her thighs, pressed them together, as Bell lowered himself to his knees. He didn't break his gaze from hers all the way down until he sat on his heels.

The gesture was more informal than what she had shown to the Horned God, as well as what he'd shown to her, but it wasn't patronizing either, the kind of thing a man might do if he believed she was a child. It didn't bring him to her level. It brought him lower.

Even without the formality, Bell had to understand what that action meant. Just as it was unthinkable for a Horned God to bow to the ground for a faerie princess, it was unthinkable for a jinni like Bell to kneel—except for one purpose. And no one had ever knelt before her for that purpose.

"No one has ever knelt before you for that purpose because you couldn't accept it, because your nobility chooses to prize magic built through years and years of self-denial. I'm not partial to such magic myself, as you might imagine. My kind is far too fond of pleasure and the power within it to deny themselves anything freely given."

"I'm not freely giving anything, and I can't imagine that *I* am what you've wanted since Maya disappeared."

He tightened his hold on his thighs for a moment, digging his fingers into the muscle, almost too hard. "That's a low cut, even for you."

"I didn't mean to hit the mark quite so deeply."

"But you knew you would hit a mark." Bell sighed, but he still didn't look away, and he loosened the tension in his hands. "You sought a mark because you're afraid."

"What am I afraid of?"

"You're afraid I'm right. You don't understand how the damage done to your face hasn't translated to having to ring the bells of Notre-Dame or terrorize young ingenues in Paris Opera basements. It limited your prospects among those offering their hand to join with the royal family, but it didn't eliminate them, even if no other offer would have been as lucrative. And now that you've joined Arcanium, diplomacy no longer has to be considered when it comes to whose proposal you accept."

"No one is going to ask a disfigured circus aerialist to marry them, Bell. Even if someone forges an obsession with one of your freaks, your circus is too impermanent."

"You're free to get married, of course, but I'm not talking about marriage. You are no longer part of your parents' ring. They signed you away, and you signed yourself to me. You're no longer subject to the obligations of a princess. You were prepared to yield your celibacy magic to your husband only last night. What difference will it make if you release it now with anyone of your choosing?"

"If I break my fast with one of your people, does that tie my celibacy magic to Arcanium through my wish?" She couldn't think of why Bell would be so inclined to get her to sleep with someone in his circus unless he could get a piece of the magic released in the act.

"I don't need your power, Sera. I don't need your magic. I don't even need your performances. If you are in Arcanium, it is because it pleases me, and it pleases me because I want to help you, not because of anything you can do for me. I didn't bring you into Arcanium to ask you into my bed, although you'll find I will not refuse you if you ask it of me. I won't be offended if you don't. Not many do." He took her hand, brushing the sensitive inside of her wrist, his flesh feverish against her cool skin. "I will use none of the magic that you release. It's unnecessary and irrelevant either way."

His caress of her wrist brought the arousal awakened by the sex demons back to the fore of her thoughts.

"Then what is the purpose of this?" she asked, her throat tight.

"You're going to be here quite a long time. It would benefit you to shift your perspective now, because others will start to show their inclination to take advantage of you. You have every right to do the same, to see something you want and consider taking it—respectfully, of course."

"You presume far too much," Sera said.

"Oh, I'm sure I do. But my overextended presumption doesn't extend to the fact that joining a freak show circus didn't condemn you to a hundred more years of building celibacy magic in the absence of any other option."

Sera withdrew her hand from his so fast that the edge of his fingernail caught the skin. It didn't bleed, but the skin flushed behind the scrape. "*No one* wants my face in their bed."

"Now who presumes too much?" He smiled sadly, settling back. "There are only a handful of my cast members who cannot have the sex they want, because I have removed the possibility of it or because they are too ashamed of themselves to try. You do not even begin to reach their level of shame. For the rest, if they abstain, it is because they still need time to recover from what was done to them in Locke's Arcanium. I don't want you to believe that you are an exception among my people, condemned ever after to suffer for another's cruelty."

"I've no interest in fulfilling someone's fetish for the incomplete," Sera said. "I'm not a tally in someone's notebook or some novelty they can win in a carnival game."

"It will be easier for you to deny those who offer themselves to you if you believe that they can't want what they tell you they want, rather than tasting what you desire with a face you never thought you'd have. But you would have gladly submitted to a husband you barely tolerated and who barely tolerated you, even with your unmarred beauty. In Arcanium, you don't need to be content with *tolerating* what you take into your bed. I discourage that kind of sex, and it would disappoint me if that was all you thought you were good for, to get anything at all."

Sera stepped back again, avoiding the subject altogether because it caught in her already-tightened throat like a stone. "You were wary to allow me into Arcanium, suspicious of me as I am of you. Why suddenly pursue my best interests?"

"Because you became one of mine, and I care for mine, especially when they enter Arcanium of their own free will."

When he took her hand again, it was less suggestive—something warm to hold without fear of being flung into the past. It was a relief not to tense just to hold someone's hand, and she wondered again what his body would feel like over hers, what it would be like to have his jinn fire against the coolness of fae flesh.

She clenched her teeth against the fantasy, nearly as vivid as reality without even experience to pull from. "And you care for your people by peeking into their darkness and making sure there is something there for you to watch? Is that how you find your pleasure now?"

"How I find my pleasure is for me and those I find it with, no more. But my people are so much more content when they find someone to fulfill them, whether that someone is a stranger or a lover to keep in their darkness. I am conniving and calculating, but my aims are far more altruistic than other spiders in their cultivated webs. I am no different now in Arcanium than I was as a god who reveled in Dionysian delights. Your kind have invoked me and my ilk in all your feasts. You don't know the pleasure of lips to skin, my dear, of heat against and inside you, but you have heard it, viewed it and you know what it can be. Why deny yourself because you feel you deserve to be denied?"

Sera backed away, wishing she could retreat into deeper darkness than the sun allowed her, wishing that she could return to her RV, with its blackout blinds and blankets. But of course she didn't wish it aloud. "I can't deny what is not offered."

"Will you deny it when it is?" His tone gave her no ambiguity to cling to.

"It shouldn't make a difference to you. I will walk your circus with my naked face to the world and dance without a mask. That should be enough. What I do with my magic and my body is my own."

"Yes, it is. Remember that. Not your father's or mother's to sell, not a husband's to use. I cannot give you away, and no one can force themselves upon you without the full measure of the Ringmaster's wrath. It is *your* choice."

Sera didn't affect offense or disapproval. On the contrary, with her arms crossed over her chest and her head deep in the hood, she probably seemed petulant and defensive. But he would know better. "I'm not one of your young women, Bell, easily manipulated because she has only seen a few mortal years from only one perspective. I have the benefit of hindsight and more years than your oldest human. I would have thought you'd know better than to treat me like a child."

Bell laughed and rocked to his feet without having to brace his hand on the ground. "To me, you're all children. Even with my years, I am not perfect, and you are not so wise. But alas, it seems wisdom must inevitably be gained by experience, no matter how freely the wiser dispense their own."

"You have the wisdom of jinn. What use is it for the rest of us?" She willingly followed him as he continued to lead her into the circus proper.

"My wisdom is the wisdom of ages. I've been god, monster and man. What I seem to you now is not what I was a hundred years ago…or three hundred. There were times I was more human than this, living among them more completely. And I've been worshiped in temples with oil and incense. I've been both beloved and reviled. I've never been fae, but I have feasted with them, long before your birth. You are so young and so new. At fifty-three, you have more knowledge but not much more experience or maturity than a human woman of twenty. In that respect, you are almost the youngest I've allowed into Arcanium, and even Caroline had more experience in bed than you have now. There are all kinds of experience and wisdom, my dear. You'd do well to be willing to learn than believe you already have everything you need."

"Do you learn?" she asked.

"Every day."

He took her hand again to place it in the crook of his elbow. A human-sized man wrapped in tight leather and walking with her—a tiny woman hiding in a sweatshirt hoodie and wearing no shoes—like a gentleman seemed a perfectly odd thing to do in an oddity circus, yet she was far more comfortable with Bell this way than with him on his knees before her.

"Walk around Arcanium, observe how my oddities and performers play the crowd and how the crowd plays with them. Whether or not you want to be seen, people come here to look at you. This is a time of constant validation of experiences through social media sharing, which means you'll be taking a lot of pictures with people. Some of the captions will not be charitable. Even when people see something interesting they like, they often feel obligated to publicly denigrate it. I'd advise you not to search for yourself online, but I assure you, if they ask for your picture, it is because you interest them."

The cast of Arcanium gradually exited the big top tent, some eating breakfast burritos or bowls of cereal or drinking orange juice. They glanced at her, this time with recognition. Some nodded at her or at Bell. Bell acknowledged them in return.

Carlo walked out with an armless black man who wore harem attire that matched that of a woman with hair tipped in bright orange and yellow. When Carlo saw Sera, he lifted his chin in greeting. She didn't greet him in kind, but her dearth of response didn't seem to bother him. Perhaps he could tell, even with the shadow of the hood, that she wasn't comfortable. It was different, being disfigured in sunlight. The night in which she had lived for so long made everything dreamlike, even when lights were on.

"Repulsive things can be interesting," she said. "But they're still repulsive."

"Have any of my people recoiled from you?"

"Do they recoil from anyone?"

"Not many, and most of them are gone now. Even then, someone will come through the circus and fantasize about the cast members who most often repulse the ones around them. You, my dear, are nowhere near my most repulsive. If you had come to Arcanium far more damaged, I would have healed you into something very similar to what you've become. You're a lovely woman, Sera, even with the cavity he created. I've been told that being able to see into people's minds, pasts, presents and futures and feeling what they feel is no substitute for living it myself, but I think I would know better than you what it is possible to find desirable."

"Because your lovers have always been so unattractive."

"They've always been attractive to me. You might not always agree. You only have maybe a hundred years of suspected lovers to consider, but I brought people into my bed further back than that, princess, and I as good as invited you."

"Do you invite just anyone?"

His laughter vibrated through her from where they connected at their arms. "Not as many as you think. I imply rather than request, and I sense other people's desire, even when they decide not to follow through. I don't take the rejection or disinclination to ask personally, even if it is sometimes personal. Jinn intimidate, and I am not universally loved."

"I'm shocked."

"You wouldn't be the first," Bell answered with his own amusement.

They passed Oddity Row, a collection of tents that led to a courtyard covered with translucent red canvas shade. Underneath, tables displayed Arcanium-branded merchandise and crafts made by the cast to support charities. Next to the courtyard and against the canvas of the big top tent, platforms had been set up under elaborately painted wooden backgrounds, perfect for taking pictures with friends and freaks.

"I'm not trying to lure you into my bed under false pretenses, my dear," he said. "I'm not asking you to become my consort or concubine. You believe no one could love you. I'm willing to show that's not true. I'm offering you a moment. But if you don't take that moment from me, I will be far from the only man who asks."

Sera wasn't interested in perpetuating the same arguments and answers with him when she had already made her feelings clear. Yet the more he spoke of it, the more pronounced the dull, persistent, pulsing ache between her legs became. He had to know how speaking of it affected her, which meant he had to be doing it on purpose to keep those feelings and desires fresh, shallow and strong in her mind, instead of allowing them to fade or allowing her to push them away, the bastard.

Bell finally released her arm as they rounded the big top tent toward the carousel, Ferris wheel, tilt-a-whirl, bumper cars, elephant and camel rides and the midway.

"Visit our food booths for something to eat, try your luck with the games, ride our rides, whatever you fancy. Then come to the big top for the performances. I want you to witness the standard we set and think about what you want for your own performance, whether you'd like to join one of the groups or maintain a solo act. We change performances all the time to keep things interesting for our fans and for ourselves."

"I don't know your people well enough to work with any of them."

"You've met Carlo, of course. The rest of the acrobats and aerialists actually come from other circuses. Arcanium gives the strange among them the chance to shine in a way they can't among others just as or more skilled. Of course, entering Arcanium gave them an advantage in skill they couldn't have anticipated." Bell appeared ridiculously pleased that he could cheat in competition with more popular and prolific spectacle circuses. "When they choose to leave, they'll all retain the skills they've gained to earn their way into circuses they've always wished they could join—provided they haven't royally pissed me off, of course, and most of them are too professional to piss me off. It was almost anticlimactic, letting in so many voluntaries to rebuild my power. Then again, the most recent involuntary tried to kill us all, so I appreciate the ease of my voluntaries more these days."

Sera stopped walking, forcing Bell to turn around. "*Tried* to kill?"

"She didn't succeed. And she won't try again."

"Tried to *kill*? You *all*?"

"She tried to poison us. She now runs the second oddity food booth, but I'll kill her slowly and painfully if she tries again. There is no future where she succeeds. Why would that give you pause, pet? Poison wouldn't kill you."

Most poisons weren't enough to break the chains of immortality, but they could be enough to melt some of the links into undefinable shapes until healing magic beat them back in place. A faerie would still suffer.

"How close was it?" Sera asked.

"She premeditated the whole process. I saw it coming from a mile away. You needn't worry that it will happen again. While I am not vengeful by nature, revenge can be sweet." The tilt of his head, the narrowing of his eyes and the crinkling of the skin at the corners told her that there could be revenge on her behalf that would be just as sweet. She found that oddly comforting. If she had more violent magic within her, she might have exacted her own.

"Perhaps I can help you with that," Bell murmured, curling a finger around a pink lock of her hair. "If you release that chastity magic that I haven't the foggiest how to manipulate, I can teach you to manage what you've been given."

"So now you've abandoned appealing to my wayward desire and instead appeal to my practicality. Interesting tactic." The side of her mouth that had been crushed still felt strange when she smiled. It would take longer than a day to adjust to the way everything moved against each other, the shift of her cheek against her gums. The reminder killed her smile. Daylight made it more difficult to ignore what Bell could see.

"I've a great fondness for practical women."

"And hounding them, apparently."

"I've been told that, too." Bell smiled, more gently than a smirk. "Have fun. Experience this circus as my guests experience it. If anything happens, I have eyes and ears everywhere. Trespass needs to be made for me to punish, but anything can be taken back. Try not to expose us as actually magical rather than a circus of exceptional illusion, please."

"I'm not a child, Bell. Do I seem foolish to you?"

"Shall I answer or just back away?" Bell backed away even as he said it, the sincerity in his expression dissolving into the charming, con-man fortune teller she recognized from when he'd let her find him. "Be good…but for goodness' sake, don't behave."

* * * *

Nothing happened.

She'd expected someone to sneer at her face or try to treat her like the oddity that she was, but there were some benefits to being the size of a child. Most of the people over five feet couldn't see into the hoodie very well, and she angled the hood to hide her left side in particular. Some children saw, gaped at her with the unfiltered wonder and horror of the young, but by and large, those who could see her were less inclined to ask her to take pictures with them, so she managed to get through most of the circus without being noticed. People weren't paying attention to other guests as much as the cast unless guests' cosplay was particularly festive, and Sera had hidden her wings. Not her collar, though, which was at least part of the reason why the children noticed her as well—the flash of color, sparkle and shine within the shadow. She could have asked Carlo to help her take it off the other night, but that would have required her to bring herself low and close. She could've asked Bell, but she hadn't wanted to bring herself any closer to him either.

The collar had been emblematic of ownership passed from the king and queen to husband, but the wedding hadn't happened, so it was not the shackle that the bracelets had been to her. Its weight was more welcoming. She couldn't see the colors, but she could almost feel them, and they made her happy when clothed in cruder—albeit more comfortable—garments.

Between the Skelly frontwoman who ran one food booth, despite having tried to poison the whole circus, and the one run by the odd chef, who was so clearly hellborn that Sera couldn't understand why people flocked to eat what he served, Sera avoided the entire oddity food fare. Instead, she chose from the standard menu that the golems served, because a corndog from a zombie seemed like the better option.

At least it was a good corndog. She took it with her into the big top tent, where she selected a seat at the very back. Like most short people, she would have preferred one closer, especially when tall people decided to sit in front of her and she had to move. But Sera managed to find a person-window that didn't fill in before the lights went out. Then she settled against the wooden structure of the back of the bench, unlike the poor groundlings in front of her who had to sit up on their own power. The fact that Sera couldn't have back problems did nothing to diminish her enjoyment of a small bit of luck, that she could forget about her face in the darkness and push her hood back to give her skin some air. The contact she wore even allowed her to experience darkness the way the humans in the audience would, unable to see the rest of the people in the bleachers as clearly, and the spotlights didn't blind her when they switched on.

"Ladies and gentlemen, welcome to Arcanium, a circus of oddities and awe, a festival of freaks and fortune, a carnival of fools with money parted."

Bolstered by the speakers surrounding the bleachers, the Ringmaster's voice resonated with sinister intensity. The words were those of any emcee, but the way the Ringmaster spoke them belonged less in a family circus and more as a voiceover in the haunted funhouse.

Sera hadn't had the stomach to enter the funhouse. It wasn't that she was scared of haunted houses. There wasn't much a human being could do to scare her. But the aura coming from the mobile buildings every time the door opened strongly suggested that what was inside was quite real and not entirely human. Demons couldn't hurt her here, but she couldn't pretend they were anything other than what they were. Humans laughed when they left the building because they didn't know that, under different circumstances, they wouldn't have left at all, and their adrenaline rush wouldn't have been part of any illusion.

She might visit the funhouse another day, when she was more acquainted with and trusted the ones who haunted it. Right now, the demons—including the Ringmaster—were unknown quantities to her. So the humans could laugh at the Ringmaster's jokes if they couldn't hear the underlying menace. Sera would remain silent and careful.

The Ringmaster finally stepped out from behind the red curtain, as dark and baleful as his voice, the eye of a hurricane in the middle of the ring, where he took his place on a wooden platform. He wore boots instead of hooves, leather instead of fur, but Sera could see at a glance that this was the satyr of the circus, not the Horned God. He wasn't one of the horny, Pan-descended satyrs of forests and vales, infatuated with nymphs and dryads. He was a cloven-hooved son of hellfire and blood, a devil if ever she saw one, even wrapped in complete human form. And unlike some of the other demons she'd idly passed—the pale-skinned tumbler who had laughed at her, the odd chef in his black coat and hat, the vengeance demon with her long hair and water-soaked clothes—he did nothing to conceal or contain the evil he carried with him, as smoke followed fire.

"We have not terrified you away yet, I see. We must rectify that error before the evening is out. I am bound by contract to remind our guests that any children under the age of thirteen are not permitted here in the big top tent, and should you linger too long in a place you are not wanted, you risk the wrath and bottomless hunger of our clowns. It will certainty bring a smile to our faces."

At the clowns' introduction, five individuals ran or tumbled from between the red curtains. Two came out with bright orange, curly hair, brown steampunk leather costumes and faces painted like monsters to hide the fact that they actually were. The other three wore black-and-white harlequin leather with as much in common with harlequin skin as harlequin design.

The girl was the one with the sewn-together mouth, and the two men who accompanied her had painted their faces as alarming, monochromatic counterparts to the monsters, but the girl and at least one of the men were unmistakably human. Sera couldn't tell with the third, who was like a blank space where a word should be. She suspected Bell had a hand in the muddiness of his origins. All she could tell as the clowns ran around the ring was that the girl and the female monster were startlingly similar—all the more apparent with heavy face makeup—and that the two black-and-white men were as devoted as lifetime guards to the sewn-mouthed girl.

The Ringmaster unhooked the whip from his waist. The fall slid over the sawdust before he brought it forward and snapped it so hard that everyone in the audience winced. The female demon laughed with her mouth closed and leap-frogged over her partner toward the center, but the Ringmaster snapped the whip just next to her cheek. Had he lesser skill, he would have split her face open, but the female demon backflipped away unharmed.

The clowns and mimes danced to the rhythm of playfully creepy string music, the Ringmaster's whip and the lean mime's riding crop against the sewn-mouth girl's backside as they did flips and handsprings, tumbled over the dust and over each other. Their routine was what could generously be called organized chaos that somehow came together into something frenetic, tense, entertaining and occasionally humorous, as a clown routine should be. The number of hours required to practice such careful timing seemed unthinkable, even to Sera. Jinni-boosted skill was one thing. Arranging such a routine among creatures who couldn't speak took something more important that Sera doubted Bell had provided.

The tumbling and dancing were ribald without being overly sexy, the kind of thing that adults would understand and teenagers would start to get but which would go straight over any still-stray-child's head. The steampunk clowns smiled and the lean harlequin mime grinned, but neither the stronger man nor the sewn-mouthed woman did, unexpected solemnity to counteract the exaggeration of the steampunk clowns, an unexpected sincerity against the sexual humor. The sewn-mouthed woman rocked against the men with utter seriousness, hooked arms with the steampunk woman in a whirling dervish, avoided the Ringmaster's whip only for the lean mime to snap the switch on her ass, then avoided the Ringmaster's whip again to get switched on the other side.

Only once did the Ringmaster snag one of the clowns, the steampunk woman, with the fall wrapping around the woman's neck like a black adder. He dragged her on her toes to the platform and jerked her up, her feet dangling in the air before the steampunk man ducked under her petticoat to lift her onto his shoulders, and the Ringmaster reluctantly released her with an ironically merciful flourish to the crowd.

The lean man kissed the sewn-mouthed mime's neck before the stronger man swept her over his shoulder and carried her away after the two steampunk clowns.

The Ringmaster's platform moved from the center of the ring toward the curtain, turning just in time to avoid backstage. A narrow spotlight switched on to catch the Ringmaster next to the cast's entrance.

"Still here, ladies and gentlemen, even when we show you exactly what might be in store? Perhaps you'd like to know what happens when the clowns get their teeth into someone who doesn't follow our warnings. Because sometimes monsters don't kill you. Sometimes they just want a little meat from your bones. A drumstick here, a wing there… They'll take whatever they can get."

From the false ceiling of the big top, the domed jungle gym descended to the ring's center. Underneath, Carlo held on to the bars with his hands. The armless dancer, Okeyo, in black cotton trousers a few shades darker than his skin, hung on by his knees.

Unlike the clowns and mimes, they both smiled, their teeth bright in the spots, in on the joke. If it was the five hundredth time they'd heard themselves presented as cautionary tales, they didn't appear bothered by it.

Halfway down, Carlo and Okeyo both abruptly let go with one limb to suspend above the netless ground—Carlo on one hand, Okeyo on the bridge of one foot.

Before the jungle gym settled on the ground, an electric violin screeched like a sustained growl through the speakers, and Okeyo somersaulted onto the dust. He shook himself as he rocked forward to stand under the cage of the gym. Carlo lifted himself up to his chin with one arm, then grabbed the bar with both hands and flipped himself upside-down into a handstand.

Okeyo moved like a snake through the bars to reach the outside, his movements sinuous in one move, jerky in another. His dance slipped seamlessly from ballet to contemporary to breakdancing, each more impressive by the lack of arms to balance him. Carlo didn't dance so much as climb the gym in unique ways, a mixture of gymnastics, trapeze artistry and exquisite timing to keep from hitting any of bars as he flipped, twisted, swung and released, faster and faster as the music sped up. Okeyo and Carlo weren't necessarily moving in tandem or to the same routine, yet though they split attention, they never quite stole it when the other had a more interesting moment. The electric string music was more playful than that of the clowns, with a bass riff that thrummed all the way through her from the bleachers to the tips of her hair.

Sera wondered whether they'd ever considered a more choreographed program with each other, perhaps to emphasize the complementary missing limbs that the Ringmaster had called attention to.

At the very thought, a black leather harness dropped from the opening in the ceiling. Carlo flipped himself into the air, grabbed the leather then quickly maneuvered himself into it.

In the fae world, this particular harness would have been indicative of indentured servitude, paying off a life debt by the giving of one's life completely, even one's body. In the human world, Sera understood the implications were not nearly so literal, but the whistles that followed Carlo strapping himself in suggested that the harness meant something similar, in a certain symbolic context.

Okeyo twitched and slithered to the other side of the gym to stand directly behind Carlo as the gym slid back toward the curtain. The harness moved back with it, and Okeyo moonwalked back as well.

Then the music shifted into something more modern mechanical, cyberpunk rather than steampunk. The lights dimmed and shifted to darker spotlights and neon all throughout the room.

The two men looked nothing alike—different skin tones, different body types—but they moved in perfect tandem. Okeyo was the more experienced dancer. Sera's own experience allowed her to recognize a skill learned the hard way, because Okeyo's body worked much harder than one for whom the skill was gifted. But because he was more experienced, he could read Carlo's body in front of him and make the adjustments necessary to make it seem like they were one. And he had taught Carlo well beyond the skill that Bell had gifted, because somehow the movement of Carlo's hips wasn't interrupted by the end of his thighs where Okeyo's flexible legs began.

Okeyo was so close to Carlo that his chest was against Carlo's back, his mouth against Carlo's neck, the dance and positioning less innuendo now and more explicit, especially with the way their hips moved and Carlo tugged on the straps of the harness.

The music and the routine ended with a mechanical groan like thunder. When the lights came back up, Carlo waved to the audience as Okeyo unhooked him from the wires. He dropped to the ground onto his hands, then waved again before following Okeyo, who mugged for the crowd, back through the red curtain.

Darkness fell again, and the small spotlight returned to the Ringmaster as the applause slowly died.

"If the clowns spare you from their wrath, we have other ways of punishing you for your transgressions. You might find yourself in our funhouse, another tortured, tormented exhibit, your misery cheap entertainment for those who pass through. But you might just be fortunate enough to be put to work.

Without a safety net, of course. Every single one of you is…expendable."

The lighting lifted to expose the ring once more. The three albino women had appeared in the center, and three trapeze bars in a line had lowered from the ceiling, too high for the women to reach alone.

One woman ran toward the other, who dropped down to one knee with her hands cupped for the other woman to step into. The second woman lifted the first to spring her toward the center trapeze. The first woman grabbed hold of the bar, swinging hard back and forth as the third woman ran toward her. The second woman springboarded her up to the center trapeze as well, their hands almost overlapping on the bar. They weren't related, but their bodies seemed identical, with identical rhythms, until the third woman released the bar and flipped across to the next trapeze.

That left the second woman alone on the ground. She ran toward the third woman and grabbed her ankles. The trapezes lifted a few feet to keep the second woman's toes from trailing the ground. She and the third woman built the swinging momentum between them as the first woman tucked her legs over the bar and reached out.

The second woman flipped from the ankles of the third to grip the first woman's hands. On the pendulum swing toward the other end, she kept the momentum built going to flip again to the other trapeze. It took a few beats for them to start swinging in uncanny rhythm once again, but as soon as they did, the routine shifted into a synchronized aerial act.

Each woman did the exact same dance, to the fraction of a second indistinguishable from each other, their hair loose and wild, their eyes a piercing blue that Sera could discern even from the back of the bleachers. Their bodies became white angels in the air, ribboned scarves fluttering from their white latex body gloves that somehow didn't rip or limit their range of motion, no matter how flexible they proved themselves to be—not quite contortionist like Selena, the demon with whom Sera had crossed paths while walking the circus, but as flexible as Okeyo at least.

They concluded their performance by doing what they'd done at the beginning, only backward. Safe on the ground, they bowed to the audience.

"It is not just the clowns' appetite or forced labor that you should fear," the Ringmaster warned as the Triplets exited through the curtain and the lights and music changed into something trance-like with a pulsing beat that quickened Sera's heart to meet it. "In a circus of nightmares, sometimes the most dangerous thing is something that seems like a dream."

A woman wearing nothing but a scant bit of black leather that barely covered her emerged from between the curtains with a man in his own limited costume, putting to the test anyone who might have broken the rules. Because if the clowns and mimes had been bawdy and Carlo and Okeyo had been suggestive, the sex demons pretended nothing. Their dance, something between a snake charmer's seduction, a harem dance and a reimagining of the tango, brought them together as though they wore nothing.

The pole that Bell had offered Sera lowered into the ring as the man and woman did everything together except make out and fuck in front of everyone. At the same time, three hooded king cobras slithered from behind the curtain, swaying in time with the woman, their attention on nothing but the two sex demons in the ring. Sera had heard that some sex demons were natural snake charmers, because the world wasn't ironic enough, but she'd never seen the phenomenon in person.

The incubus shoved the succubus against the pole, which nestled right between her breasts and seemed to invite her leg to curl around it. If anything, their refusal to kiss or outright simulate sex against each other—even with the incubus's obvious interest, which was barely held down by the laced-up leather common among the men of Arcanium—made what they did do all the hotter, foreplay as potent in the ring as it could be in the bedroom.

They teased not just each other but the entire audience, especially as they started circling the pole, counterparts to each other, this Amazonian woman and giant strongman. Yet as they lifted themselves from the ground in shows of strength and support, holding on to or curling against each other, the unexpected nature of their dance created an oddly delicate beauty—delicate in spite of the bulging of the man's gleaming muscles and brute strength, in spite of the way they both seemed like they'd fall out of their costumes at any moment.

From the first wave of magic from them, full-proof and unhindered as hurricane-force wind, Sera gasped, barreled back against the wooden brace of the bleachers. She recognized manipulative magic like fingers on her skin and inside of her, resented the intrusion even as she closed her eyes and bit her lip against a moan. At first, she thought the reddening of the light in the room was a creative decision, but as waves rippled from them with the beat, the color deepened and darkened, turning the room thick with red haze.

Sera saw their past less clearly than she could from direct touch, but their magic was a connection to them nonetheless, powerful and dense as it was. Memories surfaced within the crimson fog from every encounter they'd ever had that had sparked such a similarly strong surge—some in unfamiliar places with four walls and a ceiling that couldn't possibly be in Arcanium, some together and some with Neve before and after she had become the Patchwork Pirate, heavily scarred but no less beautiful for it, even to a faerie's eye.

They were *almost* like her own memories, intangible yet *almost* sensory, limbs entwined and moans *almost* in her ears. Sera had never seen sex so blatant and uncovered before. She'd heard it plenty, and she'd stumbled upon it a few times, but she'd immediately averted her eyes before her guards had extracted her from temptation. She'd even caught two of her guards together once—both male, which was why her parents hadn't removed them from their positions immediately.

But she'd only had glimpses, not these extended scenes of desperation and revelry, sensuality in every gesture, every caress, in tenderness and violence, in the demons' knowledge of decades and the human woman responding to their experience as though every touch was new, her desire overpowering.

Sera had known this would happen eventually, but she hadn't expected to be in such direct line of attack, nor had she anticipated how hard it would hit, how completely. She'd thought she would be able to resist, that the years she'd spent building her chastity magic would prepare her, but in the wake of the sex demons' crimson magic, she became flotsam in their tide, a mountain reduced to sand.

She'd thought her magic had grown strong, rooted in the tempering of her lust, but Sera felt small and weak under their spells, ready to sacrifice what she had built in an instant if she thought anyone would take what she offered. But they wouldn't want to look at her and she wouldn't know quite how.

"Seems irresistible, doesn't it?"

The whisper behind her startled her into a soft cry, but no one noticed. They'd fixed their attention upon the sex demons testing the limits of their strength and the far more tenuous strength of their costumes.

Carlo had vaulted over the back of the bleachers to dangle himself next to her. "They're not always this strong, but I always come back here to watch the crowd when they are. They were teasing themselves to a fevered pitch backstage. It's like torture when they do that."

Startled from her reverie, she heard over the music the far more recognizable sounds of people engaged in surreptitious sex. Blinking out the contact allowed her to peer more keenly through the haze.

People clustered close together on the benches, wrists twisting in unmistakable ways, lips meeting lips or neck, some people trying and failing to hide how they'd moved their mouths between someone's legs or how they'd moved their whole body to someone's lap.

Carlo grunted lightly as he dropped himself to the bench in the dark, but he regained his balance quickly. "Does it affect faeries like it does the rest of us?"

Sera grasped the edge of the bench, all too aware of the warm breath that brushed her ear, of how close Carlo had to come to her to keep from disturbing the rest of the crowd, although she wondered whether it was even possible to disturb them at this point. The dance routine was taking too long, as though the sex demons knew they had to last a few extra minutes to give everyone a chance to finish and put themselves right before the music faded. She doubted, though, that anyone who wasn't taking advantage of the darkness would mind a few extra minutes of an incubus and succubus on a pole.

"Why are you here?" she said through gritted teeth.

"I told you. They amuse me."

"No, I mean why are you *here*? With me."

"Because you're a still point in a writhing sea. When you've got good vision in the dark and know what you're looking for, you notice it pretty clearly. So do you feel it, or are your kind immune?"

"What difference does it make?" To shift away from him would be an admission. She tightened her grip on the bench.

"I told you, they're driving me crazy. I was hoping to find someone who wasn't." His breath was hot, his soft voice husky. His voice blended with the music—only proximity allowed her to discern it. With the music, the magic and his body so close to hers, still in leather and harness, the heat and the purr of his voice made her imagine what she'd seen in the sex demons' memories as her own, with Carlo's body over hers, skin pressed to sweat-slick flesh, the flex of his hips, his fingers in her hair as she raised herself up to meet him. She saw it so clearly that it shivered all the way down to her bones, her bound wings fluttering in a vain attempt at balance, although it wasn't her body that had lost its ground.

"Get away from me." It wasn't accusation, but Sera couldn't hide the urgency as she shoved herself away, feeling like a fifteen-year-old at her first peacetime ball. She gasped for breath, taking hold of her desire and pushing it down, trying to find strength in it the way she always had. But it didn't feel like strength this time.

"Hey, sorry." Carlo held up a hand, establishing that he would keep the space she had made between them. "Was I too close? I thought you were… Sorry."

A few people turned, glaring at Carlo because Sera had sounded so brusque. He reemphasized that he wasn't pursuing her, and the rubberneckers went back to their hit of sex demon magic.

"You hide it well." Carlo slid just close enough that he could be heard, not so close that she could feel the heat from his body.

"I've had practice." That was all she had to say about it, and he didn't pressure her to say anything more, just settled next to her to watch the tail end of the performance.

The incubus and succubus wrapped themselves around the pole and each other in a sensual cocoon, withdrawing their magic, although not all the way. The only way to rid it completely would be to finish off the sex magic, and the only way for them to do that was to feed.

"It would be a wonderful way to die." The Ringmaster appeared unaffected by their magic, but Sera knew that was likely a front. No satyr, hell- or earthborn, would be able to resist. It would just raise a different kind of desire in the hellborn. His rich baritone found notes that mimicked tenderness, intrigue. The audience would never know what had awakened in him. Perhaps no one, even the woman he had chosen, would ever truly comprehend it. "If we have adequately scared away those who shouldn't be here, then let us continue in this deliciously wicked vein."

With the sex demons out of the ring, the crimson mist dissipated, but the effects did not.

Sera leaned back to murmur in Carlo's ear, "How long does it last?"

"The show? Three more acts."

"No." She closed her eyes. "How long does the magic last?"

Carlo pulled back a little, searching her face as the lights brightened. "It doesn't end. If it's got hold of you, it's not going to let go."

* * * *

Sera would have liked to say she enjoyed the rest of the acts.

The veteran husband-and-wife acrobatic trapeze team, Lazarus and Magda, worked with Seth, their dark hair and olive skin contrasting with his pale, freckled, blond youth, yet they somehow went together, the definition of their muscles similar, lean and powerful, each touch unflinching and familiar. The act relied on heavy use of Magda's long, roped braid of hair for a particularly effective hair-pulling routine. Then Chelsine presented a single-woman act that included juggling and fire fan-dancing as well as fire-swallowing. As a finale, Bell engaged in a knife-throwing act interspersed with real magic masquerading as illusion with contortionist Selena.

But though most of the audience had settled down, their lust sated within the darkness of the sex demons' performance, Sera couldn't settle. Now that she had the sex demons' memories and her own fantasies, so vivid she could practically taste salt, she couldn't shake them. The magic had seeped into her skin, been inhaled into her lungs, leaving her sensitized and irritable because her hands wanted someone else's flesh to touch.

She kept telling herself that this would only help her own magic, but she didn't think it would, because the lust was magically induced rather than natural. And even if she decided to forsake the chastity magic, she still wouldn't have an outlet. She certainly wouldn't trust anyone else's judgment while under the same influence. The magic would fade, and someone would have to wake up next to her as she was rather than whatever red haze they saw her through now. A desperate ploy to convince herself that she wasn't hideous would only backfire if she gave into the impulse, because she would have to wake up with herself as well.

As the lights came on in the big top, Sera pulled her hood back over her head and turned away from the people in the bleachers—who didn't care to notice her—and Carlo next to her, who now had reason to be concerned. But more than anything, she just wanted him to leave, because she didn't need his concern or the temptation, ashamed though she was that he tempted her at all.

Sera put her contact back in and, without acknowledging Carlo, climbed down the bleachers.

"Well, don't leave me in suspense. Did you like it?" Either Carlo hadn't gotten the hint or he'd decided to disregard it, but he didn't walk too close to her this time, not least because he had to be careful where he put his hands, lest his palms find popcorn kernels or peanut shells. "Did it meet your kind of expectations?"

"It was as promised." The one thing that surprised her about the performances was how much skill was involved. She'd expected more overt illusion, but most of that had only been in Bell's act. There had been no shortage of magic, but nothing that humans would recognize as magic. Perhaps that was why Bell wanted her in the show—because she would bring more than just the improbable into her performance. She could do the impossible—or what they called impossible.

"That doesn't sound promising," Carlo said.

"I wasn't underwhelmed."

"You sound underwhelmed."

"I'm distracted."

Carlo clearly didn't mind that he was still going through the circus in bondage gear. Though people watched them with unconcealed curiosity, they didn't appear to judge what they saw, as though a member of the cast trailing someone who looked like a guest wasn't unusual. From what Sera had seen, the cast mingled with guests during the open hours, but what Carlo was doing now as the circus wound down was more personalized attention, looking the way he did. Sera tried to see if any of the other cast were doing the same thing, which would explain why no one seemed surprised, but her contact made it difficult to cut through the shadows. She sighed in exasperation.

"Was that your first time? With that particular… effect, I mean?" he asked.

"Yes." She ran her nails through her hair underneath the hood. "What am I supposed to do with this?"

"You do something about it or you learn to live with it. It sucks, I know. Doesn't really matter what you do or who with, as long as everyone's a consenting adult about it. Guests, cast, that sort of thing. The crew isn't necessarily off-limits, but they seem to be dead from the waist down, so..."

"Of course they're dead from the waist down. They're dead from the waist up, too." Sera headed toward the food court. Carlo followed her with even more space between them, as though the fact they were going to the same place was a mere coincidence. And perhaps it was.

"I never did understand how they worked." Carlo climbed onto a picnic table to sit on the bench while she got another corndog from one of the less esoteric food booths. It wasn't quality fare, but it was quality fair food.

When she returned, she sat on the same bench, leaning back against the tabletop. "You've been here for eight years. Did you never ask Bell?"

"Bell and I don't really have long, involved conversations all that often."

"Because he prefers to fixate and obsess over the women?"

Carlo hesitated a beat then grinned. "More or less, although not exclusively. No, it's not so much that he's not interested in me. He likes broken things, but when I came in, I wasn't broken. I think that's why he tried to attract more voluntary veterans while rebuilding Arcanium—so he wouldn't have to get so attached."

"But you're broken now."

"What makes you say that?"

"All of his people who were taken into Locke's Arcanium are broken." Sera didn't meet his eyes as she replied, because she didn't need to see what she already knew to be true. "They're hell on Earth. No one expects you to be anything but broken, no matter how well-adjusted you seem."

"I seem well-adjusted to you?" He laughed, this time without humor. "I don't feel well-adjusted."

"You would know better than me. I can only tell you how you seem."

"You seemed well-adjusted until it came to the sex magic. But that takes some getting used to, so we'll let it go this time."

"I'm not well-adjusted. I'm adjusting."

"It's not the end of the world, Sera. It certainly wasn't the end of mine."

She finished off the corndog. "Maybe it depends on the part you're missing."

"There are a few more parts I could stand to lose," he muttered. "I don't hate Sasha and Mikhail for being what they are, but, God, I don't understand why they have to spread their misery *this* much."

"I thought you were used to it."

"I said that you could either do something about it or get used to it. I didn't say I've done either of those things."

"Why not?" Sera knew why she wasn't doing something about it and why she wasn't going to get used to it any time soon, but Carlo had had plenty of time to do both.

"If I'm going to bare my soul with those kinds of details, you need to satisfy some of my curiosity, sweetheart. You could have pretended that your face had been like this all along, and I wouldn't have been any the wiser. Then you say something happened but that you don't want to talk about it. Pro tip—once people know there's something to know, they want to know."

"I don't want to know that badly."

This time, humor crept into his laughter again. Sera hadn't expected the relief she felt from it.

"You know, you don't seem all that strange. If it weren't for the wings and the way you curtsied to the Horned God as though he were the king of kings, I wouldn't have known you were fae at all."

"That's literally the most offensive thing you can say in a faerie court." She tossed the stick from the corndog into the trash without getting up from the picnic table. "But really, in a circus where the abnormal is normal and you're in contact with demons every day, how strange could I seem?"

"I didn't mean to offend."

"It didn't offend *me*."

Carlo nodded to the shadows behind the food booths. "You have an admirer."

Sera squinted to see, but the night was too dark. She huffed impatiently, then removed her contact again. Without the impediment, the whole night world opened—the world she was meant to be in.

And within that world, with a stretch of antlers and moonflash of fur and flesh, the Horned God emerged in his patient, timeless way into the light. He paid Carlo little heed, a single lingering glance of acknowledgment that might have seemed haughty and dismissive to someone who didn't understand that any acknowledgment at all was as precious as an eclipse breaking through a winter ring.

The fur at his waist was thicker because guests still lingered in the circus, speaking with cast members or getting their last pint of ale or last order of fried mushrooms or grasshoppers before the gates closed. No one else in this forsaken circus had the slightest notion of what was before them. They ignored him as just another oddity, something to stare at and dismiss, especially since he seemed to ignore them in kind.

In spite of them, Sera pushed herself from the bench and fell to the ground again to genuflect. If the whole world was going to overlook him, she would not make the same mistake. She would show him that she understood what he was and appreciated the honor he bestowed to those who would run him out of his own forests, who didn't know what they disrespected and destroyed.

But before she could lower herself completely to the ground, he stopped her with his fingers on her chin once more, lifting her to her feet.

He shook his head, forcefully, like the stag he could become, his meaning plain. He didn't want her on her knees before him—whether because they were in Arcanium and such behavior was suspicious, if any behavior in Arcanium could be suspicious, or because he had chosen a humbler life. She'd chosen the same humility, but the distance that a god had to fall to join Arcanium was so much farther. It was unthinkable that he required and accepted no worship at all, even from her.

The light brush of his fingers shifted into pressure, and for a moment, she saw a time when he *was* worshipped—the dryads lowered their branches and slipped from the trunks of their trees to prostrate themselves before him, reaching out to touch his hooves in adoration, for his presence in the forest made them flourish.

When he released Sera from his memory, she fought not to cry from the swell of his satisfaction and pride that ripped from her as though it had been her own.

"It's the least I can offer," she said. "You can have that again."

He shook his head once more, antlers catching like sunbeams in the brighter light.

"Please. It is your right."

He touched the place on her chin that dipped into the cavity, then slid her hood away. Sera flinched, reflexively reaching to pull it back on, but the Horned God created a crown with his fingers and set it on her head. From his touch unfurled a tangle of jasmine. The diadem she wore for special occasions was delicate silver and crystal, but this was the rarer of adornments, his natural magic like the scent of the jasmine he had conjured, heady, intoxicating. She struggled not to close her eyes and lose herself within it. The press of his fingers on her head brought her his memory of meeting one of his Spring Maidens, bedecked in flowers and beckoning him into the same scent that seduced her now, their love breaking the cold stasis of winter.

"I don't deserve this." She was all too aware that they were causing a scene, albeit for a limited crowd, so she tried to keep her voice quiet. However, if the Horned God didn't feel the need to hide such an action, far be it from her to question his willingness to be seen. "I am the last child, and I have renounced my least-honored crown. I am nothing."

"No." The word took a great deal of effort for him, so instead of speaking more, he stroked her cheek to bring them back in contact.

"Not least. Not nothing. Who told you that you were worth mere gold, wildling queen?" In the place of memory came his real voice, bigger than her small body could contain. She gasped as it rang through her more

strongly than the biggest bell in any bell tower someone like her was fit to ring.

"I was always worth what someone would pay, for how I could be of use," she said. "That is why they bear children at all."

"They are fools."

"You don't know what I am, my lord. I am no maiden of spring, and I would never have been queen."

"They have forgotten."

"If things have changed since the laws were first passed down, that does not mean that they are wrong."

"If you had to wish yourself into Arcanium to flee what they have done to a daughter of their own ring, they are wrong."

"Then why are *you* here?"

The Horned God framed her face with hands that smelled like good soil and wet bark, scents she already missed from home. She inhaled the forest and the flowers, briefly submerging herself in the memories—hers and his—that he awoke in her.

The Horned God smiled slightly, leaned in to press his mouth to her forehead. Not quite a kiss at first, but it warmed into one.

"It is not such a bad place to land."

An arrow in his side, a bullet in his chest, chains pulling through rings in his nipples, shackles on his wrists, blood on windshield glass... Visions swept through her like debris floating on the surface of a river, of despair and of pain she couldn't imagine. And yet, in spite of those memories, he was steady, calm, still warm in the present with her. She shuddered as he withdrew, pain remaining phantom inside her.

"Never bow to me."

Carlo watched the Horned God fade into the shadows once more. “I have no idea what's going on, but I kind of love it. It's like a soap opera in a language I don't understand. That's the most I've heard him speak since he came to Arcanium.”

“He said one word.” Sera managed to keep the tremble from her reply and to keep from falling back onto the bench. She made it seem like she simply wanted to sit, not that she needed to.

“Still more than I've heard him speak since he came to Arcanium.” Carlo tilted his head to peer at her face. “Looks like you heard a little more. You okay?”

Sera nodded, but she had to wait a few minutes before she could hope to stand again, so distracted that she didn't even think to raise her hood.

Chapter Five

When Sera had entered Arcanium amid Bell's suspicion of her, she could never have expected that he would be so accommodating, that he would value her input and creative decisions rather than force his own. He joined her during practices to help her pin down a song and a routine in Arcanium's vein, gave constructive ideas and made adjustments to the silks and the lighting at her requests.

But then he would have been suspicious of the demons as well, and he'd welcomed a good number of them into the circus—not just within the crystals he kept in his fortune-teller tent. As fae, she merely added another note in his chord.

The humans were wary around her, but with Carlo's continued easy interaction and her willingness to interact during rehearsals, their chill gradually thawed. They didn't need to know her well, and no one really made an effort to do so. They just needed to trust that she wasn't going to attack or denigrate them, neither of which she showed any interest in doing. No one blinked an eye when she came into the big top to practice, any more than they did when Marina entered with Sin and Kari.

Within three weeks, by the time Bell finally let her into the performance line-up, it was as though she'd been in Arcanium for months.

Attention was its own magic, sometimes. When she was doing the splits on a moving pair of aerial silks wrapped around her ankles, the audience was that much less likely to look at her face. They did, however, look at her face the rest of the time. Getting used to the pictures taken, the stares, the pointed fingers when she walked Arcanium as a cast member without anything hiding her from their view was a lot more difficult.

Her big top performance was a little over six minutes, mostly contained within the ring, and when it ended, she could go back behind the red curtain where no one else had to see her. But out in Arcanium, she was expected to be seen, show off her oddity and accept any attention it gathered, whether positive or negative, without retaliation. She was expected to smile with the part of her mouth that could still smile, tolerate strangers' arms around her shoulder as she stood still for a selfie, the brushes of people's fingers against her wings to figure out what kind of material they were and how they strapped onto her, through her hair to figure out whether it was real or a wig.

If she was in the vicinity of the outdoor jungle gym that Carlo and some of the other acrobats used to perform—as well as providing an extra play location for the children—Carlo sometimes beckoned her over to do some of her own milder bar tricks.

Children loved her wings, loved her hair, loved when she played with them on the jungle gym. And why wouldn't they love her? She was a faerie princess. Many of them sported wings and crowns of their own, cheap though they were. Their casual adoration was at times endearing, other times insulting, but she had to remind herself that they didn't really know what she was. To them, she was a children's character, close to their own size and approachable, as real to them as stories. They hadn't thought through what magical creatures really meant in their world or how the fae could be dangerous to them, because the old tales had been sanitized for their enjoyment rather than their fear.

Sera wasn't interested in dispelling their illusions. They'd grow out of believing in the fae eventually. Then it would be a whole different problem, because when the awe was gone, people lost some of their respect. She didn't much enjoy being dismissed as a character actor any more than she enjoyed being dismissed as a doll.

In the big top tent, though, she didn't have to impress the older teenagers and adults with her successful cosplaying skills or gross them out with the alien terrain of the missing half of her face. In the big top tent, their awe came not from the way that she looked but what she did.

She'd chosen music that was less minor key, metal or punk than most of the other acts. Arcanium had a reputation for sexy horror to maintain, but when people looked at her, they didn't see dangerous. They didn't see horror. They were fools, of course, like people who picked foxglove as though it wouldn't stop their heart. To them, she was tragic fantasy, a fairy tale gone wrong. Her musical choice was more symphonic, with sweeping crescendos within a full orchestra, driven less by beat and more by dynamics.

She came out into the ring, her one eye bright and wide and open in the periwinkle blue light dotted here and there with lavender and pink. Her pale blue romper was filmy, suggestively translucent, although no one could quite see anything to complain to management about. The halter gave her full range of motion, allowing the stained-glass rainbow of her wings to draw the attention they deserved in a sea of the wingless.

The aerial silks descended from the heavens, on the same track as the trapezes. She and Bell had agreed they needed to be thinner than average silks, because she was discernably slimmer and lighter. The skills she displayed could get lost in swaths of fabric—like a woman tangled in bedsheets, yes, but at the expense of seeming less impressive—and the broader silks tended to catch on her wings. Once Bell had thinned them to a better proportion, the cast members who watched the rehearsals had agreed that she seemed less lost, her manipulations and her body more visible and her wings had to fight less to be noticed.

As the silks started moving in circles along the aerial track, Sera climbed them by her hands alone, swinging from side to side in a way that made her journey upward more difficult, because her weight kept trying to pull her down. There were easier and more secure ways to the top of the silks, but she *could* climb up by her hands alone, so she did.

The track allowed the whole audience to get a closer glimpse of her during her routine, though at no point was she obscured. Centrifugal force pulled her outward over the first row of the bleachers while she spun around, one of her legs outstretched behind her. Again and again, she climbed then unwound to the base of the silks in almost dead drops before the twist around her ankle caught her just on the outside of the ring partitions. She lost some drama with her lighter weight, even with the thinner silks, but she offset that with her falls and the determination of each position she held. Almost violent force was needed to keep from losing momentum during those moments of stillness, when tension built in her muscles just waiting for release.

As sexual as Bell liked to make the big top performances, he'd accepted every effort she'd made to keep the routine sensual rather than sexual. With the sex demons' magic still moving through the tent, the sensual was more than enough for her as well, bringing to the forefront of her mind what the silk dance was supposed to mean.

But the sensuality that moved through her only heightened her performance, her limbs supple, creating strong lines and curves even to her own eyes. When she was in the midst of movement she associated with her old world, it was easier to forget that she wasn't beautiful, that her face was the jarring flaw that made her performance part of Bell's oddity circus rather than something pure and lovely on its own.

The first four-and-a-half minutes of the song showcased technique. The audience knew, though, with the sudden quiet then steady building of the orchestra, that something more amazing was coming. Everything she'd done had earned gasps and soft expressions of amazement and wonder, especially when she came so close to them that the silk fluttered in their faces. But a performer didn't offer their best tricks at the beginning without the artistic arc falling flat. In spite of all she'd done, the disappointment would be all they remembered.

The volume suddenly fell out of the music before rushing back in with a burst of sound. Sera wound the silks around one ankle, dropped then opened her wings. In full flight, they wouldn't be seen as clearly—a blur of glimmering color, like sunstone and opal turning to dust behind her. To human eyes, she would seem to hover in the air, drawing the silk behind her as she flew ahead of the track. She had to stay steady, because they had to assume it was some kind of harness they couldn't see, even though the ring lighting expanded as she flew right above the middle of the bleachers with no structure under the silk costume and no glint of transparent wire.

It was precisely what they'd come to expect from Arcanium, whether new guests or regular fans—impossible yet somehow possible and all-the-more awesome because of it. The fact that it would impress them more if she weren't actually flying was a point of amusement, but the added thrill of being able to fly in front of humans coursed through her with the pulse of her blood. In Arcanium, she could get away with being exactly what she was—like Bell, like the demons and like the Creature and the Horned God before her.

She brought herself back into the ring with the softening of the song, curling herself around the silk and winding the fabric around herself again for one more drop all the way down to the floor. She landed in a crouch with her wings spread and unencumbered. The landing wasn't gentle on her feet or her shins, but whatever damage she did to herself repaired quickly.

Sera closed her eyes through the rush of applause, waited for darkness that to the audience would seem complete. Then she ran through the curtain before Bell and Selena's act began.

* * * *

Outside the big top, the circus crowd had thinned considerably. Families with children younger than teenagers had already left, of course, per circus policy emphasized through signage as well as circus criers fifteen minutes before curfew. Having the clowns as the first act in the big top performances gave people a grace period of up to twenty minutes, but then the clowns had free rein. Their pheromones suffused the circus, excitement ripe, sharp and wild through the night air.

The oddities who didn't perform in the big top still milled through Oddity Row and in the courtyard. The midway was also still running, the rides still active. But performances among the guests had ended for the night, and without children to amuse, Sera was less useful after dark.

She was hungry, thrown by the schedule that open hours demanded of her and restless, with nothing to distract her from the new silken layer of sex demon magic wrapped inside her, multiple weeks' worth now.

Instead of going by the food booths—which she would definitely visit later—she walked until she reached the iron fence at the edge of the circus. The iron pushed against her magic, sour as poison gas. As long as she didn't touch it, she was fine, and it acted as a natural wall around Bell's magic, spells that had woven like a spiderweb dome around the entire circus. And like spiderweb, it was flexible, remolding itself when circus traveled, then expanding again wherever they landed. Fragile spider-silk balloons followed the voluntaries whenever they'd leave the safety of the circus.

Not many people did so, though, even during the week. Both old and new cast were far more likely to call food and entertainment in. Between Wi-Fi, the food booths, Skelly karaoke and a book club, no one really *had* to leave Arcanium.

Sera walked the fence line. The borders of the circus reached farther than the end of the midway and Oddity Row to leave room for portable or public toilets well away from the fray and to give the caravan distance from the guests. From where she walked, the carnival lights of the circus were visible, the music from the midway and rides audible, but they were distant, faint. She felt far enough away that it was like she wasn't in Arcanium at all.

The fence edged against a wooded area. They weren't quite woods, given how close they were to the nearest city, but places where trees had been preserved along a flowing creek. Sera could smell coyotes, rabbits, even a bobcat who passed close to the water. Controlled wilderness, not the forests of home—close enough for her solitude. The restlessness didn't disappear, but it lessened without anything to latch onto. There was no one out here to desire, no one who'd featured in any of the lurid fantasies she'd thought she'd outgrown several decades ago.

She'd been right that resisting the sex demons wouldn't do anything for her chastity magic. She'd tried to bolster it with each new wave, like pushing rocks into the sinking foundation of a home, but in spite of the struggle, she'd noticed no discernable difference, which was reason enough to forsake the effort. She'd already been prepared to forsake it on her wedding night. There was no practical reason to continue holding back.

No practical reason. She'd been praised for her practicality for most of her life, but that didn't mean she wasn't still a creature of flesh and bone, as susceptible to flights of fancy as anyone, especially in a world like this that encouraged them.

She knew she couldn't have what she wanted. She couldn't even imagine it, and she could imagine it even less with her face as it was. Every time she fantasized about a man—sometimes one she knew from the circus, others some interchangeable stranger—they recoiled when they looked into her face, turned away from her before they could kiss. Yet another experience she'd never had before and now never would, even in a sex-spiked circus.

She was trapped in Arcanium by her own wish, voluntary but basically in protective custody, caught in the liminal space between dream and reality, suspended between worlds with nothing to ground her, no foundation on which to stand. All she had was untapped desire that was of no use to her, building stronger and thicker with each coat of demonic magic, her blood pumping raw and hot under cool skin.

The walking didn't help as much as she would have liked. What worked best was when the incubus and succubus left the circus altogether, but they'd only done that once so far. Traveling was also a little better, because their effect on the circus was far more diffuse, like the nose-wrinkling scent of diesel. The distance she had at the edge of the circus wasn't far enough. Bell's magic kept it contained the same way the big top held the haze. She couldn't see it out here, but that didn't diminish its power.

"I never expected to find you here. But I suppose that's why you came."

At first, she thought the voice came from the other side of the fence, from the forest, because it sounded like it belonged with the moan of wind and the creak of branches, but no one was there. She turned toward the lantern glow of the caravan.

Salem stood silhouetted in the amber, a shadow draped in fur and leather.

She could scream, but he moved faster than her, and although she knew Bell could reverse whatever damage he did, Sera remembered how slow she'd been when she'd woken up from the last bit of damage. Just because there would be no lasting consequences didn't mean there would be no consequences at all.

She didn't scream, and she didn't move. "How did you find me?"

He advanced on her slowly. There was no need for him to use his speed when there was iron fence anywhere she could run, and she wouldn't be protected on the other side if she flew. "I was motivated. We are not married, but we are still betrothed, and you are still bound to me. You know it, too. It is why you still wear the collar."

"That doesn't answer how."

"Once I knew what I was looking for, you were easy enough to track. Arcanium makes no attempt to hide itself. It's harder to track a woman flying rather than walking through the woods, but your wings left enough of a dusting of magic for me to follow."

She shrugged, nonchalance unquestionably performative, but a performance she could afford. "So you found me. You can't hurt me, and you can't take me away. You can't do anything to me here."

"Arcanium is not impregnable. I'm here within its spells, and I am unharmed."

"It doesn't have to be impregnable, and Bell doesn't have to be infallible. He just needs to be more powerful than you."

Salem crossed his arms under the drape of fur over his shoulders, still as expressionless as tree bark, but in the glint of his eyes she recognized the intelligence that she could not underestimate. His burst of violence had been efficient and clean. Then he'd planned far enough ahead to guarantee that her healing could not do its job, all for the purpose of getting what he wanted, and if she hadn't run, that's exactly what would have happened. For someone as calculating and practical as he—as she'd believed she was—it was her running that had been the unexpected variable.

Perhaps Arcanium was not the most unpredictable escape, once one accepted the premise that she would run.

"You found me. Wonderful. You can report to the queen and king that they must renege on the contract they swore to without my consent or approval, which certainly wasn't necessary but would have saved everyone a lot of grief. I'm sure it will hurt their purses when the gold that crossed their palms has to be returned, but surely you can find a breeder just as suitable. Why waste your time and energy tracking me down? There are other princesses all over the world. For the right price, any one of their rings would offer you the same as mine."

"The payment has been made and the contract signed. There is no reason to search for another bride when one can serve my people's needs now. The sooner we can produce children for my race, the better."

"You should have thought of that before you decided to disfigure me just to keep me with you. I found my alternative, and there's nothing you can do about it. The longer you spend pursuing me while Arcanium's spells protect me, that's valuable time you could spend finding someone more suitable. And this time, maybe work a little more on incentivizing the bride as well as the bride's family. I didn't need much, and you couldn't even give me that. All you were willing to do was take as much as you could from me. See how well that worked out."

Sera cried out as he grabbed her arm so tightly that she went through the full cycle of bruising and healing under his grip.

"You are bound not just by ink but by blood magic," he said through clenched teeth. His eyes reflected nickel in the moonlight.

"My father's blood, not mine," Sera snapped, fighting not to show any further fear. "It's incumbent upon him to satisfy the debt. If he has failed, all he needs to do is return the payment or hand over the bride. To return the payment undercuts my family's honor, but so does handing over an ugly daughter, so you screwed them either way. And I don't see my father or mother anywhere."

"Arcanium cannot protect you from spells already written."

"I think you'll find that it can." Bell spoke from out of their peripheral vision, but when they both turned their heads toward him, he stood only a few feet away, as though he'd been there all along. "As dungeons strip away binding debts and contracts, so does Arcanium.

Remove your hand from Seraphina, please, or I shall remove it completely."

Salem opened his hand and took a step back, neither defensive nor impudent. He obeyed the letter of Bell's law alone.

Strangers considering the two men would believe Salem stronger, no contest between them. But Bell stood without tension or fear that a man bedecked with fur, teeth, claws and bone and who could become a bear four times his size glared at him, although his expression was still blank—to be confused with serene by the ignorant, perhaps, or merely solemn. But Sera couldn't help but wonder whether that blankness ran deeper behind his clear, blue eyes.

Bell's serenity was far from blank, the shrewdness behind the glittering gold of his eyes substantive. "I've known a few of your kind—wild creatures who valued solitude but also loyalty. Not one I knew was cruel. Don't blame your disregard for your bride with the state of your diminished nation. A sleuth chieftain's son should not be so callous when so dependent upon another to achieve his ends."

Salem remained a dark statue, somehow barely lit by the same amber light that limned Sera and Bell. "You should care less for the politics of other races, jinni. And Arcanium is no sanctuary. If it pretends to be, it is only delaying the inevitable. I will not have my bride playing victim in a demon's playground."

"What an admirable imitation of kindness," Bell said coldly. "Demons have tried to take Arcanium over the last two hundred years. Only one succeeded, and he's unconscious now, tormented, until the time comes to snuff him out like a tallow candle. The oversights in the previous web of spells have been seen to, and you, sir, are in no position to unravel them by brute force. You're just one man, and your magic is tied to your skin. You haven't the means to try to take her from me."

"You're not going to be able to keep her. The fae weren't meant to be confined. Humans crave submission to a higher power, and demons know nothing but chains, but a faerie will want freedom."

Sera stepped back slowly, putting Bell between her and Salem—not because she was afraid that Salem would grab her or hit her again but to show her choice. "Then you should have known better than to try to chain me to a cabin in the woods full of your unwanted children."

The Bearskin stopped for a moment, his reflective gaze on her rather than Bell, as though Bell wasn't his primary concern at all—which was either bravado or a poor understanding of what jinn were.

Sera stepped to the side, her wings spread, so that Bell's body protecting her couldn't hide what she had become. Glitter in her costume, glitter on her face, glitter in her hair—it wasn't such a terrible thing. And she still wore the wedding collar. After a week of not asking someone to remove it from her, she'd grown accustomed to the weight. The gemstones reminded her of the home she wanted to remember rather than the home soiled by the bad decisions of a spoiled monarchy.

His attention weighed heavily on the collar, as though he would have preferred his hands around her neck.

"It doesn't have to be that way," Salem finally said.

"Even if you mean that—and I don't think you do—it's too late. You beat me down once, which would have been bad enough. Then you took the time and effort to make sure that the damage would remain until the end of time or my death, whichever came first. At least here in Arcanium I have a chance of eventually getting my face back, even if just when I leave."

Salem straightened, raising his chin in an unexpectedly imperious gesture. "So you do plan to leave."

"She'll give me years before I allow her out again." Bell didn't check her reaction behind him. She'd already known the cost. "Everyone pays me their time, the princess included. And so will you if you stay in Arcanium much longer. We make exceptions for lovers, but you, sir, are no lover, and the circus is about to close. You're a match for the clowns, but at your age, you're too gamey for them anyway. Do you think your stoicism will stay as steadfast in the face of my succubus?"

To Sera's surprise, Salem deflated slightly.

Bell clicked his tongue, his smile not quite touching his mouth but crinkling the corners of his eyes. "I thought not."

"Everything okay here?" Carlo asked.

The acrobatic team, demon and human, had detoured from their way to the caravan. It was not unusual to see Bell or anyone else talking to outsiders, but perhaps they'd been concerned about the way Bell had separated the man from the faerie. Sera was oddly touched that they would go out of their way, even the Albino Triplets, with whom she'd had the least interaction due to the demon among them.

There was no mistaking the break in Salem's expressionless expression when Sera turned back toward him—utter contempt. For a member of an endangered race at a tipping point because of human encroachment, such contempt before humans was not necessarily unexpected or unwarranted, but he reserved a particularly pointed derision at Carlo, so low to the ground and missing his legs. If he thought taking half of Sera's face would depreciate her value, what must he think about Carlo?

"He was just leaving." Bell picked at the sawdust under his nails, didn't even grant Salem the respect of meeting his eyes, showing his own brand of contempt. The air around him hummed as it did right before a lightning strike. Surely Salem could sense that he was as small to Bell as Carlo was to him. Smaller.

"This isn't over." Salem gathered his dignity into armor around him. He still appeared impressive, would be to the humans who could not see Bell's magic in comparison. "You have my bride. I will return."

Bell glanced up. "I hope so. It's a bit outmoded, but I've been dying for a dancing bear."

Salem's lip curled away in a reflexive snarl, but Bell had made his point. He backed toward the fence. The iron wouldn't abhor him quite the way it abhorred her, not unless he touched it while transforming. His skin contained his magic much more effectively. It didn't seem to affect Bell either, or else he wouldn't have surrounded himself with so much of it. Sera envied them that.

"I would die before you could parade me like a pet," Salem said.

"That would be your choice—death or a wish. Consider this fair warning if you try to breach this circus or steal my aerialist. Are we abundantly clear?"

Bell didn't stop Salem as he pulled himself up by the top of the fence, vaulting over without stabbing himself on the protective spikes. A few of the acrobats murmured in admiration at the strength required to jump over a fence by muscle and sinew alone. Sera would admire him more if it didn't make her think of all the things he could have done to her if she'd stayed with him—all the things he could still do if he got his hands on her again.

Bell turned his back on the place where Salem had disappeared into the forest. "Take heart, child. He is far from my most formidable adversary. I knew the moment he entered and kept my attention on him as he walked the circus and watched the performances."

"He's been here this whole time?" Sera had neither sensed nor seen him. She questioned the worth of her instincts if they couldn't even discern when her attacker stalked her through a bordered space.

"He kept his distance and his peace. There was no reason for you to notice him, fur coat notwithstanding." Bell seemed more amused than alarmed, but Sera wasn't comforted.

"You let him stay *this whole time*?"

Some of the acrobats had already started heading back toward the caravan, satisfied that the confrontation had ended, but Carlo lingered behind. Sera didn't begrudge him his curiosity, and Bell didn't reveal any details that were hers to share, following her cue, protecting her in more ways than the physical. For that, she hoped he felt her gratitude in the midst of her irritation.

"I had no reason to remove him from the circus or bar him entry," Bell said. "He came with the express purpose of finding you. He would have taken you if he could, but he knew he couldn't and he did nothing to disrupt my circus. Stalking doesn't get one expelled from Eden, otherwise I would have to expel plenty more. I protect my own when stalkers cross the line, but I never set any law that unpleasant people cannot attend. Demons in the guise of humans, spies, PIs… All have entered the gates of Arcanium before. As long as no violence is done and my people are kept safe, they're allowed to enter, to look but not touch. If I were more restrictive about those I let into Arcanium, you wouldn't have had a sanctuary to run to."

Sera withdrew slightly in dismay.

"By virtue of association, my dear, and an abundance of caution. I wasn't cold to you when you arrived out of some rite of passage. You could have gone either way, haughty thing. You know well that calculation has its own risks. There are some I've had to keep outside the borders, of course, those whom I know have hurt my cast when it was Locke's Arcanium and who came to hurt them again. Salem had no intention of harming you when he entered the gates, and I was curious."

"You were *curious*. Oh, well, that makes it okay that he *did* hurt me, intentionally and with considerable malice, for the same reason he came here. And you let him in anyway."

"Because he didn't hurt you in Arcanium and because he had no intention of hurting you here—only in taking you, if he could, which he couldn't. So he left," Bell said, rational in a way he must have known was maddening. "I obey the laws of the dungeon, too, Sera. I can change those laws, yes, but then I must follow the laws that I change, and this is a law I have no intention of changing, because it has served me well. Locke may have found his way in because I let him enter, but it was not that law which allowed him to take Arcanium. That loophole has been closed. You are safe here."

"From him," Sera pointed out. "But what if he comes back with thirty more Bearskins? A hundred? They have a lot at stake as well, and he has his hopes pinned on me."

"If he comes back with the intent to take you in spite of me, he will find himself unable to enter."

"And if he comes back with even more?" Desperate creatures did dangerous things. Immortals were no different. Because desperation was so rare for them, they often did even more dangerous things than mortals to avoid even the possibility of mortality themselves.

"Arcanium is prepared."

"You thought Arcanium was prepared before."

"You came to Arcanium for a reason, Sera." Bell stroked the crooked line of her jaw with his hands as though she were whole. "I am humbler now but even more confident of my circus than ever. Trust your own judgment, if not mine."

For a moment, a vision surfaced of a woman with long, dark hair and bare legs walking down a sidewalk, passing under a streetlight and into a sea of cars.

Bell shut the memory away like slamming a door, though he didn't jerk his hands away, didn't punish her for letting his own guard down.

"I won't tell you to get some sleep," he said, "but do get some rest. He won't return tonight. Sasha will be patrolling the circus, and he knows better than to risk crossing her path."

This time, curiosity got the better of her. "What did you see?"

"Salem may be less connected to the emotions that you and I enjoy in abundance, but desire doesn't have anything to do with those emotions. He would have enthusiastically replenished his race's numbers, even if he hadn't cared whether you were satisfied in the process."

Sera wrenched her face from his touch. "Then he *would* have hurt me again. And he plans to hurt me if he takes me away. Is that not enough?"

"You quite mistake me. He would have had no interest in hurting you further. But you would have fulfilled duty alone. He would not have taken care of what you need—what you don't even know you need, because you refuse to take advantage of more than the haven of Arcanium." He patted her cheek gently then nodded to Carlo. "Her act reads well from the crowd, doesn't it?"

"As pretty as the gemstones in her collar," Carlo replied. "I can tell they're real, because they would be gaudy if they weren't."

She furrowed her brow at the affront. "I don't want to be gaudy."

"Didn't I just say it wasn't?"

"It's either gaudy or it isn't, whether it's real or not."

"And with that, I give my leave. Good night, children." Bell bowed to them with his customary flourish, somehow both ironic and unironic, then headed back toward the big top, leaving Sera and Carlo alone in the middle of entirely much-too-empty field between them and anyone else.

Chapter Six

"So this is in no way awkward," Carlo said. "Hungry?"

"I was trying to get some energy out, not put it in." Sera continued her walk along the fence border of Arcanium.

Carlo hesitated then decided to join her, with enough space between them that suggested he'd leave her alone if she asked. But although Carlo couldn't do anything against Salem, Sera didn't really want to be alone. She could see in the dark, but darkness was still where dark things lurked.

"You handle it better than most of us." Carlo resolutely stared ahead of them as she glanced over. Although she didn't mean to look farther down, she couldn't help it. The way most of the men's leather pants were laced was specially designed to hold a large man in, like a luxury chastity belt. It made sense for a circus that tried to be welcoming to families with small children. But Carlo's weren't the only leather pants tested by biology. They held but showed enough to titillate those who knew what they were looking at, looking for.

No more salacious than the Olympics, perhaps, but it was difficult to unsee, especially with the incubus magic running through her veins like dark red silk.

"And the rest of you handle it by..."

"Finding someone. Or someones. Most of us have at least one person here that we can...you know, exercise all the restless energy out on."

"You don't have to use euphemisms around me," Sera said. "We both know what you're talking about, and I much prefer being direct."

"Okay. You just seemed a little squeamish about the whole thing, and I didn't know if you'd go all shy Catholic schoolgirl with the dirty talk. Most of us find someone to fuck. Not everyone has someone. Not everyone is interested. Some people don't fuck with people on the inside. Some people *only* fuck with people on the inside. Some people will fuck just about anyone who asks. No one fucks the sex demons except Neve, because she's the only one who doesn't die from it. The Ringmaster only has Kitty. Other than that, it's Woodstock and a swinger's party around here. By all accounts, Lennon's got himself a whole harem."

He was right. She felt like she went all shy Catholic schoolgirl when he talked about it as directly as she'd asked, but in a circus like this, she couldn't afford to keep blushing about it. She was just glad Carlo probably couldn't see.

"Bell's got only one rule. Everyone needs to be a consenting adult. Well, two rules. You can't kill anyone with the kind of sex you're having. You can make it kinky as hell, but unless you're the sex demons punishing trespassers, there's no death involved. You know, with all the variety we get around here, I don't think we've had an actual necrophiliac. Go figure."

"Is there any other way?" Sera asked. "Any at all?"

Carlo stopped pretending they were just on a walk. He settled down on his stumps and waited for Sera to realize he was no longer with her. "What's going on? Bell says you refuse to do what needs to be done. You wouldn't be the first or the only, but people usually have reasons. And it's going to be tough, whatever reason it is, because no, there isn't another way. I don't know if you've figured out that rubbing one out doesn't help, but in case you haven't, it doesn't. The only way to break the sex demons' hold on you is to have sex, which sucks when you don't want sex. Believe me."

Sera crossed her legs and lowered herself to the ground. For the first time, with his head higher than hers, she had a better understanding of how Carlo would be with legs, if ever he chose to have them, and he impressed Sera as one of the few who wouldn't change the circumstances of his oddity. He'd had it since birth. Very little of what he did was an accommodation or adjustment. It was simply the way his life was.

The closest analog in her own experience was living with wings. Some of the humans asked her how she sat, whether the wings hurt when they bent, how the physics worked, whether they would damage them by touching them. Sera answered all their questions with the bewildered simplicity of someone who'd never had to ask, much less answer those questions before, because she'd always been around people who were either fae or had grown up around them.

"You don't want sex either?" she asked.

Carlo stared down at the ground, but his gaze was a thousand miles away, and the animation in his face dissolved into weariness. All the dips and grooves deepened and darkened like bruises, rifts, scars. "I'd like to say that answer's an easy one, but it's not. The fae understand transaction, yeah? This for that, quid pro quo?"

Sera nodded. They weren't always conning others, but trickery and trade usually comprised their interactions with humans. Sera hadn't entered Arcanium with the aim to manipulate or degrade the humans she would have to live with, but she recognized in herself the impulse for an even exchange—or one that favored her, when she could gain it.

And in Arcanium, it was so difficult to gain. Bell had arranged the balance of power to favor the weak. Smiling for photos with guests wasn't exactly in her nature, but it was her job now.

"Well, *I'm* not usually like that, but I'd feel better with some of that Latin shit right now. Who was the man just thrown out of Arcanium? Because he did this to you, and I want to know why." Carlo didn't quite look up as he stroked his fingers through the air where her face would have been, had it been whole.

Sera almost stood up again to return to the caravan alone, abandoning the dark, low pull of her need and the undeniable draw of curiosity, as much a sickness in her kind as his. But he had almost all of his answer anyway from what he'd heard. He didn't want new information, just confirmation. She couldn't control the flow of that information anymore, not now that Salem had found her and had his heart set on taking her back.

"It was an arranged marriage. I wasn't expecting anything especially advantageous to me. In my mind, I had accepted whatever my parents decided. Then, even my low expectations were dashed. All the years I'd spent developing my mind, developing my magic, making myself diplomatically useful, and the only thing he wanted was a womb to produce enough children to replenish a race. All else of the time, I would languish alone, raising the children who were too fae before sending them to my ring, where I would never see them again. All children useful to him would be taken from me as well, to be raised by his people. If he had wanted *anything* else of me, perhaps I would never have come here. But I couldn't tolerate a life like that."

"You wouldn't mind being his personal breeder if you just had something else to do?" Carlo asked incredulously.

"I told you I had low expectations."

"Are underwhelming arranged marriages common for the fae?"

"No." Sera swallowed, unsure if this was something she should share. "Just its royalty."

Carlo finally looked up. "That crown's real, too, then."

She nodded. "For immortals, children beyond the first two are rarely about establishing heirs in case of sudden mortality. My parents were obliged to produce children so they could forge advantageous marriages. It's a fact of our lives that I knew from a young age. I watched my sisters and brothers resist the inevitable, and I thought I had them beat, because I understood the reason for pairings of strategy rather than compatibility. I was willing to accept a lifetime of grief for a little something in return. My parents knew that. Perhaps they should have better remembered our own nature before they saddled me with someone of no use to me and for whom my whole life was of no use, only my body—and not because he found it desirable, even then."

To say what she'd been thinking in an exhausting loop for weeks to someone impartial to the ways of her kind, who couldn't see into her mind to know her life, provided unexpected release. Nausea roiled in her belly, but she felt like a boil had been lanced, pain that would eventually ease.

"When I tried to correct the grievous error that my parents had made by presenting an eminently reasonable argument that Salem must have believed would sway them, he came after me in his bearskin and struck me. Then he made sure that the healing magic we carry within us wouldn't repair the damage. If he'd left it alone, everything would have gone back to normal, but he… And my parents still wanted me to marry him, because he'd devalued me and what they'd received from him in exchange for the match was more than they would get from me now."

"Wow. Wow. Really, Mom and Dad?"

"I ran away to the circus—the first rebellious act in my life—in my wedding dress and collar, because Arcanium is protected and no one else wants an ugly faerie. It's like biting into a tofu corndog."

"Okay, first, ew. Second, really? There was nowhere else in your world you could go? Like, none? No brothers, sisters, uncles, gay best friends, nothing?"

"Nowhere except the circus that some people in my family freely and happily took advantage of when Locke took over. Somewhere they'd find so contemptible, they'd never look for me there." She fidgeted with the ruffled hem of her romper. "I didn't think Salem would care enough to track me down. It's not like there's a shortage of faerie wombs he can buy from those who will never get a chance to run away. I wouldn't wish it on them, of course, but I'm not going to sacrifice my immortal life to him just to save someone else's. At least humans know they can die and that it ends eventually. Marriage for life means something quite different for the fae."

"So you *are* immortal? A forever kind of thing, like demons and jinn?"

She nodded.

"How old does a princess get before they're married in your world? Because you look young, like Caroline when she first joined up, fresh and untraumatized. Sometimes you talk like you're older, the way demons talk about the old days, and sometimes you sound like you're going to college any day now. I'm pretty sure the demons look any age they want, and no one really ages in here, so it screws with your head."

"I'm young for an immortal, which is a funny thing to say, because any age is young for an immortal, I guess. But when you live forever, don't lose your fertility and age really slowly, there's no rush to marry. Most don't start thinking about it until they're fifty. Royalty, by law, have to wait that long, to control how soon diplomatic betrothals are fulfilled."

"God, these sound like the stories you tell when the kids ask you what it's like being a faerie princess. You mean you're not just making this shit up?"

"I embellish, and I leave out the boring details. No one wants to hear about the maps."

"There are maps? And they're worth noting?" That managed to make him smile all the way to his eyes, rather than the tight smile he sometimes gave when he just wanted to put people at ease.

"Don't get me started on the maps. There's a reason arranged marriages are so necessary in monarchal politics."

"You memorized all the maps, then. To be a good daughter to your king and queen parents. And you did that for fifty years without rebelling once?"

"I watched my brothers and sisters rebel. It didn't do them much good." She leaned back on her hands, her wings tucked on the grass behind her. "Then again, neither did not rebelling. Look where both of those got me."

"Ever have one of those moments when you realize the games are rigged and the house always wins? I have those days, too. Because staying in Arcanium is the best thing for me. I know that. I could always find a job in haunted houses, I guess, or the fading circus circuit, the freak shows that are dying out. I could be a male stripper. Maybe I could get a TLC series, because I'm photogenic as hell." The sincerity of Carlo's smile died, becoming more of the grimace again. "But I can't imagine leaving. And that's not necessarily a good thing. It's like a fish trying to hold on to the bait with the hook still in its mouth."

He patted her leg, which meant her alarm must have showed. "Bell's good people, Sera. Don't worry about that. I still trust him. It'll take demons another thousand years to get one over on him again. I don't think I'll still be here then anyway, even if we're conditionally immortal in here and, like every other person with an expiration date, I'm afraid of what it is. Bell's not the hook or the one reeling me in."

"What I'm afraid of is obvious." She gestured to her face. "What do you fear?"

"Really? I thought that was pretty obvious too." He searched her for some kind of guile, but she had none to offer. "Your family went to Locke's Arcanium. You know what they did to us. I don't know about fae, and the demons seem no worse for the wear for some reason, but humans don't bounce back from that as quickly, if at all. Some of us left, and I'm pretty sure some of them had Bell wipe their memories, because I don't think Jane…Joanne—I don't know which was the real name—I don't think she could function in the real world as she was. It doesn't matter what the sex demons do to us. Really, the fact they still send out the same vibes as always… It's a slap in the face."

"Because you *don't* want sex."

"No, because I *want* sex. Ever since I first came to Arcanium, it was like being in the middle of the most appetizing buffet and I'm the hungriest I've ever been. I've always been fairly indiscriminate in what I like, and Arcanium takes that and ratchets it up to a hundred and ten almost all the time. Before Arcanium was taken over, that wasn't a problem. I always had an outlet. I had Misha for a good four years, but after Locke… I don't blame him for leaving. I don't blame any of them for leaving. I wouldn't have been able to fuck him anyway, not after what we went through. Do you know what Locke did to me?"

Carlo twisted his upper body, shifting his shoulders to bring the scars on his arm and shoulder into the dim light. "He took my arms. He took mine like Christina's and the Voodoo Torso's, then suspended us when we weren't being used. He'd remove the hooks when we'd been sold, and for a time, our backs wouldn't hurt so much, but that didn't matter, because everything else hurt, and we couldn't do anything to fight back. If we weren't muzzled, we were ring-gagged. I come back here, I keep all the memories, I don't leave and Sasha and Mikhail are right back to doing what they do. I know they can't help it. Having Neve as their personal plaything would test the resolution of a saint, but goddamn it..."

Carlo slammed his fists into the dirt, which made Sera jump. He must have realized that the sound and sight of a blow wouldn't do much for her either. He offered his apology in demeanor, if not in word.

"The energy they send off when they know they're going to get a good feed and while they're getting it is completely different from when they've had to hold back. They used to be starving all the time and that was difficult, but this new energy is hot and sensual, sexual, mental and emotional as well as physical— not just wanting release but satisfaction. And I don't know about you, sweetheart, but I'm getting it from both the incubus and the succubus, because I swing both ways really hard. Always have. So I get the full measure of Sasha's power and the full measure of Mikhail's, and I was already a horny fucker before I joined Arcanium. It didn't used to bother me, but now when I... It's much harder to enjoy when I flash back to everything they made us do. I can't change that I need it, and I can't change that it makes me sick."

"You've held back all this time, since Bell took Arcanium back?" Sera had only been in Arcanium for three weeks and she was struggling. Resisting for that long seemed unthinkable for someone who knew what they were missing.

"No, I don't have the strength for that. I'm just a man, and as cliched as it is, a man has needs, though I'm not so misogynistic that I don't know a woman does, too. I don't know how much a fae needs, since a sex drive exists because reproduction is our form of genetic immortality."

"What do you think we fill all our time with? We get bored just like you. But that's usually reserved for after marriage, which is especially enforced for royalty, because we benefit from resisting until then. Not releasing that creative energy builds up our magic, strengthens it, focuses it, helps us find our aptitudes."

Carlo broke from the clenched tension that had tightened his entire body. "Wait. You're saying that you're over fifty years old and you've *never* had sex? I started having sex at fifteen."

"Yes, yes, I know. You humans have all your religious strictures against sex, but you do tend to have impulse control issues. We have plenty of desire. We just control our drive better. Maybe because we're immortal. Maybe because we're just different."

"You've *never* had sex?"

"No. Even if I'd wanted to, I had armed guards to protect me."

"Jesus. Do they do that with the men, too?"

"Most of the time. Not everyone waits until marriage, but the royal family is expected to because it increases our worth. Just another reason Salem would have devalued me. All that work to build up magic he had no intention of letting me use out there in the middle of nowhere."

"Yeah. That was the problem. Your husband not *letting* you."

Sera didn't appreciate the more-righteous-than-thou tone that threatened to become more obvious than the hint she was already getting from him. "Look… I broke the marriage contract, okay? I ran away to Arcanium instead of going through with it. I got out. I don't know how long I'm going to be able to stay out if my husband-to-be actually intends to pursue this. Pursuing me at all suggests that his priorities are not what they should be."

"You've never had sex."

"You're not leaving that topic any time soon, are you?"

"Fifty *years, no* sex?"

She rolled her eyes. "And yet somehow I survived."

"But did you really live?" At her glare, he laughed. "I'm mostly kidding. I'm stunned, but I'm kidding. What about the rest of it? You've kissed. Someone's copped a feel. You've held someone's hand. Seriously, none of it?" he asked when she shook her head at each.

"Armed guards, man."

"You couldn't even convince one of the guards?"

"I had eunuchs and mercenaries. They kept each other honest."

"I..." Carlo hunched slightly in thought. "I honestly don't think we've ever had a virgin in Arcanium before. You're as rare as the necrophiliac."

She hit his arm with the back of her hand.

"You were about to go into a wedding night with absolutely no experience whatsoever?" he said, still mostly musing to himself.

"It doesn't have to be perfect. We have forever to get it right. Besides, our sex education is far more comprehensive. We don't abstain from sex because of fear of disease or pregnancy. It's literally better for us to do so. Anyway, even if the fae abstain, we often marry outside the race—a Bearskin, for instance—and they sometimes have different mores. Shapeshifters in general tend to operate under less inhibition. It's a benefit of being half-wild, I suppose. So he would have known what he was doing. He just...wouldn't have cared whether I did or not. I didn't have much expectation for that either, although Bell says he wouldn't have hurt me or tried to."

"There's a vast canyon between 'this sex doesn't hurt' to 'this sex feels fucking awesome.' I can't believe that you, of all people, with actual magic inside you, would be content with 'my husband isn't that big of a prick and he doesn't hurt me in bed.' You're literally building negative expectations. Do you know how sad that is?"

Sera sighed and slid her hands out from under her, lying back on the grass to stare at the stars. Arcanium didn't put off nearly enough ambient light to impede her view of them. "The life of royalty is often one of practicality. Choosing your path based on what feels good is the luxury of the common." She glanced over when he scoffed. "It only sounds bad, but it just means you're not royal or noble. I could call you serf, rube or peasant, if you'd prefer."

"I kind of like 'peasant'." He sidled closer to her, now that her head was farther away from him than it had been and he still wanted to look her in the eye. "So, no sex, no kissing, no hand-holding. What about, you know, personal stuff? Is that allowed?"

"They didn't have a guard there making sure I didn't masturbate, but it impedes the chastity magic. It doesn't stop it, like actual sex. Just slows it down. If you're already abstaining for the purpose of building your magic, then there's no reason to masturbate either. Frustrating? Yes. Worth it? I don't know. It's not like I'm using my magic much here either."

"Maybe you should. Bell does all the time. Lennon literally turns into the full, noodly-appendaged water demon that he is during the Funhouse events and no one bats an eye, because this is Arcanium and they believe it's all just a really good illusion. If you do it right, you should still be able to do what you do without people starting to really think you're a faerie princess."

Sera propped herself up on her elbows. "You're smarter than you look, peasant."

Again, a genuine smile. She liked it being there.

"I've just been here a while. I know all the tricks. You're still figuring everything out, but if you can figure out faerie maps, you can figure out Arcanium. You're already doing some of it by telling real stories as though they're fiction. There's no harm in getting the scoop from the vets, though." He shifted closer again, sitting instead of settling on the stumps. "So, there's literally been *nothing*. You have no sexual experience whatsoever."

"Only what's in my head. Other people's sexual experience can be...quite illuminating."

"Illuminate me. What's that supposed to mean?"

"Chastity magic enhances a faerie's magic. Sometimes, it just gives you more across the board. Other times, it focuses extra on an aptitude. My mother is precognitive, which makes it all-the-luckier that I was able to escape. She must just not have been looking forward, didn't expect me to do it any more than anyone else did. I'm post cognitive. I see people's pasts, experience everything as they experienced them. If I touch someone deliberately, I can control where it goes. But sometimes a person touches me accidentally, and I get a random flash."

"Then I apologize in advance. I don't think I've been all handsy, which just goes to show how much I've changed right there," Carlo said. "But I'm pretty sure there've been accidents."

"Not long enough to make a difference. Don't worry. I haven't seen anything, except maybe…Misha, you said? It was really brief."

"You little perv… You saw that and you didn't tell me?" Though there was sadness in his voice, he tried to show her that he wasn't mad.

"In my experience, people don't want to know what you've seen. Even if it's innocuous, they're aware that you could find something less innocuous if you touched them again. Before I knew my own power, I saw many things that a young faerie should never see long before I understood what they meant."

"You could always work with Bell, then, as some kind of mentalist," Carlo said.

"I can't tell fortunes. I can only tell them what's happened, not what will. I doubt Mrs. Talbot wants me to mention her affair with the soccer coach or that Mr. Samuels wants to hear about his time in Iraq. Not everything I see is of that kind of significance, but when people know my power and anticipate it, the very memories they don't want me to see tend to rise to the surface. It's useful in politics, less so with paying customers."

"Can you block it?" he asked.

"Not yet. Not well, anyway. I can make it…fade back, but not entirely. I have time to learn how to control it. The aim until now has been to build it."

"Your magic must be so buff now here in Arcanium."

"Unfortunately, sex demon magic doesn't really let me do that, which makes all of this frustration pointless." She huffed and sat up completely. "But the point is moot. I have to live with it anyway."

"Why? Because you're missing a part of your face?" Carlo shook his head in annoyance. "I already told you that's not going to bother anyone."

"How many people have propositioned you since I arrived at Arcanium?" Sera asked.

"From the outside? Five. In here, I already have an arrangement with Lazarus and Magda when I can't tolerate it anymore. It gets the job done, and they're really kind about it. They get to have their bit of excitement every fourth Sunday or so, and I get to sleep soundly for a few nights. But I also have a reputation, in and out of Arcanium. Inside, people know things have changed, and they don't ask anymore. Outside, they didn't get the memo. They're usually good about when we turn 'em down, though. That's also part of the circus rap here. You can always ask, but you gotta respect when they don't want to. You, on the other hand, Miss Priss, are new and still a bit distant. You're warmer to the kids than you are to the adults, which is fine, because we actually need more of that around here. You might be little, but you're still kind of intimidating to the adults."

"I intimidate you?" Sera bit her lip through a smile.

"You're in good company. It's an intimidating circus. And you have really good posture."

"Well, among your five requests and your regular meeting with a couple, I've had exactly zero people ask me."

"Would you have said yes?"

"No."

"And people usually get that vibe. Not everyone respects the vibe, but they recognize it. Sera, you're a four-foot-five bundle of dynamite. You're insanely beautiful and look like you'd stab a man in the groin, which would be easy for you because you're closer to most of them. That's not a bad combination at all. But you haven't asked either."

Sera started to stand, frowning. "I've already told Bell not to do that, and I need you to stop, too. I don't need pity flattery to make me feel better when I see what I look like better than you do."

Carlo closed his fingers around her forearm.

It was the first substantial touch that he'd given her, unexpected. His eyes widened as he realized what he'd done, which brought the very memories he didn't want to share right to the forefront for her to see.

The vision was in a bedroom like one in a fancy hotel, luxurious yet impersonal at the same time. A normal-looking bed. Carlo with his arms removed and nothing but a harness for the demon woman to hold on to while she rode him, her long, claw-tipped fingers down his forced-open mouth. He was aroused, painfully so, with a ring around his cock and balls, but it was purely physical, a product of systematic stroking, sensation and the sex demons sending out their ever-increasing sexual frustration. He was helpless and confused and angry and sick, and he knew that it wasn't going to get any better when the golem cleaned up after the demon woman and the next buyer came in for their scheduled time, and the next, and the next, before he was hung back on the rack once again. There was no respite, no relief and any release could never satisfy, because it was never on his terms, never his own arousal that brought him there. And when it was over, there was only the pain, because Locke never let it get so bad that they died.

Carlo jerked his hand back. "I'm sorry, I'm sorry, I'm sorry. I don't even know what you saw, but I'm sorry."

Sera inhaled sharply, as though all the air had left her lungs, then coughed when she choked on her own swallow. "No, it's… It's shocking, yes. It always is. I've been dealing with this since I was a child climbing into random people's laps." But being a child who didn't understand the gravity of what she saw from random people wasn't anything like being an adult with full comprehension of what she was seeing and feeling—and her power a hundred times stronger. "How long has it been?"

"A year. We were there for six months, but when you're in pain, time slows to a crawl and slips through your fingers at the same time. It felt like years. And it doesn't feel like a long time ago. Sometimes, it's like just yesterday—and sometimes it's like tomorrow."

She'd known what was happening there, the way she knew bad things happened on the other side of the world. Experiencing it, even secondhand, from someone who had been there was like stepping into another reality.

Sera couldn't keep her legs steady. She dropped with un-fae gracelessness back to the ground.

"Jesus H. Christ." Carlo rocked forward to help her, then back, because he didn't want to touch her when that was what had sent her over in the first place.

War was usually what toppled her in fae realms. The fae didn't war often, but when they did, it was bloody, gruesome, even sadistic, because some people learned there was great pleasure in snuffing out the life of something that could have lived forever. It wasn't like killing humans. They only had so much life. To kill a faerie was to extinguish infinite potential, and to the wrong person, such a kill intoxicated with power. She'd tasted that power from others, but it had never inspired her to taste it for herself.

What Carlo had shown her was different. It was like war. It was like hell. It was the things that happened on the edges of both, in the places where no one was looking when the firebombs went off. It was intensely personal and depersonalized, pure human frailty when he seemed so substantial now—fear, despair and ghost ashes on her tongue.

"I'm sorry. Really sorry. The last thing I want is to share that with someone."

"How can you stay? Reminded of it every day, seeing the people who went through the same things, wearing a harness, having people touch you..."

"It's not all tainted," Carlo said. "You'd think it should be, that I couldn't ever wear leather again, that a comfortable bed would send me back to those rooms. I can't wear a muzzle anymore—anything over my mouth—but the harness here is...freeing. It's worlds away from suspension hooks. Its very purpose is to make sure it doesn't hurt when you hang. And I stay because...because not a lot of people out there get it, and even after everything we went through, other freakshow circuses aren't going to be nearly as safe as Arcanium. I can run as fast as the average person, and my hands are as calloused as your feet, but I'm not so arrogant within the inspiration porn of my story that I think no one can hurt me. I'm seventy pounds soaking wet. I can't kick, but I'm at a convenient height to be kicked. And queer boys get it even worse. Arcanium didn't suck me into Locke's hell. It was just the venue.

The ones of us who stayed… We're dealing with it. Bell talks with us if we want to talk. He doesn't quite get it—Maya was always right about that—but he tries and he cares. And if we really need it, he brings one of the demons out from the crystal chest for us to beat with nail-studded clubs, which I'm sure you really didn't want to hear."

Sera shook her head, but not because she didn't want to hear it. Anyone who had chosen to indulge in Locke's Arcanium had lost her respect well before Carlo had given her the glimpse she'd never wanted.

"Look… Part of what makes this work for me right now is a certain amount of denial. I have talk therapy with Bell and Troy and crystal therapy in the big top when I get angry. Can we get back to your problems, please? Don't think they're small just because they're not as bad as what I went through, because I can already tell you're going to try to brush it off like that. You were bound in marriage to someone who would keep you locked away, barefoot and pregnant, for the rest of a life so long I can't even fathom it. And when you weren't okay with that, he smashed your face in and took away something that you thought was essential to being what you are. I didn't lose my legs yesterday, but being born like this doesn't mean you're okay with it from the get-go."

He lowered himself back down, now that he was sure Sera wasn't going anywhere. "Acceptance is a process. You don't have to be there yet. But even if people's first reaction is shock and awe at part of your face being missing, their perception eventually fills in the gaps. Just like if I were to take a magazine picture and rip off part of the face. Does that make the model less gorgeous?"

"It's not the same thing at all, because you know the face is still whole." Talking about her own problems did help distract her from his, but she wasn't keen on where it was going. Her insides climbed over each other, wrapping around her lower spine like rope.

"Sweetheart, people want to fuck Skinless. They want to fuck Dez, the other Torso, although he's not allowed yet. They want the Horned God. They want Okeyo. They want me. Each one of the Skeletons has their own set of fans. Even the odd chef has someone. As far as I can tell, the only other person in this circus who isn't paired off is the Gentleman, because he freaks everyone the fuck out, and I can't even figure out if he can have sex or wants it. Brace yourself." Carlo reached out to her, like Bell had. "You don't see anything when Bell touches you, do you?"

She shook her head, although her neck threatened to creak when she moved it. She leaned back from his advancing fingers, but only a little. "He let his guard down once, but he can block me completely. It's nice."

"You could see something when the Horned God touched you, though. There was something going on between you that I wasn't part of, right?"

This time, she nodded, just as Carlo's fingers brushed her unmarred cheek.

Anxiety, more fear than arousal, paralyzed her.

He drifted his fingertips to the other side of her face, the alien terrain of the cavity, where eye socket and brain matter had been. She still couldn't quite process that there was nothing where there had once been something, that her skull was now whole in an unnatural shape, that her brain had rebuilt in a compressed, asymmetrical space.

"Do you see anything now?" He traced the length of his finger down the center of the split.

"Almost. Distant. Incomplete." Little bursts of emotion and image, like photography flashes and the immediate emotional reaction that accompanied them.

"Will you let me kiss you?"

That he asked at all was as surprising to her as what he'd asked. If he had been as prolific a lover as he'd suggested, when was the last time he'd asked for anything, instead of having favors thrown at him like flowers?

"I told you that I don't need your pity." She'd intended to snarl, but the sob she'd been holding back since she'd run away from her family ring finally broke through.

"I'm not pitying you. I'm showing you that you don't need to be pitied." He was closer now but careful, more heat against her than skin. The intention of his touch mattered, because though it resembled what Bell liked to do to her, it drew her arousal forward, beckoned her with those fingers—dusty, dirty, with the scent of sawdust and grass and the fingerless gripping gloves he wore during his performances. They were rough working hands, big and strong because they'd had to pull double-duty for him.

All at once, she wanted those hands all over her, so much bigger and rougher and hotter than her own, undoing the halter and pushing the romper down until it was just the rasp of his callouses on her, while she gripped the harness to force him to stay against her. His mouth on hers…

Sera twitched, because in her mind, she saw herself plain as day, as she was, with his sweet roughness angled to kiss her. The very thought of his perfect imperfection tainting itself with a mouth that wasn't even whole repulsed her so hard that she could have been stricken by someone's fist.

"It's just a kiss."

Even his words had heat. Hearing them, she could believe in all the people who had taken advantage of or surrendered to his charms. He would be charming beneath someone, charming above them, as comfortable in either role if it satisfied.

He caught her gasp against his lips.

Chapter Seven

Nothing, not a single memory not her own that had passed through her mind, had prepared her for the force of her own arousal—the sound wave of an explosion that would have knocked her off her feet had she been standing.

She deepened the kiss much sooner than he expected. He had no chance to restrain his groan when she pursued his tongue with hers, but he adjusted his speed to meet her with each pass, until their moans were so in sync, vibrating between and within them, that she didn't know which came from whom.

She would have thought the indentation of the left side of her mouth would have made the kiss awkward, but she had never been kissed any other way, never known what it was like for her own mouth to be kissed, only other people's. That she'd only had her first kiss when she'd been rendered unfit for the fae kingdom burned, but the flood of lust that the sex demons' magic had built in her overwhelmed that burn with rivers of fire.

He withdrew to soften the kiss, which left her smoldering but without a wind to send it raging through her. Instead, desire filled her head with smoke as he lavished attention on her upper lip, then her lower with a gentle slide of his tongue, which he clicked when she tried to taste him again.

"See? You can kiss just fine. Don't need all your mouth for that," he murmured against her chin before kissing where his words had warmed her. "I've stroked the broken side of your face as much as the untouched side. Did you even notice?"

She hooked her fingers under the leather straps of the harness to pull him back to her, surprising him again. The unfettered sound of his arousal was as intoxicating as her own because he was her first but she was one of dozens of his, perhaps hundreds, and she could still make him want her more powerfully than his own thoughts.

Sera tasted fear because the harness trapped him, but he let go of the ground to move those beautiful, strong hands over her. She took the weight of him instead, which wasn't a lot for a man, but she was small and light, and he was so wonderfully solid. Not dense yet somehow hollow, as Salem had been in their few physical encounters. Carlo's flesh gave under her palms, his muscles inconsistent and strong of his volition rather than a blessing of birth like all the immortals she had known.

He explored her, too, touched the parts of her that hadn't been broken as though to remind her that they were still there, that he still desired to touch them. He palmed her breasts, caught her nipples between his fingers to squeeze them hard, slid his hands down over her abdomen before grasping the curves of her hips, farther to her ass. He'd called himself handsy, and now she understood why. He liked flesh in his grip, savored it the same way he savored her kiss, reveled in what flesh he found wherever he found it. Sera seemed to soften, pliant, pliable, though the fae could be intractable to the wrong sort of touch.

She let go of the harness with one hand and wrapped her arm around him, urging him over her leg until his hips pressed against hers.

The lacing of the leather held him in and minimized how obvious his erection was to guests. But when she brought it against her body, there was no mistaking it for anything other than what it was. Carlo broke the kiss, his breath quickening and harsh to her ears.

"I'm sorry." She loosened her grip on the harness and around him. Without her bracing him, he had to lower one hand to her leg to balance himself, but he still straddled her thigh, and his cock still pressed against her, the leather hot and delicious against her skin. "I didn't mean to push you when you..."

His head fell, his forehead against her shoulder, the thin fabric of the romper fluttering against her sensitive breasts as he panted. "It's almost been a month. I need... I would have needed this anyway. God, little thing, you're sweet as fuck. No one's told you that before, but you'll hear it more after this. I promise."

"Carlo, I don't..." She searched his body language, the part of his face she could see, for whether she'd been too much, whether he would leave for the acrobatic couple, leave her here like this, with the smoke of her lust so thick in her head that she could barely breathe, barely see in the dark. Her eye wanted to roll back, and she fought not to let her hand slide down to grip his ass again, as firm yet soft as it appeared, even better with the leather over her palm.

But in spite of the magic that wove her to him, she resisted. She'd never had to resist someone kissing her, touching her, *wanting* against her hip, so close to where she wanted him to do all the things that had only ever been in her head. But she'd resisted enough in her life that she didn't draw him closer. Neither did she push him away, and to further confuse her, he didn't push himself away either.

"I don't know what you want," she finally said.

His laughter huffed over her collarbone. "All of the knowledge, none of the experience. I've never been with a virgin before, even when I was one. Everything you're feeling and the sounds you're making, sweetheart, the way your body's moving…it's honest. Nothing choreographed. Nothing performed. Nothing cruel."

"You credit me with too much. The fae can be manipulative, even in their ignorance," Sera said, guarded, but her breath caught when he turned his head to bring his mouth to her neck above the collar.

"And I can't?" he groaned into her. His muscles tensed in a roll down to his hips, where he rubbed his erection against her. In this, he was gentle, suggestive rather than aggressive. "Are you manipulating me, Sera? Because if you ask me, your body is singing. Listen to that moan, darling." He ran his tongue up the length of her neck to the edge of the cavity and even into it to the corner of her mouth.

Everything inside her seemed to clench, pulse. If she hadn't known from others' experience, she would have believed that was her orgasm. That there was more, higher, stronger, frightened her—such power over her that she could willingly hand over to another person, a man, a human.

Sera slid her palm up the dip of his spine to the thick wave of his hair, where she tangled her fingers and tugged at the scalp to guide him into another kiss.

She had a vague sense that they were out in the open, that anyone lingering in the circus, outside the fence or walking to or through the caravan would be able to see them—if not see, then hear. But that didn't concern her, and apparently it was the farthest thing from Carlo's mind, too, because he made no attempt to modulate his reactions either. She couldn't hold herself back, even if she tried. She had nothing from which to draw that would help her achieve some measure of control when faced with what he was making her feel.

"Is the grass bothering you?" He panted in her scarred-over ear—unlike her eye, it still functioned fine, though misshapen. "We can move somewhere more comfortable if—"

Sera spread her wings and lay back, pulling him down with her. The grass was dry, and she sensed the low presence of ants, beetles, earthworms beneath, but she was a creature of the wild. It didn't matter how luxurious the fae had made their homes. They could sleep under the sky in any weather, and they still often walked barefoot to commune with the earth that had borne them so long ago. There was nothing about it that could turn them off or away. Even poison ivy wouldn't dare rash their skin.

Over her, he adjusted his position until his erection pressed directly between her legs, rubbing too lightly against her clit, the leather briefs and her thin romper now far too many layers for her. For all the fire inside her, she wanted nothing but skin, the silk of the costume too coarse for her desires. She reached behind her neck to undo the knot of the halter.

He caught her hands just as she was about to pull the strings free. For a moment, she thought she'd gone too far—just a kiss, he'd said—and that she wanted more than he was willing to give. That he'd planned on stoking her fire to make her more receptive for someone else to quench it felt like betrayal, the very manipulation she had warned him to expect from her.

But Carlo pulled the strings loose instead and slowly drew the top of the costume down, baring her breasts, her abdomen, almost below her hips, except Carlo's erection still pressed there, and the rest of her entranced him for now.

"We wear such small costumes that you wouldn't expect being able to see everything would make a difference. God, look at this juicy little piece." He cupped the underside of her breast to bring the peak to his mouth, catching the nipple between his teeth—a startling jolt of pain that zinged straight down between her legs. She rocked her hips against him, searching, needing, begging for something she knew but still didn't quite understand.

He left that nipple hard and stinging and turned his head to take the other all the way into his mouth, kissing it with soft tongue and soft lips that had her moaning high, holding Carlo's hips to keep him against her as she tried to urge his erection closer, urge him inside. Even if she only had theoretical knowledge of what should happen, her body whispered, sang, screamed for it—an instinct for pleasure that she could not have anticipated, even after all her years among the fae and their trysts.

"Are you a screamer? I think you're a screamer, princess." Carlo raised his head from her breasts, replacing his mouth on her with his thumbs and forefingers to keep her nipples aching, keep them hard, as he pushed himself down her body. "I think Arcanium ruins us all for real sex outside of it. This is the worst place to have your first fuck, sweetheart. You'll never be satisfied with arousal that hasn't been bolstered by sex demons. I don't know how Kitty and Victor leave and screw their outsiders without any of the kind of satisfaction we get in here. It's the difference between a firecracker and a firework, and darling, I'm going to make you explode. Take over for me."

He pinched her nipples harder to indicate what he wanted her to do. She untangled her fingers from his hair with reluctance, but she was too entranced not to do what he said. It wasn't the same, her small, smooth fingertips in contrast with the broad roughness of his, but because she was doing what he told her, it meant more than if she'd done it on her own.

How could she have never done this to herself before? No one would have known when she was alone in bed, under her covers, the eunuchs on either side of the bedposts to watch over her. They'd never bothered her, because they'd always been there. She barely saw them, and they never wanted her. Surely they wouldn't have been able to know. Surely she could have...

But she was doing it now, and she squirmed in the grass, her wings fluttering, trapped under her body, each flutter humming through her in subtle vibration, like bumblebees flying by her ear.

"So soft. So lush. God, touching you is like touching silk. Silk's got nothing on you." He had plenty for comparison, because he gripped the gathered silk of her costume and pulled it down with him, baring her completely. He muffled a groan against her abdomen, just under her navel, when he discovered that the romper was all she'd worn, just that thin material between them—and now nothing.

He tugged the costume all the way down then let her kick it off before crawling back between her legs. He gripped her thighs, jerked them open wider. When she lifted herself up on one elbow to look at him, conflict warred in his expression. He smoothed his palms over her thighs in what seemed like apology. But with his gaze on hers, she parted her legs farther, lifting her thighs up and bracing her heels in the earth.

He lowered his mouth to her left thigh, just under the indentation of his thumb in the flesh. "Whatever happens, don't hold back."

Sera shuddered, her elbow slipping on her wing. The fall onto the ground briefly stole her breath, but as his seeking mouth drew higher and higher up her leg, she found all new reasons not to breathe. Between the tweaking of her nipples and the aching of everything between her legs that he wasn't touching, she wanted to scream, so she did, a raspy, growling, wild cry to the stars that inspired her to pinch and twist the tightened buds even harder. He held her down, his hands on the handle of her hips, but he still had to work at it.

He ran his tongue up the length of her folds, drawing away before he could reach her clit. Her cry caught on the gasp of suffered denial. She released her nipples, leaving them hard and hurting, pointing toward the sky, as she reached to either side of her. She grasped at grass and dirt to keep herself grounded, because the swirl and smoke of her head made her feel on the edge of madness.

Now the tip of his tongue traced over each side of her folds. Her world narrowed, quivered, on that point, as it traveled up the length of her to the place she wanted him, needed him, needed his wet, hot, insistent mouth—like a kiss but more, to send arousal zinging to every part of her yet focused on the place being kissed in a never-ending loop. She knew what was coming because other people had felt it, and oh, how she wanted it for herself.

All at once, he swept his tongue, his lips, even the dangerous edges of his teeth up her folds and closed his mouth over her clit, all soft, all heat, all delicious suction. Everything in her body went tight and firm, her spine arching from the ground. In a rush as violent as waves crashing into cliffs, she came, each break the explosion that he promised. She clenched her eyes shut so tightly that she saw explosions there—fireworks, fire and water at the same time.

She'd lived through memories, awoken from dreams that had left the eunuchs at her bed shifting because they could still feel some pleasure, although not the same as that of the mercenaries who exorcised theirs well away from her. But none of it had prepared her for the sexual silk, each layer that the incubus had wrapped around her, swirling out in a burst of deep, dark red. Sera brought her hands to her head, dug the heels into her brow, fingernails into her scalp, and cried out over and over as Carlo's rhythmic sucking conjured a pounding disrhythm that jerked her hips up to meet his mouth.

She felt his smile as he called the first orgasm through her then the second not far behind, galloping effortlessly at the opportunity to finally be released. One would think such a thing would be accustomed to restraint after all this time, but at the moment it was offered freedom, her lust reached out its dark tendrils and grasped at everything it could find. It found Carlo, sank into him like the smoke that had filled her head, sank into the ground, into the grass, curled around the iron fence—even as the iron tried to reject it—sucked away at the spiderweb of spells around her.

It didn't damage them. They were too powerful to damage. They recovered as soon as her lust absorbed them. But even through the third orgasm Carlo wrested from her, she had her own moment of fear—that this wouldn't end, that it would go on for as long as she had resisted, and this was why a wedding night after the ceremony could, in fact, last an entire week, with silence spells around the suite. Fear that Bell would come after her for damaging the spells of his circus. Fear that the explosion would reach well beyond the boundaries of her skin and that the whole circus and the country surrounding it would be destroyed in a blackened crater around Carlo still licking her through each successive peak of her arousal.

Carlo eased from her clit with one last, lingering caress of his tongue and crawled over her body again, kissing and biting the flesh with relish, as though he liked the idea of marking smoothness that would seem uncanny on a human being.

He licked a circle around one nipple before crossing his arms and resting his chin on his forearms. "Hello, princess."

Sera didn't have words. The orgasms were over, and the incubus' magic had been satisfied, but she was fae. She didn't wear out. Her body found its equilibrium as fast as it healed.

She realized she could do this and more all night, all day and into the next night without stopping if she had someone who could keep up with her.

"You're not finished," she managed to say.

"Oh, I'm sure you have plenty more in you, but if you want someone to lick you all night, a demon would be best. When you compete with demons, you do learn to offer a lot of the things they do without the help they have to do it—you're welcome—but in the end, I'm just a man, and my tongue's tired."

"No, *you're* not finished."

In his position, the laced-in bulge of his erection had settled against her mound. He had occupied his hands with holding her down, and if he'd come without touching himself or her touching him, she couldn't feel any wetness through the leather, but his cock seemed unchanged from when he'd moved down her body.

Smugness faded into the same conflict she'd noticed when he'd shoved her legs open.

She brought her hands to his face, the sandpaper of his late-day shadow against the lines of her palms as she searched the last few minutes of his memory—the taste and smell of her, how much he appreciated hearing and feeling how he satisfied a partner, how she was stronger than she looked, because he struggled to hold her down, although she wasn't much bigger than him, really. How aroused he was, the confines of the leather doing its best to hold him but the blood-swell of his erection so tight and thick that it was nearly painful—a familiar sensation for him over the course of years, well before Locke took Arcanium.

He wanted to *take* her. Not make love to her, if that's what people wanted to call slow and tender. He wanted to fuck her like a goddamn animal, every which way a body could bend, and he suspected she could bend quite a few more ways. It's what he had loved to do before, and that hadn't changed. The problem was what had attached itself to that desire, like images overlaid with each other.

There had never been malice in his roughness. He'd always made sure his partners wanted the kind of sex he liked to give or take—Misha, Maya, even Bell once, out of his own curiosity and Bell's willingness to satisfy it.

But now he couldn't take it, because it reminded him of pain so bright and metallic that it could have been blades in his ass, down his throat. Once, one of the demons had even brought knives and stuck them into his abdomen while they'd taken him.

And he couldn't give it, because he couldn't shake the fear that he was doing to them what had been done to him, what had been done to so many of them. Fucking the demons that had visited him hadn't been satisfying, hadn't been domination. His cock would be rubbed raw by the end of it, burns and blisters on the sensitive flesh, sometimes disease, depending on the demon.

Sinking into Sera wouldn't be like that. From what his tongue had tasted, she'd be as soft and strong as she felt on the outside, not as hot as the human women or demon women he'd had, almost cool in comparison to his heat. He craved knowing what her pussy would feel like around him, dreamed and daydreamed about it, just the thought almost enough to bring him over—if sex demon magic only worked that way.

He wanted to fuck her and watch how she writhed, because God, she was sexy when she relinquished control of herself. He wanted to fuck her and kiss her, because he could kiss her forever, all that new responsiveness mingled with the understanding of what she had to do, what she could do, curiosity fueled by more years of knowledge than even he had, and all of the willingness to try. He could give her more firsts, be the one branded in her mind before any man like Salem or Bell. Men of magic and power, yet she'd given *him* this gift, and that turned him the fuck on like crazy.

He wanted to do it. He wanted to give her every gift in return until he'd finally gone completely limp with satiation—which happened so rarely, between the two sex demons—and Sera was soft against him in the dirt.

His desire was not in question.

He *couldn't*. He couldn't with Magda or Lazarus, and he couldn't with her.

"I can feel you rifling around in there. It's not fair when Bell does it either." But the set of Carlo's mouth and eyes remained solemn, searching, as though he understood what she was seeing. He wasn't trying to hold the memories back, crinkling them like paper. He made no effort to resist. Perhaps it relieved him that she would know—know how desirable he found her, know why he still couldn't give her everything she wanted, and it wasn't because of her.

She peeked back at what happened whenever he met with Lazarus or Magda—or both at the same time—then returned completely to the present.

As she sat up, Carlo adjusted himself over her, one hand in her hair and the other on the ground, peering slightly down on her, gaze moving from her eyes to her lips and back. He grunted slightly at the sensation of her movement against his erection.

Sera played lightly with the nipple ring, then drew her hand over the sunflower tattoo, tracing down his harness to the edge of the leather briefs that he wore. She found the top of the lacing that held him in. The head of his cock twitched where she searched with her fingertips.

"Let me help you."

Carlo briefly tightened his grip in her hair, tugging against her scalp and making her gasp again. As though he couldn't resist her when she did that, he leaned in to kiss her, his tongue meeting hers in an agonizingly slow glide that had her clenching all over again, because he tasted salty and musky strong, and she knew that what she tasted and smelled on him was her.

Then he drew back and nodded.

With nudity a fairly accepted state in her world, and with her intimate collection of other people's memories stored on the shelves of her mind, she knew what to expect as she pulled at the tight knot at the top of the briefs. A testament to the effectiveness of the lacing, when she loosened the laces enough to push the briefs down, he was bigger than she'd assessed—not as large as most demons, more flushed and somehow more fleshy than the fae.

If there was one thing that could be said across the races, it was that a cock at rest was rarely intimidating or lovely, even among the prettiest creatures. But a cock thick with lust was a sometimes ugly, sometimes beautiful, sometimes ugly-beautiful organ that held so much power and weakness all at once.

Even a human cock seemed sculpted of something harder and denser than itself, with visual texture that she'd never seen on a faerie—a raised network of vessels, subtle ridging, the circumcised head somewhat new to her because the fae never removed foreskin.

Among the many races, some adorned their genitals, and Carlo had chosen to do so, with a ring right at the base of the shaft, silver and gleaming against his scrotum. She wondered for a moment whether he'd had that done before or after the abduction but decided it had nothing to do with anything either way, any more than the tattoos and piercings elsewhere.

She took in the sight of him, all her own yet somehow unreal. This whole night seemed like a dream—so far from where she'd seen herself only a few months ago.

If her mother had been angry that Sera had refused a marriage, she would have been furious that Sera had run away. If she'd been furious that Sera had run away, she'd be livid Sera had run to Arcanium, one of the few places where they would have no power and already a sore spot for their ring. And if she'd be livid that Sera had taken sanctuary within Arcanium, how would she feel if she discovered that her daughter had released her chastity magic for a human man? One who her race would call inferior because of what he was missing, although Sera knew well how mistaken they would be about that. Missing his legs didn't make him any less of a man.

It certainly didn't keep him from being there with her when she brushed her fingers along the shaft, testing him the way she would test hot springs with her toes. And oh, he was hot. Confinement in leather and a deep flush of blood conspired to bring him to fever. His breath caught, his taut abdomen twitching and his cock twitching with it, away from her fingers and to the side, though not to escape.

He kept his hold in her hair. With the other hand, he grasped her thigh behind him, so that their bodies made a V. She could see him better, and he could better see her touch him. Also, this way, he couldn't touch himself or guide her hand. As much as she had yielded to him, he yielded to her, passing unimaginable power into her hands as wisps of memories—mostly good—moved through his thoughts in an aimless jumble.

His incoherence came from her, because of what she had done, because of what she was doing.

She slid her fingers around him and tightened.

The groan that wrested from him, his head tossed back, hummed through her. "God, fuck, yes. Your hand is cool, cold. It's...like nothing I've ever... Closest I ever got was a hand job in winter after he'd come into the trailer from taking a long walk outside. It doesn't hurt. Most people new to this—most women, really—are always afraid we're going to break if they squeeze too hard. But you knew better, didn't you? Just like that, oh God, yes, torture me just like that."

Of all the things she'd seen in people's memories and from her early attempts to spy, she'd never encountered this stream of consciousness commentary before. It was distracting on the one hand, but each husky word was its own moan, and she was intrigued—intrigued what else might come out of his mouth if she kept going.

With her fingers still tight around the shaft, she stroked him, savoring the movement of unexpectedly soft skin over something so rigid. He bucked but not too much, just enough to show her that he liked what she did, the slight twist. Just as he groaned again, she drew her hand away and brought her palm to her mouth. The way the light hit the tension of his neck, the prominent Adam's apple bobbing when he swallowed, the hollow of his throat, was enough to make her mouth water. She used that to slicken her palm, just in time for him to watch.

She started slowly but as tightly as before then tighter, relishing the heat and hardness and the pulse of blood, the constrained twitches in her hand.

"Now do you know how people look at you? They see your face the way it is for a few seconds, maybe a few minutes. Then they see the rest of your face, and they see your small, tight, *perfect* body, and all they want to do is wrap their arms around you in their bed like a doll as they take you from behind. Not so they don't have to look at you but because you're the tastiest little spoon they're ever going to have. You have your pick of men if you put off a more welcoming signal to any of them staring at you when they think you're not looking. Even the assholes—the ones who couldn't see our perfection even if they had rose-colored glasses—if you want them to fuck you for some reason, you can always turn your head so they can't see what they think disgusts them, even though they don't mind rolling in it when they get the opportunity. They always finish the fastest, the ones who think they're better, because they secretly know they're not worthy of what they're sticking their dick into. You can wear a goddamn paper sack over your face if it bothers you. But you never have to be without lovers—not in Arcanium, not anywhere. Anyone who wouldn't have you because they think an incomplete face is ugly doesn't deserve anything, least of all you."

Sera honestly didn't know how he managed to be so coherent when he clearly wasn't paying attention to what he said, as though there was a direct connection between his brain and his mouth that didn't require consciousness to mediate. She wondered if he talked in his sleep.

Which wasn't to dismiss the effect of his words on her, a confused mix of arousal, disquiet and reflexive distaste at the mention of how she looked, because she'd forgotten for a few minutes and now she had to remember all over again.

But she loosened her grip to quicken her pace, and Carlo's eyes closed. He clutched at her thigh, tugged harder at her hair as he panted through his impending climax. Sera took all of this in, the sight and sound and feel of him, aroused again. She couldn't shake the images and imaginings of him moving over her, inside her, using his grip in her hair to jerk himself into her. She wanted to take the cock in her hand, guide it down to her cunt and hope he couldn't resist, a slave to how close he was. She bit her lip against the impulse, because it would be cruel, and it might dip his arousal in cold water far more effective than her cool hand.

"Fuck them all. Fuck Salem. Fuck the haters. Fuck them by not fucking them. They deserve it. Damn it, Sera, I'm coming. I'm…"

She thought he would kiss her again, but instead, he leaned his forehead against hers, groaning through each pulse of his orgasm, which struck her chest, her belly, then spilled over her fingers as she continued to wring his pleasure from him, unrelenting until he released her thigh to cover her hand and still her.

She almost kissed him, but she questioned the wisdom of such intimate contact after he'd satisfied the sex demons' magic. The fall of energy, the fall of mood, it could all mean that he no longer wanted her touch, that for all the streams of words of how desirable he found her, he wouldn't even want to look at her anymore.

"Is that enough?" she murmured.

He pulled her head back and adjusted his weight over her to guide her back to the ground as he kissed her in reply.

She let go of his cock, slid her hand over his harness and the heated skin of his back. They were both already filthy with dust, dirt, grass, the wetness of her arousal between her thighs and his seed smeared between them. It didn't matter how much worse it became. He rocked his hips, rubbing his softening cock through the cooling cum, and consumed her until they were still, barely kissing so much as breathing each other in.

"Well, that was a pleasant surprise." Carlo kissed her lightly one more time, then pushed himself up and off of her, laughing slightly at the state of himself.

"Surprise? You seemed absolutely sure of what you wanted." Sera stared up at the sky, skin cooling without him holding heat against her, inside her.

"I'm not surprised at you, love. I'm surprised at me." He stroked her hair from her forehead then waited until she made eye contact as he brushed his thumb over her forehead in an undeniably tender gesture. "I feel good. I still feel good. That hasn't happened in a while. Don't get me wrong. Magda and Lazarus love their unicorn time, and I get what I need from it, but it can't be edifying when your third partner only comes around when he can't hold back anymore."

He sat to reach for his leather briefs and grabbed the crumpled pile of her romper to hand to her as well. "It took a lot of trust, Sera. I don't know what you saw, but I get the feeling you saw too much for me not to trust you. Which is another negative, and I'm sorry. I'll say it the right way. I trust you. Please don't abuse that. I'm not the only one in Arcanium who takes that seriously."

"I won't tell a soul." Sera lifted herself up on her elbows, finally looking all around them. In spite of their volume, no one who might have noticed or watched them lingered now that the show was over, and she couldn't say for sure if anyone else had seen them. It had felt as though the world had narrowed to sensation and desire, a column of existence unbroken by anything but their own insecurities. "Are you okay?"

Without the warmth of his touch, the weight of his body, she struggled against the abandonment her sensitive emotions threatened to make of the fact Carlo was a foot away from her. A rush of dread followed, that the taste of her own passion, of the passion that she herself inspired, had made an irrevocable connection to a man she didn't know she could trust in return—the last bit of irony that made up her life now.

"I'm better than okay, sweetheart." He offered a hand to help her sit up. "Are *you* okay? You seem shaken. Am I failing at aftercare here? That's absolutely shameful of me. In my defense, it's been a while, and I've never been with someone who'd never had sex before. Never been with a faerie—at least not this kind. This is new to me, too. Come here."

"I'm not going to break." But she didn't resist as he moved behind her, an arm around her waist, his chin tucked at the base of her neck as he stroked her skin—in comfort rather than for sex, though her body had trouble discerning the difference, still excited, still wanting more.

"Don't knock aftercare. It doesn't have to be a down-and-dirty S&M sesh for sex to cause a mood drop. It's normal. That's why these things usually happen in bed instead of outside in the middle of spring grass." He laughed a bit as he held his filthy hand out in front of them.

A warm breeze rustled over them, conjuring the mess away, until all that was left was whatever dirt and grass they rested against.

"So you have that cleansing magic, too." He kissed her shoulder. "Not going to lie, kind of loving it. Damn useful."

They reclined there for a while, Carlo stroking her through the odd shudders in her belly, every hesitation and resurfacing of her uncertainty, glimpses through his idle thought pictures, most of them good, aftermoments with other lovers—only a few flashes of when the demons who'd bought him had tormented him with gentleness before stabbing him with the hooks he'd been hung by.

Whenever those would pass through his head, she'd worry taking care of her was doing more harm than good. But she'd shift and he'd hold her just a little tighter, as though he knew she knew what he was thinking and didn't want her to believe it spoiled the moment, any more than memories of past lovers he no longer enjoyed.

She looked back at him. "A paper bag over my head?"

"What's that?"

"You said if I wanted to have sex with people who didn't like how I looked rather than people who don't care, I could wear a paper bag over my head."

"Did I say that? I don't know half of what I say during sex, sweetheart, but I'm sorry if that one hurt."

"You were more annoyed I might want to have sex with someone who made me want to wear a paper bag over my head, but still…"

"Don't have sex with someone who doesn't want to look you in the face while they're fucking you. You can fuck in any position you want, but anyone who insists on not seeing you while they do? That's a huge red flag." He caressed her lower lip with his thumb. "Because you're no one's pity fuck. They should be grateful to you. Okay? You never have to feel desperate. There are people waiting in your line, and they'll worship where you tread. A few of them will even worship your feet. That man didn't take everything away from you like he thought he did. Like you thought. And he's the one who came hustling after you, not the other way around. Don't forget that."

Chapter Eight

Alone at one of the few tables that wasn't illuminated by the portable lights, Sera sat with a tray of food, because she was always ridiculously hungry after a day's circus work, and apparently sex and magical emergence worked up an extra appetite.

She'd offered to get something from the food booths for both of them, but Carlo had said he'd make his own dinner and he would leave the door unlocked. She didn't know what to do with that. Without skin contact, she lost what insight she might have had to his motives, unsure how much he was being polite and how much he really wanted her to play doll in his bed.

Her mood still threatened to drop lower than the ground under her feet. That wasn't a state she was inclined to share, even if he was willing. She'd distracted him and he'd distracted her, but distractions weren't solutions. With the sex demons' magic briefly broken and her lifetime of sexual tension similarly shattered, she was left with a unique clarity.

She didn't regret what had happened. She didn't regret having come to Arcanium, didn't regret her time spent with Carlo over the last month, didn't regret having sex with him first. She felt different with her chastity magic no longer a series of delicate golden chains running through muscle and bone, shifting in almost imperceptible whispers under the surface of her skin. She was freer, lighter, her magic like smoke seeping from under a tipped-up bell jar but not dissipating from her control. It was as though she'd been caged and now the door had been opened. She had the whole wide world of her power within her reach instead of what was just beyond her bars. Her magic was so much larger, so much more malleable and compliant than it had been in the fifty-three years preparing to use it.

As she made her way through the fruit bowl, two corndogs, fried mushrooms, nachos and large soda, she tasted every little thing, every burst of salty, fried goodness, melted cheese, the maraschino cherries in a fruit salad that masqueraded as healthy. She didn't have to worry about her health—in Arcanium or out—but fair food was still a novelty to her. She'd been far more used to the fresh fruits, vegetables and grains harvested from fields and greenhouses at the coaxing of green-thumbed fae.

"I've always liked a small woman with a big appetite." With the circus closed, the pale rock god had taken on his normal chartreuse hue, his black hair transformed into tentacles. "I hear you've got other hungers being satisfied lately. Would have liked to see it, but alas, I have other women's appetites to tend to."

One thing she'd learned while living among humans and demons was the effect of a well-timed middle finger.

Lennon laughed, but he did what all the other demons did and gave her the wide berth she preferred.

So she'd been seen, heard and word had already spread. Sera didn't like that she would be spoken about—or how they might speak of her—but if she'd cared enough, she would have ensured that the sex hadn't been out in the open where literally anyone with tolerable night vision could see them and anyone who didn't need a hearing aid could hear.

As the demon passed her, her magic brushed against his.

Underneath the casual veneer, he was a seething mass of horrors—horrors that he voluntarily bound away and not just because Arcanium required it of him. It was like nothing he had ever shown to anyone else in the circus, although many assumed he revealed himself for the Funhouse events. He was born of earth and fire rather than hell, but the combination was eldritch enough to create something similar. If he hadn't shown that to anyone, if this mask he wore was the demon and man he chose to be, that didn't necessarily make the other part of him disappear.

But it said something about his character that he'd chosen to become a creature who vulnerable women trusted. His motivation might not have been completely altruistic—instincts crueler, perhaps, than they could know. But he'd sunken any malice within him like ships to the bottom of the sea. His persona had become his nature, no longer the work it once had been. Being a demon, a true demon, was often lonely, and he didn't like to be lonely. Arcanium ensured that he never was, one way or another.

He turned his head to meet her eye.

"I felt that, little girl. You've got some power in you, but it's untried, untested. I'd be careful." From anyone else, it would have sounded threatening, but she swore concern passed like a shadow through his already-blackened eyes.

He continued out of the food court and around the big top.

Living among beings who skewed their waking hours with the sun still took adjustment. She was used to being surrounded by people, but while she often enjoyed the quiet following the chaos of a circus day, emptiness was new to her. She relished the peace until about three in the morning, when she started craving company and usually had to go to bed just to combat that sense of loss. During her late nights, she would notice signs of life—moving vehicles, other lovers trysting outdoors, the clowns creeping through the circus, the shadows of the succubus then the incubus as they did their own patrols, the Tooth Fairy as she entered and exited the odd chef's booth.

But by three a.m., even the night owls had fallen quiet, and it was just her. She doubted Carlo would still be awake, so she eschewed his RV in favor of her own.

The Horned God waited for her.

How long he had been standing there, unmoving as a fantastical statue, she couldn't tell. He'd always had an uncanny stillness that he used both on Oddity Row and in the circus proper. Sometimes children climbed onto his oddity platform and played around his feet, draping him with the ribbons and flowers that had been left in baskets all around him for the purpose of interactive accessorizing. He'd since shed the ribbons, but strings of peonies and daisies and clips of sunflowers adorned the rack of his antlers and horns, spilling down his body and wrapped loosely around his torso as though he were the embodiment of a wild spring. The bauble lights cast his white fur and gray skin in gold, an explosion of color.

The question of whether he was all right died on her lips. His white mad eyes were not unkind, and the set of his lips was no different than usual, no ferocity in his posture. His magic swirled about him like dust motes in a sunbeam, calm and hypnotic. She had never seen his magic before like she had Bell's. It captivated her, beckoned her to meet it with her own to learn what the overlap would feel like.

Better than the overlap with a demon, even one who had chosen a less dark and sadistic path for the dark and sadistic thing he was. The Horned God wasn't demon. His magic with hers was like chocolate and hazelnut, a combination far more harmonious.

He broke the illusion of the statue as he lifted his hand to her, offering contact.

She rested her hand in his.

From the tips of his fingers, a garland of peonies climbed up her arm to settle around her head in another crown, but this time, a burst of more flowers nestled into the cavity of her face, an impromptu mask, petals soft on the skin.

She saw herself through two eyes from a distance, Carlo with his mouth buried between her legs as she succumbed to her pleasure. Her magic pulsed and glittered dark red around her as the chastity magic broke to set it free. It burst far out of Arcanium through the glistening silk web of the jinni's magic, although it wrapped densest around herself and around Carlo. When it reached the Horned God, it passed over him like the brush of silk ribbons on his skin. His arousal, a temperamental and selective thing, heightened to her, although it was often only half-hearted with the incubus and succubus. He swelled from the thick fur, a low groan rumbling from his chest as he relished what came to him so rarely. Spring brought it out of him more than most.

Then his memory went back to the clearing, with the Spring Maiden in their bed of moss and flowers, their bodies wrapped around and straining against each other, everything they did an action of instinct rather than art, beautiful, graceless desire, wild, mad, over and over and over.

When the Horned God lifted his head from his Maiden, her face was Sera's, with peonies nestled in the empty space and her good eye bright as a sapphire above the wedding gemstone choker.

Sera jerked her hand back. Not a memory.

A suggestion. An unspoken wish.

"You were beautiful." Without contact, his mind's voice was more distant, less overwhelming and encompassing, but she could still understand him. *"You are beautiful."*

He bowed until his antlers touched the ground then took her hand again to salute her. Before she could say anything or process what he wanted of her, he had already made his steady way around her RV to wherever he laid his head. When she darted around the vehicle, he had disappeared.

* * * *

Now that Carlo had told her how other men looked at her when she wasn't looking, she was far more aware of what she saw when she caught them. Or maybe she finally allowed herself to see it because she accepted Carlo's premise that she was desirable. In paying attention, she could tell the difference between men who looked away because her face turned them off and those who looked away because the rest of her turned them on.

She supposed it didn't hurt that she borrowed from the fresh flowers the Horned God kept about his platform to form a headdress every morning of whatever he had on hand. She made herself noticed, instead of trying to hide. People didn't just notice her because she was noticeable. They noticed that she wanted to be noticed.

She didn't dissuade the attention she received, but she changed very little of her aloofness from before, when she'd assumed their shyness was from disgust.

Carlo seemed to be allowing her to process what had happened and decide in her own time what to do about it. Like her, he went back to his behavior from before, other than more lingering glances, heavy as velvet instead of smooth as silk. He remained friendly, helpful when she rehearsed her act, making suggestions to perfect her timing and plan for future routines.

If anyone else knew what she had done and with whom, they mostly kept their peace, other than knowing looks and conspiratorial smiles. Strangely enough, putting herself in the awkward position of such public sex seemed to have solidified her place in Arcanium. The approval of a veteran human voluntary thawed what chill had been left. Perhaps the Horned

God's flowers helped as well, and the way she played with the children.

"Did you want them?" Carlo asked on the way to the big top for the evening's performance. "Children? No matter how they pull on your hair and wings, you never yell at them. And although you preen for an audience, sweetheart, you seem to prefer the children's company."

"I'm the last child of seventy-five. My brothers and sisters have all had their own children, and I'd expected to have plenty of my own. Some of my brothers and sisters who fulfilled their duty as royalty didn't necessarily want the children they were required to have, but I would have been happy to bear if my husband-to-be hadn't been such a dick."

Carlo grinned, although it wasn't a particularly happy one. "I've been rubbing off on you."

"He would have taken some children and discarded the others. That is not the home I would have chosen for them or myself. The human children here, though, do eventually return to their parents—as did my nieces and nephews. I want children, but perhaps it is not such a bad thing now to enjoy them in smaller doses and wait for when Arcanium is no longer my home."

"Yeah. Children and the clowns do not mix well. It's why Caroline, Riley and Colm do their best to scare them away at the end of the evening whenever any stay longer than they should. They'll do better lost and alone on the other side of the fence than they do in their parents' care on the inside when their parents don't believe how important it is to follow the damn warnings."

"Why allow children in the circus at all if it's such a danger to them?" Sera asked.

"For the same reason PG-13 movies do better commercially than R," Carlo said. "A wider market means more guests, more recommendations to other people by those guests, better exposure. And the presence of children during the day forces us to be more creative with what we do and how we push our boundaries."

"And other people's boundaries."

Carlo didn't break his stride. "Are we talking about guests or you?"

"Yes."

"I didn't think you were mad at me, and I didn't take it personally that I slept alone."

"I'm not mad and I go to sleep later than you do." She sighed as they entered the big top tent. "I'm just…overwhelmed. And confused. And everything's changed inside me because the chastity magic is gone. I don't know whether you notice it, but the demons do. The Horned God does. I don't know whether the different way people treat me is because of that or whether they treated me like that all along and I just didn't notice. I don't know what to feel or think or trust."

"I can't tell you what to think or feel, but I promise you can still trust me. I'm not miffed that you needed space afterward. I'm a little insecure about it, but I needed my own space, because I got overwhelmed and confused, too. I'm not like Bell. I didn't see you coming, Sera, and I don't quite know what to do with…with what I want to do to you, when all this time since Bell got Arcanium back, I haven't wanted to do that. And I'm still afraid of how I feel and what I think of when I do."

"Why are you telling me this?" Sera asked.

"Because sometimes it's nice to hear other people are feeling similar things." Carlo climbed onto an armchair that someone had considerately thrown backstage. The whole area was a hodgepodge of storage and secondhand theater furniture that wouldn't have been out of place in a yard sale or a shabby antique store. "I wasn't lying, Sera. I choose to trust you. So far, I haven't seen any reason that trust is misplaced. Have I given you that reason?"

Sera hesitated, especially since the rest of the big top cast was either there or showing up. But the incubus had done his work over the last few weekends, and he'd just entered the big top with Sasha.

Carlo smiled a little as she placed her hands on the arms of the chair to lean in and angle her head to kiss him. He cradled her face, his fingers dipping into the bouquet over her face as he kissed her back slowly and sweetly.

"You've been staring at me all day," Sera murmured against his lips.

"And I thought I was being subtle."

"Liar."

She removed the crown of flowers and the mask that dangled from it. She couldn't wear it into the ring. Bell hadn't forbidden her from creating the headdresses, though, perhaps because the dip of her broken face was still visible through the flowers.

Uncertain but carefully following the direction of her own desire, she kissed down to Carlo's neck, where his pulse thrummed against her lips. She caught the flesh where his neck met his shoulder between her teeth and sucked lightly, tasting the sweat of his skin. It awoke the hunger that usually only started after her performance. Her stomach growled.

Carlo laughed as he kissed her neck in a mirror of her, just beneath her collar. "Have you noticed the rest of them staring at you? Do you believe this liar now?"

"Yes," she whispered, breathing in his skin, the musky place behind his ear, the scent of his hair. He didn't wear cologne, but the leather, sawdust, grass, canvas and fair food that were his world had sunk into him. "I still don't know why."

"Well, people on the outside sometimes wonder what a man without legs can offer a lady. When they have the balls to ask, I always explain that I have the only leg that matters."

He surprised her into a snort that shifted into a laugh. She hit his arm as she straightened.

"Anyone else catch your eye, now that you know you catch a few yourself?" he asked.

"Trying to get rid of me already?"

"No."

The solemnity in his husky reply arrested her, pleasant heat sinking down her spine.

"Anyone catch *your* eye?" She wasn't prepared to be jealous. He'd been candid about his past lovers.

Carlo shrugged and smiled with a certain amount of self-deprecation. "Someone always catches my eye, sweetheart. But not like you do right now." He took her hand and squeezed it.

"Talk to me after the performances. I need advice." She squeezed his hand back.

"I like the sound of that."

* * * *

"You're going to turn into a corndog if you keep going like that," Carlo said, his tone far from a complaint. "But please, don't stop."

Sera had a corndog in each hand, and for the first time since arriving in Arcanium, she realized the innuendo and choked on her bite. She didn't know how she'd missed it the first hundred times.

"You do realize I'm using my teeth, right?" Sera considered her handfuls to figure out if there was a better way to eat them and decided there wasn't, so she decided to continue enjoying them the way she had been.

"I know. It's hot."

"You are so weird."

"That's why we're here, darling."

They were mostly alone now. The guests didn't congregate in the caravan area. A few golems on the edges discouraged them if unaccompanied by a cast member. Already, Sera barely saw the golems as little more than animate furniture, which she was sure was the intention. They disturbed her, but they were soulless. There was nothing there to notice unless they were needed, and she rarely needed them except to dispense food.

"Are you sure you're okay with this?" she asked.

"I could ask you the same question. Neither of us is as fragile as we seem, Sera. There's nothing wrong with being careful, but since that night, I dream about you instead of having the nightmares. I wake up so hard for you. I've been cold-showering for the last two weeks. For the first time in a while, I'm thankful for the sex demon magic, because it's connecting me to something here instead of from before. Whether we get a repeat of that night or that night is all we have, I'm good with it.

So whatever you want to do here is good to me, even if you brought me out here while eating corndogs like some kind of kinky breakup hint."

She giggled again as she tossed one of her corndog sticks into a trashcan.

"Nothing like that. Just an extension of something discussed earlier. I need your wealth of wisdom." She was only half kidding. He wasn't a diplomat, had no formal training in strategy, and he—like everyone else in Arcanium, apparently—had unconventional ideas about how relationships could work. But that was why she wanted his advice.

"That's me. Wealthy in wisdom."

"Arcanium, my world and your world all function by different rules, different social mores. You'll warn me if I slip into something even Arcanium does not accept, yes?"

"Sweetheart, Arcanium's a demonic circus. That list is devastatingly small."

One picnic table sat solitary in the middle of the caravan. She climbed onto the bench to sit on the table. Carlo vaulted up onto the bench, unbothered by having to look up at her.

"I think the Horned God is courting me," she said.

"That's shocking, Sera. Simply shocking."

"Stop being sarcastic. He's difficult to understand."

Carlo shrugged with a grin. "Easier for you than the rest of us, with your telepathic bond thing."

"He can talk, but he's been sending me images, focused memories instead of words, and I don't know how to interpret them."

"Well, what's he sending you?"

"How much of old and new paganism are you aware of?" she asked.

"I know that New Age crystals are bunk and most mind readers are master manipulators rather than actual telepaths, present company excluded. I know some of the Greek and Roman gods. And I hear a lot about Hecate. That's about it. Why?"

"Late spring is when the Maiden Goddess meets with the Horned God to celebrate a ripened, fruitful spring—a mating season, if you will. Sometimes, he meets with one of the Maidens themselves, but when the Maidens have chosen other partners, other gods, he turns to other women as well, usually creatures already in the forests—dryads, naiads, nymphs..."

"Fae."

"Less frequently, but yes." Sera rested her elbows on her knees and pressed her thighs together. Carlo kept glancing at the necklace of the costume's halter. Her nipples tightened under his regard, although they wouldn't yet be visible under the looser fabric.

"And he's chosen you to be May Queen to his horny god. I'm not seeing the problem."

Sera closed her fingers over Carlo's shoulder to send him what the Horned God had sent to her. She wasn't even sure it would work, except Carlo reeled against the edge of the table, his head thrown back with a startled groan as his cock shifted in his briefs.

"Jesus, woman. A little warning might be nice."

Sera jerked her hand back. "Sorry."

He grabbed her wrist, though, and brought her hand back to his shoulder. "I'm not mad. Do it again. I like seeing you from a distance. And for a god who doesn't get it up that often, when he does...sweet Mother of Hades." He groaned again as she sent him the Horned God's message.

She licked and bit her lower lip as he squeezed her wrist. With his other hand, he grasped at the bound erection straining under the leather.

"Have I mentioned how many cold showers I've needed since that night?" Carlo let go of her wrist but he didn't stop rubbing and squeezing his cock in a vain effort to relieve some of the tension.

Sera climbed down to the bench, straddling the narrow planks, and tentatively slipped her hand beneath his to cup the erection and stroke up its length to the head. She didn't undo the laces this time. They unwove themselves, magic making much quicker work of them now that she knew how to do it. She usually didn't mind the long way around things, but she was afraid she'd lose her nerve if she took her time, especially under lights rather than in darkness fewer people could see through. But she wanted to be bolder, and she wanted Carlo's abandon to continue—freedom that he had made her feel, freedom he hadn't felt in so long in spite of the hooks and chains that had been removed.

"Sera…" He grunted when she softly stroked over his bare shaft, pushing the briefs away from with her knuckles but not removing them completely.

She leaned down and drafted her breath over her fingers. If she could feel it, so could he. "May I try?"

He struggled to even his breathing. Without anything to hold him back, his cock seemed to strain up toward her, the desire inside him almost like pain that ached in her mouth and her cunt, as intoxicating as anything from a faerie's table.

She sensed his trepidation, too, not because she caused memories to surface, but because he feared that they *would* surface and mar his experience of her. He wanted it to stay sweet, wanted it unbranded by a more distant past that sometimes felt as real as the present, catching him unawares.

But God, the chance to watch her, feel her, try yet something else she hadn't done with anyone, another first against which all others would be measured... Though he wasn't arrogant, he had the confidence of nights of undeniable pleasures before and after Arcanium. He remembered her first pleasure, how sensitive and easy it had been, how much she had needed it, how much she'd needed him to give it to her. This would be far from his first, but how long had it been? He wanted it, needed it so badly, and he wanted her to give it to him, could almost feel it already just from the sheath of her breath and the cool, hesitant brush of her fingers. Her cooler temperature was completely new to him. Not so cold that it did the same work as the showers. Just cool enough against his heated skin that he was aware of familiar sensations in whole new ways.

Once she was old enough to recognize where the thoughts were coming from, Sera had avoided touching so many people, even her friends, her family. She'd forgotten how *much* came through—not just distant hindsight but sight almost like telepathy, a second or two behind the passing of thoughts and feelings. To have Carlo in her magic was like lying on the shore of the sea during rising tide. It wasn't unpleasant, but it threatened to pull her under. Less so than with the Horned God, but he didn't have to be a god to have power of his own.

The more she took Carlo into herself, the more she understood how the fae could lose themselves in the sex they had, even if they weren't like her. She didn't think all of this was from hindsight alone. Some of it came from the new freedom of her magic to reach, to hold, to embrace, to move fluidly through her and him and back again, the thin air between them keen and charged as the air before a storm, rendering her as breathless as he was.

Carlo placed his hand on her head and guided her down. She tasted salt and flesh, breathed in the mist of his blood and spirit as she strengthened her grip around his erection and sank her mouth over him. He turned to the side to bite the strap of the harness to keep his groan from being too loud. Bell didn't discourage them from taking their lovers during circus hours, but he expected some effort at discretion. Sera liked that he had to fight his natural impulse to express his pleasure, whether wordless or the stream of promises, oaths and fantasies that had passed his lips without restraint.

She didn't know what she was doing. A palaceful of memories in her head, and she couldn't choose a technique, didn't know which among the multitude would speak to him, so she was as uncertain as she would have been if she hadn't known anything at all.

Carlo left his hand on the back of her head, but he didn't push, didn't guide. He just played with her hair as he clearly struggled not to push his hips up to fill her mouth before she was ready. Even when he sounded like he would explode right there, he ensured her comfort over his own, his consideration as appealing as the scent of leather and pheromones from his skin.

She sank her mouth down over the head and just a little farther, testing her limits, testing the bulbous head against her throat. The fae could choke—an ignoble death, graceless. She had to be careful as she tried swallowing around the head to keep from gagging.

It didn't work. Carlo tugged her head up with a slight laugh as she coughed.

"Sweetheart, I don't expect you to be demon or my sword-swallowing boyfriend. It's a novelty, but I hardly need deepthroat to feel something fine. You were good right up on the top there."

This time, he guided her down over the head, then slid his fingers deeper in her hair to hold her there.

"Tongue around the edge, particularly right there, where it is, on the underside. Or over the slit, but sparingly. Suction, a little teeth on the shaft just below. And your chilly hand on the rest of it, love, just like you were. Ah, yeah, that's fucking good."

Carlo brought the back of his hand to his mouth to bite the base of his thumb. Wave after wave of his arousal shot through her as though it were her own, and in a way, it was. Because she was causing it, because it pleased her to please him, as it had pleased him to please her.

Her saliva dripped down his erection, slicking the way as she quickened her strokes, like she had that first night, but this time, she hummed around the head, lashing steadily at the ridge on the underside as he'd suggested. His hips jerked on the bench in spite of his efforts to control himself.

"Show it to me again," he said through the skin between his teeth. But he let himself go to continue, "Show me what he showed you. What he wants from you. Now."

She poured the memories into his mind, living them with him—the fantasy of the Horned God buried deep within her as she moaned in the same ecstasy he had witnessed under Carlo's ministrations.

Carlo's hand in her hair clutched reflexively as he came, and he groaned, almost growled, into his hand.

Sera thought that, after trying to take him deeper into her throat and failing, she might not be able or want to swallow, but she discovered to her surprise that his seed was rich with power, almost like magic or faerie wine, and she drank it down greedily, sucking so hard that he shouted. After he stopped spending, she didn't stop sucking, and he shouted again, but this time from oversensitivity.

"Okay, that's too much. Too much, too much, too much." He tugged at her hair to urge her off.

She almost didn't let him go, even though he wasn't giving her any more. When she raised herself from his cock, he paused with his hand still in her hair, poised to either release her or jerk her back.

Sera saw herself through him—her blue eye bright, pupil more dilated than usual, her fierce, feral expression lean and sly as a fox or coyote. There was a sliver of fear in him, of memory, but it didn't linger and it didn't burn.

Instead, as Sera lowered herself to trace the ridge around the head with the tip of her tongue, stroking him more gently, he twitched in her hand, and she called to his arousal with her own. She rocked her hips against the bench, pressing her clit to the wood in an effort to tend to herself while her hands were otherwise occupied. She found the core of his desire, stroked it with her magic the way she stroked his cock with her hand and tongue. He let go of her, hands in mid-flail as she made him hard again.

"God, you learn fucking fast, princess. But there's more going on here than just good head, isn't there? It's l-like you're i-inside of me… Ohhh fuck."

Rendering a dirty talker speechless imbued her with a special kind of pride. She coaxed her own arousal up with his at the rush of delicious control, drank him down again as she moaned around his cock through the tandem orgasm, although hers seemed secondary—and empty—against his as she fed from the power in his seed once more.

"What are you, a goddamn succubus? Were you taking secret lessons from Sasha or something? Jesus, woman, I'm not… Oh, God, I'm getting hard again. Fuck, fuck, fuck, fuck, fuck…"

Wings fluttering, Sera lifted herself up and straddled his hips, catching his erection between her hand and the silk of her costume, with the piercing at the base right against her clit. It wasn't enough to stimulate her, but she sensed the tug of her rubbing herself against it singing in little zings through him and twitching him in her hand.

"Do you know what happens to humans when they stumble into one of our circles?" she murmured near his lips.

"They're never seen again?" Carlo tried to kiss her, lick the remnants of his cum from her mouth, but she teasingly stayed out of reach. He kept his hands on the edge of the table, even though she wasn't holding him down, hadn't bound him. He yielded to her, willingly riding the magic she sent through him.

"Well, yes. It's nothing personal. We have a responsibility to protect our own against those who would encroach, and your kind is as invasive as mistletoe. There have to be places where you don't belong, where you suffer consequences, and there are precious few places where that still happens. You think you can quell all land, control all creatures, compel your own." Sera stroked his renewed, oversensitive erection, twisted her wrist near the head, her thumb sometimes brushing the slit, where pre-cum slicked against the finger. "But there are still wild things in the world, my dear, and I am one of them. When a human steps into our circle, they are greeted with eminent hospitality. They feast, and they dance, and they are tended to with great enthusiasm."

She finally granted him the kiss he sought. He groaned through each pass of his tongue over hers, striving to claim her, even though she had far-more-enjoyable hooks deep within him, plying him like marionette strings. Now that she had found all the places begging to be plucked, she took full advantage of what she knew, what she remembered, what she wanted for him.

"It's rarely violence that kills them," she murmured against his lips as his third orgasm built under her touch. "It's sheer exhaustion."

He took her face between his hands so he could kiss her through his third climax, which dripped down her fingers, thinner than before. She brought her filthy hand to her mouth and moaned as he joined her in licking it clean.

"God, have you always been such a wicked girl? You acted so innocent."

She didn't know whether she was wicked, but she had power—more power than she'd known she had. Her mother had never prepared her for that, although she had tried to prepare her for so much else. There had been no way to anticipate what would happen after the release of the chastity magic.

It seemed all the more insulting now that this power would have been imprisoned in an isolated cabin somewhere, reaching out for something to grasp, nothing but emptiness for her to find—not even the wilderness itself for her, just a bed and the children that would be made within it.

He kissed her again before she could answer, gradually wrapping his arms around her, holding her against him on the bench so that she didn't need to hold herself up. It was an oddly intimate position, and she succumbed to it as much as he had succumbed to her control.

She smiled against his lips. "You've clearly corrupted me."

"I think it was all in there the whole time. You're just figuring out what to do with it. Meow, darling."

"You're okay with it? The magic inside you, I mean?" A reminder of what she was, instead of a doll with pretty wings.

"It's...overwhelming," he admitted. "But you're not mean and you're not cruel. Thinking you were tame? That's my error, not yours. I like it, Sera. You're not like them. If you're taking something from me, you're giving just as much, and I'm pretty sure we can't die of exhaustion in here. The fact you're worried that you'll make me think of them... Well, that alone shows that you're not. Stick with me, kid. I'm just fine being your teacher *and* your lesson."

He kissed her again, savoring her while his cock softened against her, because it meant there was no drive for him to push higher. And she had nothing to feed upon, so she could enjoy the slow, heated leisure in spite of her own climbing feelings. But she had all night to play, and she wasn't afraid that the heat of her desire would render her ash.

"Lesson Number Twelve— Your Horned God is interested as hell. What he sent you was the fairytale version of a dick pic, obscene emojis and a porn GIF. The message couldn't be plainer than if he wrote 'wanna bone?' on your hand. Despite the fact that he's literally one of the only cast members of Arcanium who's had no sex as far as we know, when he's hot, he's fucking hot. It's up to you whether you want to buy a ticket for that ride, but hoofed gods in forests seem like they'd be nice and freaky in the sack. And maybe, just maybe, he'll be able to keep up with you, tiny Amazon."

"You think I should?"

"Sweetheart, what's stopping you?" Carlo gathered the silk at the back of her costume, slung below her wings, and tugged her back to him. "Is it me?"

"There are provisions for divorce, but otherwise, the fae marry for life. And our life is indefinite, potentially infinite."

"I don't see a ring on either of our fingers. I'm not saying this is nothing, Sera, because it's something to me. I want you to know that." He nudged her forehead with his, and she brushed her lips against his mouth. "But we're just starting out. I've never been the jealous kind. Both Misha and I had sex with other people—sometimes with the same people, since Maya was the most polyamorous Catholic I've ever met. With Arcanium all sexually charged, monogamy is acceptable but hardly compulsory. Almost everyone here has more than one lover. If you want me to dish, I'll serve, because I have almost the full 4-1-1 on that, even the people who don't want anyone to know."

"I hate gossip. Please tell me later in lurid detail."

Carlo laughed. "If you want to stick with me, kid, I'll take the best care of you that I can. With my…relatively new issues, I probably won't even be tempted to stray for a good long while. But honey, you just got started, and you have all this energy humming like electrical wires through you, through whatever you sent into me. So, hell yeah, go out and experiment and have whatever fun you like with whomever you like. We don't have to worry about disease, and maybe the fae don't have to worry about that anyway, so the sky's the limit. For a woman like you, I'm not even sure about that." He tugged the base of her open wings.

"Are you sure?"

"I wouldn't say no if you slept with the whole damn circus. I *always* understood how Bell could just tie Maya blindfolded on a pike and watch anyone and everyone take her for both of their pleasures. You're beautiful, and the Horned God is beautiful. Watching that would be as beautiful as he imagines it. What's wrong with that?" Carlo slid his hands up her sides in reassurance. "I'm not asking to watch, love. I'm just saying that you looking beyond me for satisfaction does little to make me jealous and does everything to make me horny again. So you do you, ask me whatever you want and show me whatever makes you happy. I certainly won't tell you no to that."

Sera settled farther back, chewing on her lip. "So you think I *should*?"

"What are you afraid of?"

She rested her fingertips against his chest to send him the sensation the Horned God had given her of his voice ringing in her head, coupled with the gale-force intensity of her orgasm that Carlo had so generously provided.

Carlo tossed back his head, leaning against the table, and groaned again. His cock swelled half-erect in a matter of seconds. "Jesus Christ on a cross, babe. Maybe this is why you *do* need someone else to fuck. You Arcanium women don't quit. Only a demon and maybe a fertility god can keep up with you."

Sera smiled, toying lightly with the cock probing at her thigh. "Come now, young man. Have you ever really *tried* to keep up?"

"Even in Arcanium, three's about my max, as you can tell." Without her stimulating him with more potent imagery, he'd settled back down again, although he still sometimes twitched with her gentle stroking. "Before Locke, during a Funhouse event, I'd sometimes manage four or five, back when Mikhail and Sasha would dial it up to twelve instead of just eleven. Neve basically goes all night at these things, though. She and the Spider have literally lost count of orgasms before. I can't even imagine."

"I can help you do more than imagine," Sera said.

He tilted his head as though unsure whether she was kidding, but Sera gave no indication either way. "Not tonight. I'm beat. Maybe after you've had a night of orgasms you lose count of and share them with me, I'll be up for such a thing."

Sera expanded her magic, stretching out in every direction. She passed through Carlo, through the core of contradictions within him—the confidence and insecurity, the nonchalance and possessiveness, the arousal with shots of resentment that he had to be as susceptible to sex demons as he was. Mingled within was the genuine attraction he had to her, stronger than he'd expected or planned only a year after losing Misha and losing himself.

He half wanted her to go to the Horned God because the idea of her fucking another man was one of the hottest things he'd had in a while other than her, and he half wanted her to go to the Horned God and discover that she preferred a man who was whole.

Not whole in the sense that he had two legs to walk on. Carlo had been legless all his life. He hadn't known a time in his life when his arms hadn't been enough.

The Horned God had been just as tortured as the rest of them, put up on the same auction block, bleeding and beaten and bound when returned to his glass case in the morning. Like the demons, though, he seemed untouched by the experience. He was whole, while Carlo was missing something that had once been his. He would give everything to have it again, but he didn't have any wishes left, and that meant his memories were his forever, wandering like ghosts to haunt him. He didn't care if they haunted Bell, too. Carlo wasn't as pissed off at Bell as some of them, but ghosts kept Bell honest. He just hated that they made Sera afraid of breaking what had already cracked.

If Sera had been more experienced shielding herself from other people's thoughts, maybe she wouldn't have found herself experiencing them like newly traumatized ghosts of her own, or perhaps just last gasps of present thoughts. It was like listening at keyholes and peering under doors, an unfair advantage with a man who couldn't see into her in return.

Her magic overlapped with another.

Demon magic was black as oil. Bell's magic was golden as dark autumn honey. Her own magic flowed as red as the incubus and succubus', as the Horned God had seen it.

The Horned God's magic was multicolored, like the flowers that he conjured, bright as winter sunbeams on water foam.

"On your six," Carlo whispered in her ear. "I think he just might be able to keep up with you. And he's hard. I've never seen him fully hard before."

She clutched at Carlo's shoulders, her nails digging into the skin.

"You can't be afraid it's going to be too good." He peered at her, into her, as though if he focused hard enough, he could see in her what she saw in him. He couldn't, but he tried.

"I'm allowed to be apprehensive. He's very big."

"Have you seen what Mikhail utterly fails to hide in his leather? Or Ciarán, for that matter? As nonhumans go around here, the Horned God's a little above average, but I've taken bigger without magical help."

She stifled a laugh in his shoulder. "That's not what I meant. I meant all of him. The Horned God's usual lovers are as tall as human women or taller. They don't usually take fae."

"Again, have you seen Mikhail and Ciarán? If Ciarán can get some without crushing people into wine in the process, I think you'll be fine with an actual god. Look… I know you haven't done this before—at least what he showed you—but he's apparently done it plenty, and no one's bad-mouthed his technique yet enough for you to hear about it through the grapevine or at the water cooler or wherever the fae get their scuttlebutt. Your fiancé was about the same size. You were willing to go along with that, in theory."

"I was also prepared to tolerate sex rather than enjoy it."

Carlo lifted her head from his shoulder, brushing her hair back from her face. "He seems considerate, giving you flowers and asking quite nicely. I don't think he's going to hurt you at all. And I can't give you what he's offering right now."

"That's not what this is about—"

"I know. I told you that I'm not jealous. Okay, maybe a little jealous, but I know how much you want this, even if you're afraid of it." Carlo pressed a kiss to the corner of her mouth. "It's okay to be afraid, but you don't need to be. If he doesn't do right by you, you get to tell Daddy Bell on him."

She turned her head to kiss him again more fully. Then she sent him another wave of the memory that the Horned God had sent her, of watching her with Carlo and how that had aroused him.

Carlo groaned into her mouth, his hips bucking on the bench. "Fuck, woman. If you don't want another mess, I suggest you clean your fine self up and try marathon sex with the aforementioned fertility god awaiting your answer. Because I'm this close to tearing up your costume, and I don't think Kitty would be very happy about that."

"I made it, and I wouldn't mind at all." Sera sent her cleansing magic over them then unstraddled him, leaving him half-hard and exposed to passers-by, but there weren't many. Most of them were occupied with each other rather than the acrobatic couple at the picnic table—although some of them tore their attention away long enough to notice the Horned God, which told her that his presence among them wasn't common.

He was there for her, waiting under the bauble bulbs of the strung Christmas lights. Even the thicker fur of his daytime concealment was no match for the erection that had emerged from underneath. It spoke volumes to his self-control that he didn't worry about it occurring during circus hours. Bell would never let him get away with that cock sticking out from his fur, even though leather shorts rarely did enough to cover Mikhail and Ciarán's sheer, monstrous size, no matter how loose or binding their trousers. Sera could not imagine a human woman, much less her, submitting to what Ciarán had to offer, although those who married more well-endowed immortals had assured her that there were ways to endure it.

It really wasn't size alone that concerned her, though.

None of the others seemed to see in the Horned God what she saw. They revered Bell and their fear of the Ringmaster was a kind of worship, as peasants had once appeased gods they most feared with incense and sacrifice. But there were other demons among them they hadn't begun to understand, and like Bell, there were other gods. Sera didn't know whether it was an inherent arrogance of humanity, that they believed themselves smaller gods to hold dominion over the world, wresting power from the gods before them, or whether it came from the same egalitarian impulse to bond with other beings that left them making friends with tigers and trying to cuddle serpents. Probably a combination of both, the sweetly frustrating creatures.

They passed the god among them with as much notice as he gave to them, his gaze passing over them as though they were invisible and Sera the only other person in the circus. Except perhaps Carlo, because though the Horned God's gaze didn't waver from Sera, the attention of his magic did. It joined hers in an eddied embrace around the man making himself as presentable as an almost-naked circus acrobat could ever be.

It interested her that Carlo interested him, given that the god had granted interest to so few. But for now, his magic receded from the man to entwine with Sera alone.

He held out his hand.

He intimidated her, because although he was not as tall as the Ringmaster or Ciarán, he seemed to tower. More flowers draped over his antlers, almost making him mild, nearly concealing the benevolent madness in his wide eyes. Among the guests, he was a Ferdinand, but sometimes the distinction between demon and god was a matter of origin rather than action. His hands were the same size as Carlo's, and as strong. Carlo's torso was the length of an average human man, the god's only a little bigger. The faun legs, though, were broad, strong, and with his backbent knees and hooves, they were almost as long as she was tall.

Her hand in his seemed insignificant. But he was even warmer than Carlo to her cool body, and he enveloped her hand in that warmth.

His expression remained unchanged. After exposure to so many humans and immortals, if he were capable of expression, he would have learned to express by now. Cats were believed to be cold and aloof because they didn't have the same muscles necessary to make expressions as dogs did. There was undeniable emotion within the Horned God, though, if one knew how to find it.

With his hand around hers, he filled her head with his thoughts, more image than words, because now he knew how they thrilled her—what he felt when he witnessed her with Carlo, pride and desire, impatience and preparation, admiration for the magic seething around her and his long-suppressed appetite come to the surface with a vengeance after its generous hibernation.

He showed her what he wanted of her, and when he turned, she followed.

Chapter Nine

As Sera and the Horned God left the golden light of the caravan, the Patchwork Pirate crossed their path, flanked by the incubus and succubus.

The god leaned in toward the succubus, who raised her head to exhale when he inhaled. Neve, with her scarred face to complement Sera's, watched with the confusion of someone witnessing behavior for the first time. Perhaps the Horned God had escaped her notice as he had for the other humans.

Except the god stretched out the hand not holding Sera's to Neve, and Neve returned the gesture, fingertip to fingertip. Sera couldn't say what passed between them, if anything other than contact, but it seemed a far more familiar greeting than what the god had done with the succubus. Neither the incubus nor the succubus considered such contact an intrusion upon their arrangement with Neve, so Sera stood quietly by.

When they parted, Sera sent her curiosity to the Horned God.

He curved his lips in a subtle smile but waited until they were in the darkened Oddity Row—no lights, no guests, no cast, no crew, nothing but the singing of frogs and insects in their company. Then he whirled her around in front of him, like a gentleman at a dance. She was well-versed enough in dancing with gentlemen that her feet followed form with little thought.

They stood outside the Horned God's tent, its curtains still open and the baskets of ribbons and flowers spilled over on the wooden platform. He brought her hand up to his shoulder, bending down for her to reach, then tucked his arm under her legs to lift her up against him like a lover, her legs slotted around his hips, her arm around his neck at his coaxing.

"Bell often charges me to protect her in the Funhouse. Having her with the incubus and the succubus in the same room is too intense for anyone else. Even alone, when the demons are many rooms away, she is a force of nature."

He swept Sera's mind into a decadent bedroom bedecked with silk as red and luxurious as Sera's magic. Neve, naked and scarred head to toe, lay in the middle of the bed from which emerged the grasping, gripping, clawing hands of demons—and Sera knew they were demons rather than monsters, their magic dark, though glittering with amber. They caressed her, over and inside and everywhere at once. Wicked fingers entered her cunt with a wet sound then came out slickened with her arousal. Neve moved her body to hurry the hands on her, but they would not be hurried, and they would not be gentle, nor did she seem to want them to. Their claws made red ghost lines of the scars that covered her in place of clothing.

People stood all around, but the Horned God—viewing Neve from his central position in front of the bed—fixed his attention upon her. He so rarely desired human women. Their spirit ran too thin for his tastes. But he coveted her, this beautiful, damaged, sewn-together creation of hell and heaven. She was not for him, and he didn't always desire her enough for it to show, but sometimes he spent as he served her, while she and everyone else in the room were too distracted to notice.

Sera arched, bringing her body more tightly against the Horned God's. If this was how Carlo felt when she sent memories and fantasies into him, no wonder he'd almost come all over again. She loved making him do that, and she loved when the Horned God did this to her, filled her to the brim with desire that was not her own until she spilled over with her own and his at the same time.

"I do not often take humans, but I would take her if she desired me to do so. But she does not. That does not relieve me of my charge of protection, nor do I resent it. It is a pleasure to be near her."

"Even with her scars?" Sera asked.

The Horned God brought his hand to the cavity, caressing it like the petals of the flowers he had given her.

"Scars are memories. They do not mar you. You are complete as you were, as you are, as you will be. You will change, princess, but whatever the change, you will always be complete."

"The women you want, the women you take, they are all beautiful, my lord."

Instead of replying with words, he sent her his wish once more—entwined with her on the bed of moss and flowers in a clearing, under the moon.

Her head fell back with a high moan, but she nodded, sliding her fingers over his in the cavity and touching herself as well. The skin there was so smooth, soft, like the craters of a half-moon sanded out of definition. She still had sensation, as defined and delicious as the undamaged side of her face. The nerves there tingled with the same arousal that shot down her body. And when he drew her fingers away and licked a line up the damaged side of her face to kiss where her eye had been, she couldn't help but shiver and struggle against the impulse to bring him closer and keep him there.

"It is not ugliness. It is merely change. We all change, even immortals. Do you think that what humans and demons have done to me have not left scars?"

His hooves clopped loudly in the small tent, resonating in the hollowness beneath the platform. There was a small red velvet curtain behind the platform, a miniature of the one in the big top, and a whole other half of the tent that the guests of Arcanium never saw—a place for the oddities to take a moment of privacy away from the stares and touch of the guests.

The backs of oddities' tents did not require invitation, but it was polite to wait for one. Kitty opened her tent to all cast. Sera sewed her costumes in the large dressing room and living quarters that Bell had made for her. Neve often came out from Mikhail's or Sasha's tent. Sometimes, the Spider visited the Sphynx, although Sera thought those visits weren't for the same thing, because the Spider always left unhappy.

George, the Two-Faced Man with another face on the back of his head, had invited Sera to join his tent whenever she wanted to rest from walking the circus.

She was the other side of his coin, with only half a face of her own. George was a gentleman, human, but his other face was less so of either and he unnerved her. Unlike Carlo, he wasn't voluntary, and his second face didn't strike her as an amusing accident. She hadn't taken him up on his offer.

She had no such reservations about joining the Horned God.

When the curtain closed behind them, the moonlight above the clearing he'd shown her glowed into existence. Like Kitty's, the back of his tent was bigger than it seemed from the outside. The bed of moss, ferns and flowers was well-tended and meticulously arranged. More flowers and faerie lights were draped through the trees in a deliberate act rather than coincidence. She'd never seen him enter one of the caravan RVs or trailers. He would want to be confined even less than she. He'd had to leave the forest that was his home, so Bell had let him keep a little bit of home for himself, something that couldn't be taken or intruded upon.

He lowered her to the moss-covered ground, kinder to her bare feet than the brittle grass and dry earth on which Bell usually set up his circus. No matter how or where the Horned God turned, he never caught his antlers in the branches or garlands, always ducked his head just so, with the grace of an immortal who knew himself too well to be graceless.

From a carved wooden cabinet that didn't seem out of place in the forest—as though carved from it rather than placed within it—the Horned God removed a labelless wine bottle, blown in a style that she recognized as faerie-made.

Humans could lose their minds under the influence of faerie wine, but for her and for the god, it was a wonderfully inebriating opiate—the last breath of death, but sweet as grapes ripe from their own vine. In roughly hammered copper cups, the Horned God poured them both a small measure of oblivion.

He handed her a cup. *"You do not need to fear me. I am neither demon nor monster. I seek neither fear nor corruption. I am just as wild as you, and wild is not evil."*

"But it *is* dangerous." Still, she drank the wine, and he followed closely behind, the dark vintage staining his pale gray lips.

*"*You *are dangerous, princess. Your magic is new. It has only reached the end of one stage of its growth, yet it is already powerful, and you have so much farther to grow. I think the human man is good for you, but you are not as broken as you think you are, and he still needs to heal. Allow me to fill in the cracks and remind you what you are."*

This time he picked her up with an arm around her shoulders and another under her knees, then lay her out on his bed, soft with moss and surrounded by flowers. The scent spored around her as her body sweetly crushed them beneath her, as the god knelt above her. He took her empty cup and his own and discarded them without a thought—droplets of oblivion would only feed this piece of earth, and he had other things to focus on, such as the erection that slowly pulled up closer to his abdomen—pale in comparison to Carlo's, but flushed in comparison to his own skin tone, gleaming in contrast to his usual matte. The fur had thinned from what was required during circus hours, although his scrotum was still nearly obscured.

He seemed far more the god that he was in this private place, larger than life, his magic a glittering mist in the moonbeams, his eyes glowing white as he stared down at her. He didn't pant—for his size, he was quite quiet—but his ribs expanded, pushed against the flesh, as he struggled to control his heaving breaths, his rhythm more uneven the larger his erection grew and the closer it tightened near his abdomen, just from looking over her in his forest bed.

Sera shivered, fought against squirming under the weight of his regard, almost as pressing as the weight his body would be over her. She could sense it in the pressure of his knee on the moss next to her, in the dent he made with his hand by her head. He was as dense in form, perhaps more so, than Carlo, but he was so much larger. Insecurity in their diminutive size was one of her kind's enduring vanities, because sometimes gods and men laughed at these childlike creatures in their midst, the way they laughed at small dogs when they bared their teeth, not understanding that small things could be just as deadly—more so when they believed themselves not taken seriously.

The god took her seriously, and she took him more so. It wasn't just his size that made him greater than she but his age, his experience, the dreams of which he was made.

When he passed his palm above her body, the ghostly fingertips of his magic drew down her costume as though it were insubstantial. Her magic swelled to meet his in reflexive self-defense. She fought to quell it, even as he made her more vulnerable.

"No. Do not hold back what you are. That is what they taught you to do—settle for less so that you could satisfy their needs rather than your own. It is not man who domesticated you. Your own kind made a pet of you—something they could use then sell when they could get a

better price, no matter the cost to you. Let your magic free. You cannot hurt me. My magic will protect us, my beautiful maiden. Lovely."

His thoughts became less coherent, more images and impressions, when he lowered his palm to her bare skin. He stroked up her body, from ankle to knee to hip, sliding his thumb over the seam of her closed thighs. She parted them behind his strokes, but he didn't bring his touch between, although his nostrils flared as he caught the freed scent of her—arousal from her time with Carlo, renewed with the god, built up to a perfume as heady and strong as the flowers on either side of her face.

The Horned God smoothed his hand—as rough as Carlo's, a hand that had grasped tree bark and braced itself on stone and dirt—up her abdomen to her left breast.

He clearly wanted to go slowly, to savor her, to reassure her that he could be gentle, could give her the time she needed when she was afraid. But her magic flared out, burst like pomegranate juice in her mouth to join the wine, and she reached up to the shorter antler on his forehead and into the tangle of his hair to draw him down, with all his weight, his heat, the energy coursing underneath his mask of flesh.

She nearly burned under a body as fired with lust as a demon, except when she brought his mouth to hers, he didn't taste like one—no trace of the anise or smoke that flavored the dark magic suffusing Arcanium, nor the honey that formed its base. Between them, she tasted the oblivion wine they had shared, made of fruits so ripe they had fallen to a forest floor to ferment, to intoxicate with both decay and decadence—all part of the forest, part of the cycle of life and death over which a Horned God surveyed, encouraged, participated.

His magic was wilder than hers, but hers was so much darker, and she didn't know what to think of that. It did nothing to dim his desire, though, because he tasted her as deeply and thoroughly as he had drunk the wine, moved over her with the speed she set for him with her hands in his hair and among his antlers. He did not smile against her mouth, but he sent her how pleased he was through everywhere they had contact. His pleasure was like sinking into a bath of champagne.

He stimulated her everywhere, with his hands, with his mouth, with his hair, his fur, his heat. Her magic blocked the moonlight. His magic brought it back. They clashed and entwined, their kisses a violent battle of lust that she couldn't hold back anymore. She didn't want to be careful. She didn't want to be curious. She didn't want to be pleased. She wanted release, satisfaction, more than an orgasm or three, more than oblivion. They rocked together in the green, the god's cock trapped between them, but that didn't seem to bother him as long as skin trapped it on either side. He dug his hooves into the forest floor, shuddering the earth, bit her shoulder to make her cry out and scratch lines down his back, drawing blood.

She slithered her magic around him, pulled him around her onto the bed then under her, trapping his cock between her cunt and his abdomen. She tapped her bloodstained fingernails over his white-haired chest, over the thin, faint lines of protection spells that she assumed the tattoo artist had done for him after the abduction, because they all fairly screamed as keep-out signs for unwanted dark forces.

And yet here she was, a darker force than she wanted to believe she was, even now. He inhaled the dark red magic as he had drunk the oblivion, his bright eyes eclipsed with his desire for her. He had lost words but not feelings. They sang in the mist of his magic, hummed inside with vibrations that seemed like they would shatter into crystal shards if she didn't shatter him first.

"*Goddess*" was the only word that came through before she raised herself up, grasped the base of his erection with a hand that felt winter cold in contrast, and brought him to where she wanted him. Regardless of her apprehension that he would bring pain, she'd been stimulated enough. She'd been licked, bitten, tasted, stroked, but she wanted someone to pierce through, wanted the very pain that she feared if it meant she could stretch, grasp, take, drink.

Sera stroked her clit as she sank down over him, took him as deep as she had wanted—needed—Carlo to take her. She didn't resent that he couldn't, but this was what she had craved since the sex demons had sent their seductive magic down to her marrow, since she'd woken up in a sweat in her own bed so many years ago at the first sexual stirrings that only her eunuch guards had been permitted to witness.

She stretched around him, and it did hurt, but not the way she had expected it to. It stretched and hurt the way her muscles did after running for hours with none of the help of her wings, like they did when she reached her limbs in every direction after a long sleep, a deep, abiding burn that she willed to go on forever, because a body that healed as fast as hers relished that which could still strain.

Sera stroked herself faster as she moved over him with the rhythm she knew from memory and instinct combined, rewarded with every moment he submitted, groaning like a stag as he raised his hips to join her pace. He did not hesitate, didn't ask if she was okay or send concern through her. He understood what she wanted, and she understood what he wanted. He had shown her well in advance, and she had shared his fantasy in the dark hours surrounded by the close domestication of her living quarters.

She paused only to come. The Horned God's moan joined with hers, and he pulled her down to his chest as she shuddered and twitched around him, still rubbing her clit through the pulses of dark red magic that released from her as though she were a heart and her magic the blood. He absorbed what she gave, wrapped his arms around her as though to draw all of her into him, to feel her orgasm within.

He didn't let her stop to breathe. As soon as her orgasm subsided, he rolled her back under him to rut, hard and fast as his desire demanded. He dug his fingers into the head of his earthen bed, tilted her up with his other arm under her back. In spite of the end of her orgasm, she wasn't finished. She urged him harder, faster, begging not in words but the same way he spoke to her. Her thoughts were too scattered to solidify.

There was no deceit between them, no gentility, no trappings or trimmings, no calculations or arrangement, no diplomacy, no bitter expectations. There was only what was when everything else stripped away—lust and magic in the beautiful night, pain with pleasure, and neither of them had tired yet.

He came but he didn't stop, and she came again but didn't stop.

The moon didn't move, the forest was undisturbed, and both of them continued until they were a bloody, moss-stained, pollen-dusted, semen-strewn mess on the chaos of a bed, the Horned God's heavy breathing hot against her scalp. The tattoos that had been needled into his chest glowed a dark red, like blood in the light of a lantern, holding her magic deep within them. Moonbeams glittered opalescent under the thinnest layer of her skin, magic that he had shared with her in return. They finally fell quiet, fog blanketing the valley of their bodies together.

Sera was full, aching and satisfied, with only one wisp of a wish that there were one more person in the bed with them, tucked against her body, because he'd been a part of their night in his own way, and it felt incomplete.

The Horned God nudged her hair lightly with his nose. *"Another time."*

* * * *

She was reluctant to leave the Horned God and the piece of forest that Bell had given him. The night and the day were their own, a weekday with no responsibilities, and she could sleep through the better part of it without repercussion. But they couldn't stay in this enclave forever, and not knowing the time in a world of perpetual night disoriented her. The back of the tent appeared part of a forest, but she knew it was just the back of a tent in real-space, and if she couldn't get herself into open air to let her magic loose, the illusion wouldn't be enough.

The Horned God took no offense. Their magics had passed back and forth enough that they barely had to think to understand each other. There was nothing extraneous in their communication, and in the simplicity of it, there was no room for lies.

He raised himself from her, his fur mostly covering his cock again, although the mess they'd made did little to conceal their activities. She picked up her costume but didn't put it on, and though both of them could have cleaned themselves, neither did. Unlike many modern humans, both forest god and fae—even one raised within an extravagant lifestyle—could endure mess for a while, especially when it was well-earned. If morning had broken, she might consider cleaning herself and redonning the costume, but night would hide enough.

When they stepped onto the platform from behind the red curtain, it was still night on the other side. The only thing that told her it was likely the same night was that she wasn't famished after their exertion—hungry, yes, but not hollow as a human would be after a night with the fae. She was more than a match for a human man, but the Horned God had exhausted her, pleasantly. She could understand all the better why the humans who stumbled into rings never tried to leave, even when sated a dozen times over.

The Horned God wound his fingers through her hair to pull her head back. He nuzzled the cavity where her face had been with a humming purr.

"Again. Anytime. I have had many barren years, and Arcanium keeps me in spring."

Even tired as she was, enough to sleep for two days and nights, she stroked along the line of his cheekbone, up to the brow antlers, back to where the larger ones emerged. She didn't have to speak to acknowledge the offer. Tired, yes, but how strong she felt, like a lightning charge building from thunderhead to ground.

Of all the things her mother had prepared her for in the realm of sex after she was married, the rapid, almost rabid expansion of her magic had not been included in those lessons. Hers had already expanded twice over and, in spite of each successive release, hadn't receded.

Perhaps her mother hadn't told her because she'd never felt like this before. Perhaps not all sex affected the fae like this, because she'd never felt it in her memories. Or perhaps her mother simply hadn't expected her last daughter, with such low expectations, to ever know what this could be like. In a world of diplomatic matches determined by contractual agreement rather than personal compatibility, no one would understand what they relinquished in exchange for political stability and prosperity. Maybe that was why the nobility and royalty were strongly encouraged to build their chastity magic in the first place, because they had little chance to bolster their magic after chastity was relinquished.

After everything Salem had done, ruining her for her own world, he had not ruined her completely. She could never accept anything less than what had been offered to her here in Arcanium.

Dawn hadn't yet tinged the horizon, but she sensed it like mist, her nocturnal time almost over. She leaned back against the Horned God in farewell. Then he helped her down to the ground from the platform.

The clowns passed through Oddity Row at the crunch of dry grass under her feet, but they veered off in another direction as soon as they realized the childlike form in the dark had wings. She headed to the food court alone. The Horned God retreated back into his sanctuary.

There was usually a golem at the food booth at all times. At least, there had been so far for Sera's late-night cravings. But she'd never stayed up until dawn, and there was no golem there when she arrived at her usual booth, not even crammed in behind the counter like a hidden corpse.

"May I help you?"

The odd chef was eerily normal, by all appearances an average human man—bald, average height, average weight, wearing an open chef's coat over black trousers and a white undershirt—a uniform to throw on when disturbed in the middle of the night. She hadn't known he lived in his kitchen, but it didn't surprise her.

He looked average, but darkness emerged from him like spilled ink, throwing off her senses. She tasted rotten peach, felt thick mucus sliding down her arms, heard hundreds of hungry cockroaches chewing through a junkyard. He kept something terribly ugly within him, yet both his demeanor and manner were polite, and he didn't throw that ugliness at her—merely struggled to keep it contained. Something must have been testing his resolve, because she'd never sensed this kind of ugliness when she'd passed his booth before. Demonic energy, yes, but nothing like this…seepage.

From behind his thick-rimmed glasses, he impassively took in the sight of her. No judgment, gleeful or disapproving. Utter patience, in spite of the hour.

"I wanted something to eat," Sera replied slowly. "I overindulged."

"I've been known to encourage that from time to time." He went around the counter and through the open door to his kitchen.

She didn't follow him, but she didn't leave either. Through the open door, the sound of pots, pans and other metal things clattered faintly.

After more than a few minutes, the odd chef came back out with a wide, shallow bowl of sliced apples, Havarti and gooey raw honeycomb. In his other hand, he held a small, unmarked bottle of oblivion, identical to the one in the Horned God's oddity tent. The odd chef must have been the one to make and gift it to him. No faerie merchant would sell to someone in Arcanium, even a god.

The odd chef stepped around the counter to hand her the bowl and the bottle with a small bow. "I've been waiting for you to come to me. In my experience, the fae don't often wait so long before overindulging."

"I've indulged plenty through what the golems offer."

"But they have no imagination. I give them a recipe, and they follow it to the letter. Good consistency but no variation or imagination for special requests. If you aren't tired of it yet, you will be. Don't hesitate to request something more specialized from me or Vivian. I can access almost anything, even the sorts of things that wouldn't be on a menu. There are products that the humans of our little circus cannot enjoy in the same way which I offer to the demons and jinn of Arcanium. There is no reason I cannot extend that courtesy to you."

"I'm only ever hungry," Sera said, still wary, although she detected nothing off or untoward about the food and drink he had offered—standard faerie fare, in fact.

"I enjoy feeding the people in this circus. There is no need to skirt around me, Your Highness. I rarely bite, and while I would love to watch you eat, I have plenty of other opportunities to relish the enjoyment of my food. There's no reason I wouldn't leave you in utter peace. My only task is to serve."

"*To Serve Man* is a cookbook."

The odd chef paused, his expression unchanged. His blankness differed from Salem's, because whatever malice slithered out of him didn't seem to originate from any intense calculation behind his eyes. It wasn't a smokescreen or mask, just plainness, even placidity, although there was something…something unspeakable just behind those black eyes of his. Unspeakable—evil, perhaps—but not aggressive. With all the focus that the rest of the world put upon Bell and the Ringmaster, she wondered whether they made a mistake ignoring the other demons of Arcanium simply because they did not look or act as much of a threat.

Then the chef laughed, his smile uncomfortably large though not unnatural—a stark contrast to the blankness of before. "I haven't heard that reference in some time. I can serve man if you ask it of me, but I have to fight the incubus, succubus and clowns for the flesh. It's not my preferred meat, especially in this place. There are far more interesting things to do with it than consumption."

"You made it for Locke."

The smile faded, but Sera still didn't sense anything dangerous directed at her. "Only because the meat was provided. I didn't serve man to man, only to demon with a taste for it."

"I have no taste for it." The fae had been known to consume human flesh, but as the odd chef had said, there were far more interesting things to be done with it, and once those things had been done, the meat wasn't much use anymore.

"Then let me know what you might have a taste for, my dear, besides circus corndogs. I'm open at all hours, although I might be occupied. Please knock at the door. I will hear it wherever I am. But do not enter."

"Of course." She took her decorum cues from him, as she had at countless feasts and parties of mixed company. He wasn't the only demon to prefer honey to vinegar. They could make pleasant company, for a time, but when she'd had to endure their company in the past, she hadn't been able to see and feel their magic quite like this.

"Good night."

Sera nodded to him, her own kind of bow, although he had called her 'Highness', so he would know why she did not curtsy to the floor as she had with the Horned God.

She took the bowl and the oblivion with her to the food court as the odd chef stepped back inside his booth.

There had been press write-ups about how unusually clean Arcanium was for a traveling circus, which was imperative in a place where the exchange of bodily fluids in strange places was so encouraged. The golems would sanitize the picnic tables before anyone else used them, so she didn't bother cleaning herself before settling cross-legged on top of one of the tables.

She systematically polished off the entire bowl before opening the oblivion. She'd never had a whole bottle to herself before, small or large, and she considered the uncorked bouquet—like whole orchards in a hothouse—before taking a deep swallow. She'd had one glass of the Horned God's bottle. His desire, his magic, had swept through, used it, overwhelmed and overcome it. Now she could enjoy it on its own, experience the serene, disorienting bliss, the sultry slowing of her full and quick mind, as the sun rose and lightened the sky.

She left the bowl on the food booth counter and took the bottle with her, carrying her wrinkled costume over her arm as she walked toward the sun. It would still be kind for an hour or so yet. But the circus would be stirring soon. Even during the week, there were early risers, people whose entire lives were utter mysteries to her. She much preferred the softer edges from the sun's beautiful reflection. And she was reluctant to give the rest of Arcanium an opportunity to see what had become of her. They would understand better than most, but she loathed the thought that they would believe her tawdry.

The light on her skin exposed the filthiness left behind from what she had done, made it more real. With the help of food in her belly and the oblivion in her hand, she settled into a serene lake surface of contentment that she didn't think she'd ever known in her full fifty-odd years.

"You have given yourself."

Sera stopped where she stood, barely ten yards from the iron fence. The voice had come from behind her. She didn't look, because she had nothing to fear as long as the fence was in place and the Bearskin stayed on the other side of it.

In her moment of alarm, she hoped Bell heard her, but if he did, he didn't acknowledge her. His web of spells stayed steady, undisturbed.

"You had your chance," Sera said. "You would have squandered it, but you had your chance."

"*You* still have a chance." The fence rattled but not loudly. He must have been leaning against it, perhaps testing it. He hadn't yet jumped or climbed over. "What you are willing to do could have purpose."

"It has purpose now. Just because that purpose doesn't serve your purpose doesn't mean it's useless, and just because I don't serve you doesn't mean I am useless. An acrobat in a jinni's circus might seem frivolous to you, but what do you expect when you affiance yourself to a faerie? Such a superficial breed, wouldn't you say?"

Now she turned, facing him without shame of what she implied or what he inferred.

It could have been his proximity to the circus, to the succubus, but as he looked over her—streaked, stained and slightly inebriated—his cock twitched in his leather trousers, grew, pushing against the loose material.

"If you were expecting me to honor a contract I never signed while staying within the circus to which I bound myself, I'm afraid this might be a bit of a shock." Sera took another drink of oblivion. "But since you weren't intending to do anything with the breaking of the chastity magic nor with the development of my magic afterward, I can't see why you would be upset."

"I am not upset that you fucked one of Bell's circus freaks. Only that such pursuit is a waste of time."

"The waste here is not me, Ursalem. You wasted your own time negotiating for something I wasn't prepared to let you have, and now you waste it again. All this time, you could have regained the money that you gave my parents and paid for another faerie princess, perhaps even managed to get her pregnant. While here, I have used more of my preparation for marriage than anything you would have required of me. I converse, I dance, I smile, I bow, I love. And I don't have to fear that my children will be taken from me, because there are no children in Arcanium. You could have had me when I was whole, but you chose to render me a fraction. Arcanium accepts fractions as though they are whole, then fill the spaces with something new. Only broken places can truly accept broken people."

"My world is a broken place."

Sera huffed, skeptical of the emotion that had crept into Salem's tone, a stone tossed into the lake of her newfound serenity. "It is not like you to be sentimental."

"I am not sentimental. I was prepared to do whatever was necessary to secure you, Seraphina. My people pooled money they rarely use and therefore do not have much of for the exorbitant fee that your parents required, the kind of fee fit for a princess and all the care and good breeding that went into creating one. I wanted your lineage more than your learning, but that you could learn what was required spoke well of your mind, of what progeny could come from you. Your lineage promised steadiness, cold practicality, not the madness that comes from the passions of the common. I needed practicality, because ours is a practical problem. We are immortal but not as reparable as you. Within a few generations, the

Bearskins might be functionally extinct, with nothing but halflings to carry the line."

"I am hardly the only lowly princess of a diplomatic line in the world." But Sera fluttered closer to the fence, still out of his reach. Then she held out the bottle, just within his reach.

Salem considered the offering. He had seen her drink from it, so he would know it wasn't poisoned. When he took the bottle, she flinched, but he didn't try to grab her in the process.

"You're the one we paid for. You are far more guaranteed than any other I could try to find." He crossed his arms around the iron bars and tipped the bottle up for a few swallows.

"Surely the fate of your people does not rest upon one sleuth's antisocial son," Sera said. "It is true that I inherited my pragmatism from my mother. She taught it to me as surely as she taught more unsavory things. And I tell you that pinning your hopes on one marriage, one faerie to churn out all the hybrids your people need as variants, hardly seems like the ideal plan. As solitary as most of your kind are, you are intelligent enough to sacrifice your own comfort for the survival of your race. Why, then, does it rest upon one long-suffering man and one vain faerie princess in an unhappy marriage?"

"Because it is what we decided. Our dwindling numbers force us to be cooperative, but it doesn't happen easily or often. We pooled our resources and arranged the contract for *you*. I did what I had to do to ensure that you would be my wife when your vaunted pragmatism wasn't enough to overcome your pride, and still you managed to slip away from us. The king and queen will not return the money. They are confident that you will come to your senses or that they can take you away. We do not have strong enough alliances with other races to challenge the contract you so cavalierly dismissed. You speak of diplomacy as though it is easy for every immortal race, but we are nowhere near as garrulous as your kind. Once we have made a decision, it is exceptionally difficult to change. Our hopes are set on you. That was my choice. It is the choice I must live with, and unfortunately, it is still the choice you must live with."

Sera took another step toward the fence, her unsettled magic awakening more in caution, but Salem merely handed the oblivion back to her, with some still left. He watched the curve of her throat as she tossed her head back to drink it.

Swaying with the empty bottle, she considered Salem as he stared back at her, pressed to the iron, his cock unmistakably hard under his trousers. In Arcanium, erections were in such abundance, even under the common bindings, that she could no longer not see them when they were before her.

"It really doesn't bother you, does it? You destroyed my face because *I* would care, not because you do. You wouldn't have settled for an ugly faerie. You just wouldn't have cared. Like they don't care."

"They. Then you have more than one lover in this low place."

"It's neither low nor high, rich nor poor. Arcanium is like nothing you can imagine underneath the façade of cheap thrills. If I choose a lover here, it's none of your concern. You didn't answer my question."

"Your face would turn your kind away from you. It was meant to crush your spirit more than your skull, so that I was your only option, because you were already mine." Salem reached through the bars to touch her unmarred cheek, turning her face to the side so that the cavity would be mostly hidden to him. "No, it does not bother me. I would have even allowed you to correct the disfigurement, once you understood that I would always be your husband, no matter whose eyes you caught, because we have a responsibility, a task before us."

"We are not married, and Arcanium doesn't permit its women to bear children while child-eating clowns guard the circus." Sera stepped back from the tenderness in his touch that didn't match what she had seen, although there was no malice in the magic woven through his skin—not like the odd chef, who couldn't help his.

She searched behind his expressionless face, within the cold intensity of his eyes. Sera didn't need to touch him to see his past. Her magic overlapped his, as good as contact now.

What she found there wasn't the animosity or aggression that she anticipated. Although there was coldness—cold pragmatism, as he had described it—it did not touch everything within him with frost. There were patches of warmth, sunlight through the branches of trees, beaming within clearings.

The marring of her face was a regret, both practical and emotional. So much of his magic was tied to his body, so limited was his power. She was a forest fire to his candle flame, and he wished every day that he had not cast her away in the first place. He might have found better use for her than out of his reach in a mid-rent circus or trapped in his family home in a birthing room indefinitely.

She saw him standing in the bedroom apartment he had created for her, aware of its inadequacy in comparison to what she would have known in her opulent palace. He offered instead spare walls of wood and mortar, clean but otherwise bare floors that he wondered if he should warm with a rug. On one side angled a marriage bed, and across from it were rough-hewn bookshelves and assorted comfortable chairs that his mother had selected because he hadn't known what to choose. In the corner, a nursery had been arranged in preparation—a crib, a mobile, a lamp, a rocking chair and not much else. His wants and needs were few. He didn't know what a faerie princess needed. All that mattered to him was that she wouldn't leave. That was the reason for the keyhole in the door.

There were so many rooms to his family home—something that looked more like an abandoned logwood hotel to those who stumbled upon it by accident. But it was necessary when his kind needed space to live with each other. It was empty now, but he intended to fill those rooms with his children as they grew, with the wing he had set aside for his wife and her faerie children, with keyholes of their own, and the other wing for the children who showed propensity for shapeshifting, so that they had the space they needed as well.

He saw his snow-covered home as though from a distance, saw his own future there and called it good. The Bearskins were not a powerful people, but they were proud, their history rich with wildness, physical strength, the beauty of solitude as well as of brief or isolated companionship, close devotion among families.

He didn't have to be near the rest of his people to fear that their proud sleuth would die out, unremembered, disregarded, discarded, when none of them deserved the deaths given to them by ill-meaning hunters threatened by their presence in woods that were their own. Bearskins adorned the homes of humans who desecrated the corpses, when the skins were supposed to adorn their brethren instead. Within this spacious but humble home, the walls held hope. Cold, yes, but he was used to the cold.

He had not yet met her, had not seen her, had no expectation for her beyond what she could offer his kind.

Now, regret colored that memory, that his urgency and fear had led to violence that had only more completely severed his hope. The sight of her now, and the impression that each successive meeting gave, colored it as well, brought the marriage bed—as humble as the rest of the home, covered with quilts and a folded skin of an ancestor—fore in his mind.

The scent of her desire and the desire of the man who had covered her mingled with that of a forest. Each breath made him hard, because he wanted more every time he saw her, although she had been in greater and greater disarray—farther and farther from her ostentatious home and closer to the wild that he knew.

The image of her in the marriage bed was inexorably linked to the wish for a child in the crib, the sight of her pregnant then nursing, of children clasping her legs or his to walk, with little wings or the first hints of skins of their own. Because one thing led to another in his mind. Even his desires had practical ends. But he did desire her, and his wishes for the future had not altered, only become richer the more she refused him.

"Leave Arcanium and come with me," he said. "I can promise you more than I did. I can even put it in writing for the both of us to sign in a blood pact rather than your parents."

"Even if I wanted to, which I don't, I couldn't."

Sera felt for his people, and the fantasies he carried of her were far more enticing than she'd imagined sex with him would be. But entering Arcanium, though her last hope at the time, carried much less regret than he assigned to his own actions. "Bell's service requires years, even when voluntary. I can't leave."

"There are ways to break wishes, just as you broke the contract."

"The contract bore my father's signature, not mine. It is much easier to break from blood that is not completely your own."

She heard enough in the distance to tell her that people were not just waking up but walking around Arcanium. With reluctance, she cast the filthiness from her body, then stepped into her costume.

She bent over close enough for Salem to curl his fingers around a few twisted locks of her hair and tug her closer to the fence. At whatever emotions he noticed pass over her face, he did not pull her all the way against the iron, although he kept hold of her hair.

"I need you to let go of me." Sera straightened, not backing away from the fence or his hold. "I need you to let go of this dream that persistence alone will get you what you want or even what you need. Neither you nor I are equipped to take on a jinni like Bell. As dire as the straits are for your people, you need to let me go and find someone else. Hang your pride. Demand your money from my ring. There are others who can give you what you need, others who can give you what you want. I'm no longer available."

Salem released her hair. "What if Bell could be taken?" His hips canted against the fence, involuntarily and perhaps unconsciously. His eyes hooded as he stared down at her, at the display of her cleaner body, barely covered by the romper. And now he knew what she looked like without it. "What if Arcanium could be breached?"

"He cannot and Arcanium cannot." Sera narrowed her eyes. "He will not be caught off-guard so soon, Salem. Abandon the very thought. Do you know what he's done with Locke's audience? He keeps them in a chest, bound to lifeless stones. The cast use them for target practice, for incubus and succubus feasts. It cannot be done."

"It's been done."

"It cannot be done indefinitely, and it certainly cannot be done while Bell is still careful."

"*If* it could… If it could, would you come with me? No contract but what you and I agree to in our own?" He lifted her head by gentle pressure under her chin. "Please, Sera."

"It doesn't matter." Now Sera stepped back, away from his touch, too far for his reach. "I don't know who needs to hear this, but let it be heard. Leave Arcanium alone. If you want to return to visit me in peace, Bell won't stop you, and if you remain a gentleman, neither will I. But do not pursue me at the expense of Arcanium."

It was Salem's turn to back away, fading like smoke in the glare of the sun. "I'm sorry. It's too late."

Chapter Ten

Sera didn't know whether Salem had given her the warning to prepare her to be taken against her will or to prepare Arcanium for an assault, but it prepared her either way. He had to have understood that Bell would also know as soon as he said it, but she hadn't been able to read Salem's emotions before he'd faded, his magic too insubstantial to grasp.

She found it difficult to reconcile their last encounter with what she'd known of him. Difficult to reconcile his lack of regret after destroying her face with his new regret—at the lack of desired result from it, yes, but also that it had severed her from him. Difficult to reconcile that he had assigned to her all of his people's hope as well as his own.

Regardless of her feelings on the matter, he was one Bearskin. He would not be the threat coming for them.

Bell sat cross-legged on the rug in his fortune-teller tent, where he'd been waiting for her when she came running in looking for him. "Proceed as usual. I'll personally tell everyone who needs to know."

"The humans as well as the demons?" Sera thought of the scars still on Carlo's back, scars he must have requested to keep. If they were taken by surprise again when Bell could have given them plenty of warning…

"That's why I will tell them personally." Bell beckoned her to the ground with him and took her hands in his, urging her to relax.

"They'll blame me."

He caressed her palms with his thumbs, a steady rhythm as hypnotic as his voice, his glowing eyes. "The blame lies with me for making this your sanctuary, not you in seeking it. You wouldn't be the first to seek sanctuary only for the antagonist to follow you in. My crystal collection replenishes itself with the souls and spirits of those who come here for retribution. Before Locke took Arcanium, I kept those who tried to harm my people as my prisoners. I no longer have the heart for that, to the Ringmaster's great frustration, and to tell the truth, I barely had the heart for it before. Now, they just add color to my fortune-teller tent, if I keep them in Arcanium at all." He glanced back at the chest, at the stones that decorated the sideboard, more hanging as pendulums from the ceiling with the translucent scarves.

"One or two demons hardly compare with what I think is coming," Sera said.

"Then let this be the test." Bell released her hands to rest his on her thighs, just above her knees. "This will be the first attempt to really probe at what they believe to be Arcanium's weaknesses."

Sera covered his hands with her own. "What if Arcanium falls?"

"It won't, as you so vociferously insisted to your betrothed."

"What if it does?"

"I won't have my people taken again," he said. "There are plans in place if the borders are compromised. Even if they take Arcanium, they won't get the cast within it."

"You can promise nothing or else you *would* promise it, which means there is a possibility that Arcanium will fall again."

Bell shook his head. "I cannot see for certain because it is of too great importance to me. It's the curse of seeing forward that it is harder to see what is your own. But I make contingencies for my plans now, and I entrust those plans to the others. Take heart, child." He leaned in to press a kiss to her forehead. "Proceed as usual. I will spread the word."

* * * *

The atmosphere within the circus palpably changed, a dark pall creeping over the fields and through canvas and velvet, as pervasive as scent. Even those who hadn't been in Locke's Arcanium witnessed the change among those who had and grew more subdued.

The circus moved to another location, which had nothing to do with trying to escape. The Arcanium website and every press release listed where new and old guests could find them. Bell could take them into hiding where nothing and no one could ever find them, but as he'd said to her, everything was to continue as though nothing were wrong—easier said than done, but they tried.

No one treated her more like a pariah than before. If anything, the tumblers, aerialists and acrobats spent more time around her—in her general vicinity during open hours, eating with her during the week, hovering when she was backstage. Because most of them were human, with very little magic to read and little contact between her and them, it took a while for Sera to realize they weren't keeping an eye on her because they feared that she would double-cross them. They were trying to protect her.

Even the clowns played guard, darting through the corner of her vision when the circus was open, rustling over grass when she walked the quiet circus at night. The Albino Triplets took over when the clowns had to be elsewhere. The demon Triplet, Marina, didn't speak much except to the other two, with the comfort of years' familiarity, but her blue eyes sometimes inked black when Sera would climb the jungle gym around the children, when they would pull on her wings, when fathers would get too close to take pictures with her and their kids, when men without children would stare. Sera would have found the confusing mixture of the demon's light-streaked dark magic unpleasant if she hadn't been touched by the reason it was so close.

Carlo was one of her rare, true constants, because though his face took on a drawn, hollow cast, he changed nothing about how he treated her. He spent no more or less time with her—perhaps because he'd already been spending plenty with her prior to the threat. Every brush of her skin against his told her that he knew she was capable of protecting herself more than he was of protecting her. Like many of the human women of Arcanium, he'd aligned himself with a much more powerful entity.

Strangely, she had seen neither gray hide nor white hair of the Horned God since the night they'd shared—not so much as a point of his antlers over the caravan vehicles. He still left the flowers and ribbons out on his oddity platform, and she still heard the children talk about decorating him, but he kept himself from her sight.

She felt him, though. Oh, how she felt him—glittering, glistening invitation shot through with the warning to *wait*. Wait. Wait. Wait for whatever hovered in the air to settle, for this tension to finally break, one way or another. As an immortal, he was more resilient than the humans, but he'd had his share of captivity and pain, and he wasn't a demon. He responded to it in his own way, as a stag responded to the destruction of his home—by disappearing, as much as he was able to without leaving Arcanium.

His magic pervaded the circus as much as the dread, as much as Bell, as the darkness of the demons. This was their home, and demons and gods guarded their home with unmatched jealousy.

They traveled to yet another town with a similar field. It never really made a difference where they went. It was always so much the same—only the horizons seemed to change. She had never lived in such open air. Instincts that a princess had never needed warned her that the fields gave her fewer places to hide. Tents, even ones bigger on the inside than they seemed, would offer little protection.

* * * *

She was sitting on the top of the jungle gym, children all around her and Carlo hanging below, when Salem reappeared in Arcanium.

He stood there amid the moving throng, his gray-streaked hair loose in the breeze. He wore his bearskin trousers but with a crisp white shirt untucked, the first time she'd seen him completely covered. Others noticed him—men and women—because they noticed immortals, sensed grandeur even if they didn't understand it, as they noticed her in spite of her disfigurement. Stoic and silent, he looked at nothing and no one but her.

Sera straightened, her wings fluttering in spite of the fuss a little girl was making with the gossamer veins. At the shift in her demeanor, Carlo turned around on the bar and followed her gaze. He'd only seen Salem at night, his vision in darkness less keen than hers, but he recognized him immediately.

Carlo swung down the bars then ducked underneath. "Sera?" He glanced between her and Salem, the drawn quality in his countenance like bruises now. She hated how this waiting and what they'd been waiting for had affected him, that it had brought his past even closer than it had been when she'd first arrived.

Sera sent her magic out to all those who could see or sense it, crossed spiritual paths with demon, jinn, monster, god, even the odd human with enough magic for her to feel.

"It's time."

She climbed down from the jungle gym, absently apologizing to the children and their parents that she had to leave. She touched Carlo's shoulder to indicate that he should follow. The Albino Triplets had been waiting and watching over her while standing to the side of the jungle gym. They now stepped forward to join Sera and Carlo.

As Sera passed Salem, her wing brushed his arm, releasing a whiff of regret, although she couldn't tell how recent. When he followed her, it wasn't as part of the circus. He edged the small group of them as it grew, with more coming from the midway. From the other side of the big top tent, where the courtyard and Oddity Row had been set up, other cast members rounded the canvas. They all carried with them various levels of fear, however squared their shoulders and determined their stride.

Sera stopped in the middle of the field between the big top and the elaborate gates, open and blocked only by the ticket booths. She hadn't sensed fae magic while on the midway, but the closer she came to the entrance, the more it jolted through her, the way she felt every time the caravan passed under electrical towers.

The fae were outside the circus, standing in concentric circles around its perimeter. The iron would be singing unpleasantly in their blood, but it couldn't keep them out any more than it had her.

Most of them wore human clothing to superficially avoid detection, some with their wings hidden under jackets and others with their wings made invisible to those too mortal to see through weak illusion spells. A few wore their own costumes, but it was not completely out of place in limited numbers, given how many humans entered the circus in corsets.

Even without seeing the wings, the humans paying their way into the circus could tell that something wasn't quite right. The guests weren't magic-sensitive, but they all had perfectly decent diurnal eyes that could plainly see that a disproportionate number of solemn short people had surrounded the circus. Was it a protest on behalf of the other vertically-challenged people in Arcanium? Was it a stunt, a flash mob, a special performance that hadn't been announced in the press release?

People continued to enter the circus, though, nervously looking back at those who stared at them with contempt and dismissal. Humans would be no obstacle to fae soldiers. If anything, they would be a vulnerability for Bell, if he was dead set on protecting everyone who entered. Which was why the fae waited outside and only Salem had crossed into Arcanium. He'd acted as Sera's lure, but he kept enough distance that no one could accuse him of harming anyone, regardless of his ambiguous intentions.

Lennon, joined by the other Skellies, stepped in front of Sera, the demon threatening to push through his human façade beyond mere black eyes and sharp teeth. Sera held out an arm to warn him back.

Perhaps she was not the most intimidating of cast members to place before the rest. The Mountain, as gargantuan as his name suggested, would have been better or the Ringmaster. But everyone within and without the circus who understood what was going on knew perfectly well that appearance had little to do with power. Lennon might have been more powerful than she—she couldn't tell, with how thoroughly he kept that part of himself suppressed—but she was strong enough, and she was the reason the fae were here. She would stand front and center, bear the vulnerability, because she had brought this upon everyone else. It was her responsibility to meet whatever came head on.

"Really, Seraphina. There wouldn't have been a need for this drama if you had just come home."

Sera had never seen her mother like this, in a tailored suit a human woman would wear to work in a bank, not the attire of a matron queen.

The queen stepped to the threshold of Arcanium's gates, her hands up to indicate that she was weaponless, although such distinctions were senseless for those with magic. It did, however, suggest that she was not prepared to use it. Only a fool would enter Arcanium so brazenly ready to wield the magic at their disposal.

"You think *I'm* dramatic?" Sera said. "You surrounded the circus like faerie stones. You trapped every single one of us inside until you get your way."

"Which should be easy. All your jinni leader has to do is hand you over and everything goes back to normal. We've no quarrel with Arcanium."

"Of course you do. He has Falconell. If you hadn't had quarrel with Arcanium, I never would have come."

"And you decide to align yourself with the man who took your brother?"

"You and I both know what Falconell did," Sera said. "You regarded his indiscretions as an embarrassment when you should have regarded them as an abomination. We were lucky Father wasn't there that night. I notice he's not here now, either."

"The people of this circus were prisoners of a dungeon at the time. They trusted the wrong jinni. Their fate was his fault, not our family's." Vinia came closer, her hands drifting down to her sides. "You've made a mistake, Sera. Several, in fact. But they can be rectified."

"I rectified them when I escaped the ring and broke the contract that father bound me to. The contract I signed here in the circus? *That* is a contract I cannot break. Like you said, I've aligned myself with the jinni, instead of monarchs who intended to throw me away like trash."

"Come now, Sera. It never bothered you before, not until you were betrothed to someone who found you wanting and you couldn't stand not being as spoiled as you were in our home."

"He didn't find me wanting!" Sera struggled to maintain control of her emotions, not for her mother and the cast behind her but for the guests, to keep from calling additional attention to an already-odd situation. "He found me perfectly useful but not as a faerie wants to be useful. You willingly relegated me to the function of broodmare, a role for which I was grossly overqualified. Ursalem understands the error of his ways, Mother. Do you? It wasn't the assault that was the greater betrayal but that my future husband could do so without repercussion. Was your last daughter truly such a burden that you would disown her for something as insignificant as gold?"

"There is nothing insignificant about gold, and there is nothing insignificant about faerie children, especially with Bearskin flowing through their veins, even if it does not present. It is essential for us to carry the blood of the endangered, as we carry many. We didn't give you an insignificant task, Sera, just because you thought it was beneath you. Now, enough of this tantrum. It's time for you to leave this cheap hell and return to where you rightfully belong—in our halls, wedding the man we promised you to."

"This is no tantrum. The contract you gave to Salem is null and void. Even if you were to break Arcanium's spells to pieces, Mother, I am still bound to the jinni who holds my wish. A demon can take the wishes for himself, because he too is born of fire. The fae cannot, because we were born of earth, no matter how many you bring to take it." Sera placed her hands on her hips, tilting her head like a child. "Remember all those history lessons you had me take to become a glorified womb? Who knew they'd finally pay off in a circus?"

"If you don't come with us of your own accord, I'm afraid we *will* have to take you by force. Ursalem, do your people a service and grab your wife for us, please."

Salem stood stolidly between the two factions, either reluctant or too uncertain to choose a side. "Not until the spells of Arcanium are lifted. I have fulfilled my part of the contract, Your Majesty—more than my part, in fact, given that I found her after she ran. It is your task to deliver your daughter. I came to you in dire need of Sera's assistance, but I will not assume the risk of the jinni's wrath when you have an army behind you."

"Our circle will return your money *and* honor the contract if you take her now. I will sever the spells that bind her here." Vinia gestured to Sera more emphatically this time, the stones in her golden rings glittering daggers into Sera's good eye. "Does that make her worth the risk for you now?"

"The chastity spells are broken," Sera said.

"It is none of my concern if your tantrum brought you to the end of your growth. Your husband has no need for it."

"I'm not sharing this information because it is of consequence to my husband. I'm sharing it because it is of consequence to you. Not only was it coded into the contract that I be a virgin upon marriage to ensure the lineage of my children, but my magic is also no longer contained. I'm not the cocooned woman you sold, Mother. I know what magic binds me here, and it's nothing you can touch. To take me from Arcanium would cause me grave pain—mortal pain to weaker flesh. It would not end until he returned me to Arcanium."

"What is your pain to him, to me, as long as you do your duty?" If Salem had always been cold to Sera, Vinia brought the temperature down still more, her gray opalescent magic shivering with it. "This is why you were born, Seraphina. If you must suffer, that is due to your own miscalculation, one of a series that brought all of us here now. If Bell is the kind and generous demon he pretends to be, he will not allow you to suffer indefinitely, and if he does, then you've no reason to stand with him now. I am prepared to do what must be done to take you back, daughter. Is he prepared to do what is necessary to keep you? Are you truly worth that much trouble to him, as a faerie princess for children and an aerialist using the arts I taught you for other purposes? How you managed to break your chastity magic in here is beyond me. What real use are you to anyone now? Did you give yourself to a demon, who seeks only the corruption of whatever purity you had? Or are human standards really as low as that?"

Her mother had condemned her to marry Salem, but for Sera to hear her own fears confirmed so baldly stole what bravado had given her courage, swept it away in the silent gale of her mother's disgust. Sera had no answer, nothing but dark, pulsing doubt deep in the dark blood rushing through her veins.

A warm hand, dusted with dirt, crept into her own to remind her that, though she couldn't see those with her, she wasn't alone.

Vinia's lip curled in amused contempt. "Oh, I see. You're a true princess of the fae, Sera, yet you gave yourself to the first horny human male who would take you. Did he have to take you from behind?"

"I don't know what you're seeing." Carlo's voice was much steadier than Sera could hope of her own. "There's nothing wrong with her face."

Vinia peered down her nose at Carlo, so close to the ground that even someone of her stature could look down. "She's not enchanted. There are no illusions hiding… Ah, I see. An effort at gallantry. Or perhaps you must call her complete for you to be complete as well."

"Do you want me to list my lovers alphabetically or chronologically?" Anger tightened his grip. "Even considering your age, Your Majesty, I'm betting my numbers are better than yours. And not one of them complained."

"Then our standards *are* higher."

"Narrower. A subtle but significant distinction. Given how low Sera's expectations for sex were, I'm betting the quality of mine is better than yours, too." Carlo let go of Sera's hand to walk forward. "Don't hate the player, love. If you're not getting it good from your crowned hubby, in spite of this ice-queen gorgeousness you've got going on, you've got to speak up. Why don't we do this by a show of hands, guys? I'm not talking to the folks on the outside, although if they can hear me, feel free to contribute. All of you coming in, too, since we're just doing this willy-nilly in public for some reason. Please cover any delicate ears now. Raise your hand, anyone, if you would sleep with this woman in a heartbeat—from behind, from the front, top, bottom, sixty-nine, upside-down, whatever makes you hard."

Sera fought the impulse to look behind her, because she was already feverish at every suggestion, as though she hadn't done every single one of those with the Horned God alone in one extended session. The only hands she could see were from Carlo beside her, Salem to the side and quite a few of the fae soldiers outside the fence, despite the fae's vaunted standards. A few more raised their hands as the word spread of the reason.

Sera forced herself to keep facing forward before she could decide to dig herself a hole to crawl into and die. It didn't help that those who had hurriedly covered the ears of their children and a few teenagers were glaring at her, as though she were the one to blame for their awkward position. A few of the men entering raised their hand as well—surreptitiously if accompanied by a woman. They didn't have to raise them high for Carlo's point to be made.

"Men, women, demons, humans, gods, monsters, fae, choose your poison, none of us give a fig about her face. Her would-have-been husband doesn't care. I certainly don't. Bell insisted she keep it, because this is a place people can admit they like it. If she decides to join the Funhouse, she'll get her own set of fans following her around on their knees, begging for her favor. I've got my own loyal fans. Most of us do, even the ones *you* think are too ugly for that sort of thing. Like I said, we're probably getting much more and much better than you. So don't bring personal attacks into this, ma'am." Carlo lowered his hand, then sat on the ground as though a faerie queen wasn't staring daggers at him. "So instead of standing there making idle threats and trying to get someone else to do your dirty work, why don't *you* try to take her from us? Go on, bitch. We have all day."

Vinia took slow steps into Arcanium toward her daughter and the mouthy human who dared speak to her like a peer rather than a queen. "Even if you had all your parts, you'd be so far beneath me that corpses would decay upon you. Do you know what I could do to you, what I have done to better men than you?"

"I have an idea," Carlo said dryly. "I'm old hat at what people like you can do to me. But you're not going to do it here. If you could, you would have just grabbed her, tossed her over your shoulder and left. There wouldn't be all this talk while you…what? Poke at Arcanium's spells looking for weaknesses? That impressive army of yours is still out there. It's just you and the bear guy in here, menacing us with scary, scary words. You might be powerful. I can't tell. I know she is, and that's a good kind of scary, so I assume you must be, too. But you're afraid of Bell. Even with all of you and your respective magics here, you're all still afraid of him."

Vinia crouched, narrowing her eyes with a cold smile as she brought herself to Carlo's level. "But Bell isn't here. All of you gathered around my daughter, lambs herded to slaughter, but I neither see nor sense your shepherd. In fact, I see plenty of demons, plenty of humans, but none of his *favorites*. Could it be he's abandoned you to save his skin and theirs? So you see, Sera, you're not worth saving. You're just another acrobat with a funny face. He can create that again. You're nothing special to him."

Sera didn't look back at the mention of Bell's absence or the absence of his favorites, but Carlo did, as though startled. The subtle sag of his shoulders suggested that Vinia hadn't been lying.

Vinia rose to her full height again and held her hand out to Sera. "Now, be a good girl and come with me. Your husband is still willing to take you, not that either of you have a choice anymore. The contract is *not* nullified, and you will *both* honor it." Vinia glared at Salem. "If the jinni knows what's good for him, he will not interfere with affairs of the fae, as he never should have in the first place. Take your wife, Ursalem. That is a blood covenant command. You are mine until you honor the contract we signed."

"Mother, please don't do this. Just let me go." Some of the confidence and authority had leached from Sera's tone, and both of them heard it, because Vinia's smile broadened.

"Why would I do that when the Ursal paid such good money for you?"

Vinia grasped Sera's wrist and jerked her forward. Carlo swung up onto his hands in protest, but Vinia backhanded him, her stone rings ripping through his face and drawing thick lines of blood as he spun to the ground.

Salem calmly stepped over Carlo, no more notable than a log as he came up from behind Vinia.

"Oh no, someone hit me. Stop the presses. That's literally never happened before." Carlo swung back up onto his hands, ignoring the blood that painted half his face and dripped down his neck. "For someone so insulting of demons, you really like inviting comparison, don't you?"

Vinia exhaled sharply, turning back around with irritation, but Carlo bypassed her to latch firmly onto Salem's leg.

Salem stared down at him in utter incredulity, too stunned to do more than half-heartedly shake his leg to kick Carlo off.

Carlo only tightened his hold. "Maybe the get-up didn't give you the hint, man, but I literally have no shame."

Sera hadn't moved, mostly because she hadn't seen Carlo clinging onto Salem's leg coming in a million years and now that it was happening, the unexpected paralyzed her as effectively as any spell. The only upside was that it appeared to have done the same to her mother, who still held her daughter's wrist but hadn't tried to drag her anywhere.

"I can still walk with you there," Salem finally said, when kicking did little more than threaten to throw him off balance rather than Carlo off his leg.

"Yeah, but not as well. I may have my limitations, but I work with what I got."

Salem huffed, but rather than try any harder to get the man off of his leg, he continued as though nothing held him back. Though Carlo gave him a limp and an artless gait, Salem was Bearskin, not fae, and he focused less on the art of his walk than getting where he needed to go. It didn't slow him down nearly as much as it might have a human man of the same stature. Salem still carried all the strength of a much larger bear inside of him.

The shudder of magic across Salem's skin broke Sera's paralysis. Even under the circumstances, the admonition not to reveal his magic weighed upon him, because shapeshifting was more difficult than faerie wings to explain away as illusion. But if shapeshifting was necessary, he showed that he was prepared to do it.

Sera darted forward, away from her mother's hold on her wrist, and hooked her fingers under one of the straps on Carlo's harness. "Let go of him."

At her alarm, Carlo immediately released Salem. She dragged him slightly over the ground as she pulled him away, but he braced himself on his stumps before she released him.

"Hubby not happy?" Carlo muttered.

"He can turn into a damn grizzly. I don't recommend antagonizing the bear," she hissed back.

"You clearly don't know the bears I know."

"He only had to hit me once."

That sobered Carlo up quickly.

"Salem, he's just half a man, and the rest are chum without their master." Vinia crossed her arms and lifted her chin, the air around her glistening with ice crystals as she pinned Salem with her magic. "If you don't take my daughter for your wife right now, like you promised you would, I swear that you will lose your entire future—not because you won't have Sera to give you children, but because I will end every Ursal-blooded immortal I can find, here and abroad, until there are too few of you for even a hybrid breeder to diversify. Your world will be barren, cold, just a howling wind in an empty house and only your inadequate ears to hear it. That *will* be your future if you don't grab your hell-damned wife *now*."

Salem whipped around, slamming his foot into Carlo's face, which smashed his nose in and sent him reeling. This time, Carlo didn't rock back up again.

Sera screamed—one part fury, one part horror. Her wings hummed like those of a wasp as she tried to fly around Salem to determine if Carlo was even still alive, but Salem snagged her around the waist and scooped her up over his shoulder, holding her legs as effectively as rope. With the direct contact of his arm on her bare legs, she sensed the unbearable vibrating tension of his magic threatening to split and turn him at any minute, no matter who saw, if anyone tried to get in his way. He would do anything—*anything*—to preserve his people.

"And you, Sera… If you dare use an ounce of that magic you're building for its purpose against the woman who *gave* you that power, I'll make sure if that half-man isn't dead yet, he snuffs out completely. Then I'll take all of your children from you straight from the womb. The Ursal can keep his bears, and I'll steal the rest. That will leave you as alone as I would make *him* if he falters."

With an imperious turn on her heel, as only a faerie could do on such uneven ground, Vinia led Salem and Sera toward the Arcanium gate.

Something crashed into Salem from the side.

Sera flew off of Salem's shoulder, slamming into the ground. The bright copper of magical blood, like newly shined pots, cut through the air.

Salem grunted, staggering but not falling.

The Horned God had planted the shorter antlers from his forehead solidly into Salem's shoulder, the larger rack framing either side of the Bearskin in its own warning, because the Horned God could have struck Salem to kill and hadn't. That didn't mean he hadn't made a mark. The brow antlers were a good three inches long, and the entire length of them pierced through Salem's skin and muscle. The Horned God's forehead pressed against the flesh, which meant that he'd added in the force of his skull behind the blow. It had left him as unshaken as a ram.

Salem still grunted, struggling to remain standing and trying to push back in spite of the stiletto stabs in his shoulder.

The human beings entering Arcanium had ceased walking past them as though everything was normal. They could tell that this wasn't right, because Carlo's broken nose looked real. The blood dripping down his face looked real. The effort and pain on Salem's face looked real. Arcanium was full of illusion, but it was usually contained, shadowed, colored with lights and music to obscure that they weren't illusion. This, even for a potential enactment of some fictional vendetta, seemed extreme. Of all the disbelief Arcanium guests were willing to suspend, their ceiling had officially been reached.

The fae soldiers on the other side of the fence reached for their spell-dipped daggers, ready if any of the human guests of Arcanium decided to interfere.

The Horned God ripped his antlers from Salem's flesh, rending him more. Salem bellowed, a hollow roar that didn't match his appearance. The bear strained just beneath a paper-thin surface. As he whirled to meet his adversary, that translucent layer broke.

The bear—massive, thick-furred, a bewildering anomaly in the field—emerged from the manskin as though vomited forth. It was not a pretty transformation, but all that mattered was that it was a quick one. The grizzly stood at his full height, dwarfing the Horned God, even with his antlers.

The Horned God neither trembled nor cowered. His eyes glowed white—moonglow in the daytime—and he spread his arms in challenge.

Sera sat up, transfixed by the unspoken magic between the Bearskin and the Horned God, although if they were communicating, they kept it private. Then Salem bellowed at the Horned God, this time unfettered by the throat of a man. He lumbered forward in a charge that was much faster than it seemed, because it didn't take him much effort to barrel across the distance in a matter of seconds.

The Horned God was capable of magic that Sera couldn't begin to understand, but he did nothing to stop the Bearskin from hitting him straight on, his forehead almost completely inside the bear's mouth.

One of the brow antlers stabbed into Salem's hard palate, and in return, Salem slammed his teeth into the Horned God's skull with a painful crunch. It didn't completely crush the skull like Salem had done to Sera's face with his paw, but the Horned God screamed, high-pitched with pain that didn't allow for modulation, raking through a throat unaccustomed to sound.

Salem tried to close his mouth over the god's head, but there was another terrible sound, like punching through thick-rind melons— multiple, staggered.

Salem tried to pull back. Something caught him, kept him trapped against the Horned God's head.

The god shoved his hands against the bear's chest to push him away—at least that's what Sera thought he was doing. Then antlers emerged from the bear's shoulders, though not the way they did from the Horned God's. They stabbed through flesh, hooked the bear to the rack that the god grew from his palms. It didn't appear to be fatal, but that didn't mean it wasn't painful as the antlers grew through him, branched off and expanded. The ones that the Horned God usually sported grew as well—reaching out like pernicious vines that made trees groan, tearing through Salem's mouth and into his head.

Blood. More blood. So much of it. Sera was torn between begging the Horned God to stop and understanding that killing Salem could be the only way to stop him. He might have had a change of heart, but he hadn't had a change of mind, and Vinia hadn't given him much of a choice in the matter.

All Sera could do was breathe in the fine mist that only someone who fed from life energy would know was there—aerosolized droplets from each push of the antlers through Salem's body, from each effort Salem made to pull himself back, but the growing antlers were worse than arrows, which would hook into flesh and tear if pulled back. There was nowhere for the bear to move, backward or forward, where branches of antlers didn't block his path.

Terror made the darkness of the bear's wild eyes tragic. She couldn't find any trace of vindication within herself. He coughed, grunted then flexed. This time, cracking branches filled Sera's ears. When the god pulled back his hands, the jagged line of the partial break deepened near his palm, ripping at the skin there as Salem continued to wrench against the antlers—to break through rather than maneuver out.

The madness in the Horned God's eyes glowed brighter than a high full moon in a night sky. He dug in his hooves and completely snapped off the antlers impaling the bear.

The two men who were not just men broke from each other, panting.

With somewhere to go now, Salem pushed the antlers out the other side of his body, the holes left behind disorienting and surreal, but his magic slowly stitched through the damage. He could still bleed out, but his bear form had a lot of blood to lose before he reached that point, and he would replenish faster than any ordinary man.

The Horned God looked incomplete with broken antlers on his head and from his hands. But in a matter of moments, he shed the ones on his hands and the broken ones on his head grew anew, outpacing Salem's healing. He didn't just repair what had broken. Antlers grew from the front and back of his shoulders, down his back, down his arms, like spikes in armor going to weed.

The bear panted on all fours, waiting for his wounds to heal enough, hunched over to protect his more vulnerable insides, but the Horned God wasn't attacking. He became a wall of antlers between Salem and Carlo, who stirred on the ground. Sera nearly cried in relief that she wouldn't have to taste his death like uncorked oblivion at the back of her throat.

"How dare he." Vinia snatched Sera by the hair, yanking her to her feet. "How dare the jinni twist a man's likeness into a god. None of his freak collection deserves the honor of such an image."

Sera jerked away from Vinia's grip, then struck her face with her nails rather than using the cut of rings to draw blood. More bright copper magic to breathe in.

Vinia cried out. It wasn't that Sera had never struck someone before—nor could Sera say that Vinia had never struck her in anger—but in another life, Sera would never have dreamed of striking her mother, no matter what her mother had done. Vinia was queen.

None but the king would be able to strike her without a potential death sentence, if the monarch was particularly vindictive.

"Bell didn't give him any likeness," Sera snapped. "Congratulations, Mother. You've officially pissed off one of the Horned Gods."

"A Horned God in Arcanium?" Vinia's hand hovered halfway to her mouth, fingers fluttering in unconscious fear.

"The Bearskins aren't the only one losing their home. From one god to another, he thought Bell would give him a safe place to rest from running. And he chose me, Mother. You tried to take away the chosen Maiden of a Horned God, and I honestly don't know what he's going to do about that."

Vinia's uncertainty passed over her face, each potential decision subtly shifting her expression with anger, fear then intrigue. She seemed to calculate her error, calculate her options, calculate whether anything had changed just because Arcanium harbored something that the fae honored.

She grabbed Sera by the hair again. Opalescent ropes appeared from thin air to wrap around Sera like spider silk, binding limbs and wings until Sera couldn't hope to move. Sera's magic wasn't bound, but it couldn't tear Vinia's magic away.

"You think you have power just because you've had some good sex?" Vinia sneered. "I've had centuries to develop what you've only just begun. And if you want a chance to develop your own in the endless years to come of warming your cold husband's bed, I suggest you stand completely still while your husband kills himself a god. Even gods can make a fatal miscalculation."

"I hear queens do from time to time as well."

The humans who had entered the circus and those outside of it in the makeshift parking lot didn't just stop moving in fear or bewilderment. They froze, not so much as a breath or a heartbeat to shift them. The trees stilled mid-sway. Even the insects and birds went silent, caught in the midst of a song.

Bell stepped between the loosely regimented cast. A few of the people following him spread out to join the rest—Neve, the Spider, Kitty with the Ringmaster. His favorites, Vinia had called them. Neither Neve nor Kitty would have been intimidating against a faerie horde, but the Spider bared teeth dripping with venom that tasted sulfuric amid the coppery blood in the air. The Ringmaster walked in black smoke that spilled from him like exhaust and spread behind him in a train. It even poured from his black eyes. In his wake, the clowns darted to the sides, guarding the mimes behind them, but their giant mouths were open from ear to ear as they prepared to attack with multiple rows of lantern-fish teeth.

Vinia dragged Sera back with her, her fear from angering a god multiplying by the presence of a jinni and a hellborn demon who was doing nothing to hide what he was, even by Arcanium demon standards. He hadn't taken on his demon guise, but no faerie could mistake from where his magic flowed.

The queen stopped just on the edge of Arcanium. It didn't matter to Sera if she crossed the threshold. As a voluntary, there would be no repercussions for simply crossing the boundary, only if she were taken away with no intention of returning her. But Vinia pulling Sera across the line would officially be kidnapping. The queen was willing to raise hell when the outcome seemed in her favor, but she wasn't so foolish as to steal Sera from right under Bell's nose when she now didn't know whether he was willing to give her up to save himself.

For all of Vinia's foresight, it was apparently as useful as Bell's when it came to Arcanium. Sera's gift of sight was far more reliable. The past didn't change—perception did, but not the past. All too often, the future could be molded in too many different directions. The slightest shift off-course could change everything, and things had clearly not gone to plan.

Bell followed Vinia to the gate at his own pace, relishing the queen's reaction to each advancing step. "I believe you have something of mine."

"She was ours, and she was sold to her husband. Those bindings must be honored first," Vinia replied, resounding her imperious voice over the field as thoroughly as Bell.

"By whose reckoning? She didn't choose her blood, nor did she choose how one would use that blood connection to sell her. But Sera came to me willingly. The wish is more binding than blood, more binding than any contract. She's in my service now, and you, my dear, are trespassing. In addition to trespassing, you've hurt and harmed that which is mine. I'm afraid I just can't allow that to stand."

"You wouldn't dare harm me." Even so, the queen's trepidation quivered through her hold on the magical ropes. "Kill or take a queen of a faerie kingdom, and you'll get more than a circle of soldiers around your circus, more than a battle. There will be war on your hands."

"I much prefer peace, but war would be my obligation if you don't drop that princess and let her return to me right now."

"You would never win." Vinia jerked Sera closer to her. "You are only one jinni."

"Arcanium is not just one jinni, as you well know. Although I wouldn't need it, the war could end swiftly and surely if someone, anyone, made a wish that I could use. A few of my people still have wishes yet to whisper in my ear, and avoiding a war is excellent motivation." As Bell finally reached the gate, he considered how Sera was oriented. Her head crossed the line, but her feet were still in Arcanium. "Are you hurt?"

Sera shook her head.

"Good. But the Bearskin caused grievous harm to two of my cast members. I'm law-bound to hold him accountable for it." He glanced back at Salem. The Bearskin's wounds had closed, although he still bled and glared at the Horned God, who continued to block him off from Carlo. Lazarus and Magda had joined Carlo now, wiping the blood from his face. He seemed dazed but more or less himself. "Like I said, I've always wanted a dancing bear."

The Ringmaster stepped around the antler wall. The bear jerked up as the Ringmaster grabbed his whip, but Salem wasn't fast enough. The whip lashed around his neck, and a single powerful tug jerked him to the ground. Salem tried to escape the leather holding him down by transforming back into a man, but the Ringmaster snapped the whip down over Salem's back.

Shock made Salem buckle, which gave the Ringmaster the time he needed to snag him around the neck once more. The Ringmaster's boot on the fall kept Salem down. A zip tie appeared from nowhere to close around his wrists. He wouldn't be able to transform into the bear again with the whip digging into his neck and the zip tie digging into his wrists. When Salem tried to break them with his magic, the Ringmaster kicked his abdomen, leaving Salem gasping for breath he couldn't take.

"We'll discuss what will happen to you in due course," Bell said impassively, although when he turned back to the royalty before him, his expression and the lantern-glow of his eyes were anything but impassive.

"You can take the Bearskin, for all I care," Vinia said. "You don't get my daughter."

Bell clasped his hands behind his back, affecting boredom he was incapable of. "You have no say in either one. What you do have a say in is whether you leave Arcanium and never come back or whether you remain with me. Really, what it comes down to is how much you intend to piss me off. Because you're deathly close to slicing through my last nerve, and I've been on edge since the last time someone tried to take Arcanium from me."

"It's not just faerie kingdoms that would come after you if you steal me away," Vinia said. "We spread our children far and wide for just these sorts of alliances. If something were to happen to us, Arcanium would fall."

"I'm certainly not looking forward to the mess. I only have two clowns. I suppose they could contact their brethren to help get the entrails out of the velvet. And what on earth am I going to do with hundreds of thousands of potential cast members? I wouldn't even know what to do with myself."

"You act as though it's nothing, Bell, but we all know that you lost Arcanium for months. What can be lost once can be lost again, and no one is happy with you now. All they need is one good excuse. All Arcanium needs to fall is one person with power to slip in and bring the whole house of cards down. For your pride, you would make my daughter a concubine to demons."

Bell raised his chin, the honey of his magic as dark as buried amber. "Locke took Arcanium because of a flaw in my design that has been repaired. He ensnared the dungeon whole then used his considerable power—greater than that of your entire fae kingdom—to keep it. Yet he only managed to keep me out for less than a year. He was a prince of hell. You're just a faerie queen. Don't presume to warn me about the terrors of the night. I was there before mankind stood upright and the fae were only as high as my knee. As old and wise as you believe yourself to be, I am older and wiser, and furthermore, I am fucking tired. I will wage a war that will leave scorched earth in my wake, but I would rather tell fortunes and encourage lovely people to do amazing things while ordinary people look upon them with wonder. Locke was the closest anyone came to taking Arcanium. By the time it happens again—*if* it happens at all—should I still be entertaining strangers, your daughter will doubtlessly no longer be with us…if it is indeed your daughter's welfare you are concerned about."

He tilted his head, as pleasant as any gentleman of any time, to address Sera. "I know you think you're trapped, love, but the ropes are created from nothing, and to nothing they will return, as wispy as any illusion. You have the ability to break them."

"Sera…" Vinia caught on her daughter's name. But there was nothing more for her to say that hadn't been refuted. All that was left was the queen's arrogance and pride, qualities earned among other immortals, but those of Bell's ilk only ever passed through fae rings for their own amusement or benefit. The fae intimidated many races, including some jinn, but they didn't make it a point to invite themselves where they could not intimidate. It was all too easy to forget that there were other beings under the sky who considered them weak.

Sera found the illusion in the ropes, woven from strings of magic, and tore at them, but she had to go strand by strand, which meant her mother still had a hold on her, and even under Bell's nose, the queen rebuilt the illusion for every strand that Sera tore.

Bell could have broken the ropes himself, but he didn't. Instead, he sighed. "How about this? I'm loath to hurt the family of one of my own. In fact, I prefer those I bring into the circus to have severed most of their ties whenever possible. Family annihilation just breeds resentment, and I am, at heart, a sensitive man. You were willing to make one trade. Are you willing to make another?"

"I'm listening." Vinia's grip on her magic loosened, intrigue and wariness passing through Sera's mind like ghosts.

Sera sliced now through whole cords of illusion, then fell to the ground as the ropes dissipated into fading frost. She scurried from the edge of the circus back into it, slipping to Bell's feet. She didn't care that the soldiers and her mother saw her so clumsy. She didn't need to please them anymore.

Bell brought his hands around from behind his back. In one, he held his leather bag, from which he pulled the spirit quartz he'd shown Sera on her first day in the circus.

"If you and your soldiers and mercenaries leave and never return, I will give you your son. A child for a child. It physically pains me to yield a prisoner guilty of such crimes, but if it will save bloodshed and much tedious wailing in agony, I'm willing to part with him. I've no doubt he has seen the error of his ways."

The queen gazed at the crystal with unconcealed greed. A married middle son was far more useful than an unmarried last child. Bell was offering a higher-value prize, but at the cost of so many witnesses from their ring to watch the queen capitulate to someone whom all races despised.

Sera's mother held out her hand for the crystal.

Bell kept it out of her reach. "You need to step inside and give me your word that you will not pursue this vendetta against Arcanium. No telling your allies to act as your proxy. You go back to your kingdom and leave Sera and Salem to me, or else I take your son back and you can join him in my crystal collection. If your ring falls into chaos, on your own head be it for breaking a promise far stronger than anything you've ever signed in blood. If you take the crystal, you make this promise. Are we agreed?

The queen hesitated only a moment. She gathered her magic in preparation for some kind of double-cross once she stepped back into the circus, but nothing happened. Only when she took hold of the crystal did Sera grit her teeth against the indestructible seal of the vow, like the burst of light before the sun crossed the horizon.

"Don't make me kill you, Vinia. Take your son and never return." Bell released the crystal into Vinia's hand.

Vinia backed out of the circus and abruptly disappeared. One by one, then in groups, the fae soldiers around the fence followed.

Sera climbed to her knees, reaching out with her magic for something dangerous left behind, a curse like a bomb or an invisible beast to tear through flesh and break bone before anyone knew it was there, but she found nothing. The only fae magic left in Arcanium was her own.

"She didn't get what she wanted," Sera said. "She didn't have control. She left now, but she's only going to get more furious."

"Vinia dearly wants to retaliate, but she's inclined not to." Bell rested a hand on her shoulder. "I'm sorry that you thought I abandoned you. I wanted to know what they would do if they believed Arcanium vulnerable, a litmus test for what other immortals would try. Even without me present, Arcanium's protection spells remain strong. They would not have been able to steal it by force, and they didn't know the first thing about how to steal it by trickery, as Locke did. In the end, if any other creature succeeds again, it won't be power that destroys this place. It'll be sounder strategy than my own."

"Do you see it?" Sera knew what Carlo and the Horned God carried with them, what Vinia had pretended to fear for her daughter. She didn't know whether she had the same strength as the Horned God or the demons to endure what a less scrupulous demon would have in mind for the circus.

"I never saw an end where your mother would succeed, not even the fog that usually accompanies something hidden from me. There are a few of those when it comes to the fate of Arcanium, but it is an ever-changing fate, my dear, and I wouldn't worry for a while." He drew her to her feet then slid his arm around her shoulder and pressed a kiss to her forehead. "Go to your men. Carlo will be fine, and the Horned God is, as you know, quite resilient."

"What about Salem?"

"Mm-m, what about Salem? That's the question, isn't it?" Weaving through the frozen humans without concern, Bell walked with her toward the fallen Bearskin, still on his belly on the ground but the wound from the whip nearly healed through.

The Horned God's antlers had almost receded back to normal, as though he was reluctant to pull them in completely while Salem was still a wild card in Arcanium. He turned away from the Bearskin, though, as Sera darted to kneel next to Carlo.

Lazarus and Magda stepped back from him, the concern on their face dissipating. He was still covered in blood, but all traces of the damage done by Vinia and Salem had healed over more quickly than Salem could heal himself.

"Ow, ow, ow, ow, ow. Even when you know it's not going to last, it fucking hurts." Carlo adjusted his nose, testing for tenderness, then winced at a pain in his head. He smiled faintly at the brush of her fingertips over the dried blood on his cheeks and chin. "Don't worry, kid. It takes more than that around here to do us in. You okay?"

"Am *I* okay? They barely touched me."

"There's more than one way to hurt."

Sera sat back next to him. "I'll be fine."

"She didn't even try to pretend she didn't sell you off as a breeder. Isn't that, like, fae trafficking or something?"

"I got my practicality from her. There are downsides." Her mother had been warm sometimes, attentive, caring, patient, addressing the welfare of her children when it came to their futures outside of the ring, but not insomuch as it interfered with court politics. That was where Vinia could chill to the bone if she needed to, even more so than the king, who preferred to avoid the conflict that Vinia was willing to seek out, if it yielded more fortune for the ring. "As royal fights go, this one was…on the mild side of moderate."

"You're kidding."

"I wasn't usually a subject of the fights, but yeah."

"I'm sorry."

"Don't be. We don't get to choose our family, and I love them anyway. I just don't want to be with them right now, for the obvious reasons."

"Sure. Sure." Carlo winced as he rocked upright and took a few steps forward to the Horned God. "By the way, man, thanks for the antler thing. I appreciated the intervention rather than just a general assumption that I'd be okay."

Bell was as unfazed by the accusation as Carlo was in making it. "I knew the Horned God would come to your aid."

"Uh-huh. So, what's going to happen to the bear?"

"Do it quickly," Salem said through gritted teeth. Any strength in his voice was throttled by the leather denting the skin, but the Ringmaster didn't tighten the lash—any tighter and air would cut off completely.

"Do what?" Bell asked mildly.

"Kill me quickly."

"Well, yes, I could do that." Bell circled Salem, taking his time, because he had the luxury of it like no one else Sera had ever met. "I doubt many here would mourn the loss. However, I think we all witnessed the conditions with which you harmed my people.

Although the attack was not justified, there were, shall we say, extenuating circumstances? A guillotine over the genetic diversity of your endangered race, for example. I've let people live for worse offenses done of their own desirous will. Not much anymore, but, my dear boy, I wasn't kidding when I said I wanted a bear for the circus."

This time, Salem snarled and lunged, an attempt at intimidation that fell flat when the Ringmaster jerked him back to the ground. "You would have me dance for you?"

"Okay, I exaggerated about the dancing. I think even I would get a few frowns from animal rights' activists if I did that, no matter how well-kept you were. But if I can find a place for a stag-antlered god, I'm sure I can find a place for a Bearskin. There is an inherent indignity in joining a circus, but only insofar as your dignity is delicate. You'll find a different kind of dignity in here, Ursalem, if you choose to stay."

"Then I can choose to go?" Salem said.

"No. You have the same choice I give to anyone who trespasses in my circus and harms my own. An ultimately harmless misunderstanding I can excuse. But you might have killed my Torso, damaged my god and kidnapped my faerie, and there are consequences for that. You knew that there would be consequences as soon as you stepped forward to take Sera away. It was why you hesitated."

Salem managed to get his arms underneath him to brace himself on the ground, but he didn't lift himself up again. "You let the monarchs go."

"And if they return, they will not receive the same considerate offer. They'll just be sentenced to death.

Truly challenging them now would have led to a far graver outcome."

"My people's diminishing land and bloodlines are not grave enough outcomes for you?"

Bell nodded to the Ringmaster to loosen the whip. Then the jinni crouched in front of Salem, his balance impeccable. "You were willing to continue pursuing Sera as your bride, even when it would have been better for your line to leave her, even when you had no good reason to pursue her and she had no good reason not to attack you when you did. I understand that both of you have mixed feelings. You, uncertain why you would risk your people for someone you were willing to destroy. Her, her mother's practicality an unmistakable silver vein in her mine, because she has sympathy for your desperation and the plight of your people."

Bell beckoned for Sera to join them. Sera hesitated at first, but then she crawled between Carlo and the Horned God.

Salem watched her with something that looked like anger behind his eyes, but she didn't think it was. It wasn't quite desire, either. It quaked through her with its intensity, though, tensed her back at the same time it warmed her face, even the place he'd cratered.

It finally occurred to her that, though he couldn't rise to his feet without the Ringmaster kicking him back down, he was bowing to her—eyes on her, which could be disrespectful, but he meant to impart the significance without saying it out loud. Only a few beings in the Arcanium would understand it.

"You have a choice, Salem. You can choose to die, or you can wish yourself into my service—no more and no less than that wish, no specifics, no caveats. You put yourself in my hands, and I choose how to use you. You won't be able to leave Arcanium like Sera can, which means the woods will always be out of your reach. And as long as you remain here, there can be no children. However, rather than expecting the same length of service as I would from other involuntary members of the circus, I will tie your service to hers."

"Bell, that's not—" Sera began.

Bell cut through her protest. "You didn't come to Arcanium because you wanted to be here, Sera, but you did come here of your own will, so you have freedom that my involuntaries do not. I don't expect you to linger, my dear. And when she decides to leave, Salem, if you have served me well, you too will be released. Whether she leaves with you of her own accord as your wife to aid your people or leaves you to find someone else is her decision. After what you did to bring her to me and what you were prepared to do to take her back, I'd say I'm being exceedingly generous, don't you?"

Salem peered up at her face, at the place that he had obliterated like an eraser to pencil. There was no reflexive disgust, no resentment. He was humiliated but steady.

"If I were you, I would take this time to consider my life choices, reflect on how your emergency does not justify another's unwilling sacrifice and pay court to the woman you decided to pursue, if that continues to be the path you seek." Bell stood from his crouch. "It's possible that path will change, because you're not the only one to whom she can give her affection in this thoroughly impractical place. And she is not obligated to return any of your affections or intentions. Do you understand the choice I've given you?"

Salem nodded.

"You wouldn't be so wasteful as to choose death when your people's future is on the line...not even to save your pride." Bell leaned down to lift Salem's chin, urging him to his knees rather than forcing his belly to the dust. "Make your wish, Ursalem."

Salem swallowed back his words, but as the Ringmaster's whip unwound from his neck completely, he could no longer claim that a demon choked them away. "If the queen decides to take her shame out on my people, there might be nothing left by the time I'm done."

"Oh, I don't think that will be a problem," Bell said. "Your mother will send an envoy to the ring to recover the gold. They will proceed to seek a new solution while you are in here, because it will be necessary. They can't afford a war with Arcanium, and you can't afford to fight me on this. It puts your people in a tenuous position, yes, but it was a tenuous position that you were warned about and still you persisted. Though your trespass today was for your people, it didn't start that way, did it?"

Slowly at first, then with more conviction, Salem shook his head.

"Make your wish."

"I wish myself into service to Arcanium, to be released when Seraphina is no longer a part of it," Salem said, each word as tight as though he were still whip-bound.

"Good boy. Now, go to your trailer and get cleaned up. You'll recognize it in an instant. Then take a walk around the circus until it closes, see it from the eyes of someone who is part of it now. And for goodness' sake, don't get in anyone's way. We'll talk alone tonight, you and I, about what you're going to do for me."

Bell faced the crowd of his people who had gathered closer. Already, they had lost the appearance of guardians prepared for a battle. Relief was palpable among the veterans that Arcanium had been tested by those with real power and remained unbreached.

"As you were, children," Bell said. "No one will remember what happened, but I'd prefer not to hold this many people in stasis much longer, and more people are arriving by the minute. I can't close the circus now, but I can encourage my chefs to plan a dinner party after this weekend is over, can't I?" He raised his eyebrows in query at the odd chef, who nodded. "I think we could use a nice, relaxing party with plenty of margaritas, please."

Bell stroked Sera's cheek, Carlo's, then reached up to cradle the Horned God's face. The Horned God bent to press his forehead to Bell's, far more a gesture of affection than what he'd done to Salem—a sign of trust between both of them and perhaps a moment of communication that they kept private as well.

Bell kissed the corner of the Horned God's mouth then gathered up the bloodied, broken antlers that littered the ground near where Salem still knelt. He handed them to the Horned God with a bow—a slight one, with a lowered head, because they were equals. From one god to another.

The Horned God took his antlers then turned and handed one to Carlo.

"Thank you." Carlo appeared thoroughly confused, but even he understood that to reject such a gift would be rude and that, as gifts went, former body parts were probably a high honor from a forest god.

Sera fought a grin, even as she accepted her own token. She curtsied low without looking down then raised herself up before he could urge her to stand again.

"Up you get." Bell guided Salem to his feet and gave him a gentle nudge in the direction of the caravan. "Carlo, you should clean up, too. No crossing paths, you two. Not yet. Do what needs to be done then return to work."

Salem spared Sera one last glance before Bell nudged him again to leave.

The humans were still frozen in place, although the world beyond the parking lot moved, making everything within the circus seem like figurines in an enchanted snow globe.

"Are you sure they'll stay away?" Sera asked.

"All signs point to yes," Bell said, mimicking his own Magic 8-Ball. "You're allowed to have every complicated feeling you like about that, love." He rested a hand on the small of her back to guide her away from the open gate and back into the circus. "But it's time to fulfill your own wish."

Chapter Eleven

"What a day." Carlo joined her on the way out of the big top. "Kidnapped, deer god versus bear shifter, antler gifts, near-death experience then back to business as usual. I'd say this was a typical day in Arcanium, except it really isn't. Near-death aside, I actually feel better. I feel alive. Is this what adrenaline feels like?"

"Adrenaline would be long gone by now, but you could still be riding a high of endorphins from the pain and relief," Sera said.

"Enh, what would you know about human biology?"

"More than you'd think. We're not so different, and the fae have forty-five years to learn and relearn information."

"*Forty-five* years of school? What is this madness?"

"It encourages greater retention. We have to retain far more for far longer."

Sera visited the golems' traditional food booth for her usual meal of corndogs and soda, which Carlo watched with his usual amusement. Then she stopped at the picnic tables instead of going back to the caravan. The tension in her muscles unwound moment by moment, fiber by fiber, now that the day was over and she could finally release the events of it.

If Bell were to be trusted, she was free—bound to Arcanium, but only for a short time. She was free to let go of her fear, free to ignore or bless Salem with her favor at her whim, free to enter the Horned God's tent whenever she pleased, free to kiss Carlo in front of everyone or no one, if he still wanted to after nearly dying because of her. She could have whomever she wanted, of any race, immortal or mortal, if they would have her in turn, and it seemed quite a few of them would have her if she asked—far more than she ever would have imagined when she'd taken sanctuary in Arcanium from her own ugliness.

"Are you really going to still run off with him and have his little bear babies?" Carlo asked.

Sera finished off one of her corndogs. "Maybe. Does that bother you?"

"Yes, considering how his heel offended my nose and possibly my brain before Bell interfered. I get why he did it. I get the gist, anyway. I doubt we'll ever be friends, but I've lived around people I hated before. Misha was pretty well despised for a while. But, Sera, you know what he was going to do with you. What he already did."

"I'm more powerful than him. No contract will hold me to something I haven't agreed to."

"With everything you can do, you'd agree to just pump out children?" he said. "Nothing against the nuggets, but just babies, Sera?"

"Not just that. I won't be content with just that anymore. But you can't understand."

"Try me."

"You can't understand what it's like for your race to be dying." Sera sipped her soda but barely tasted it. "You're not part of a dying race. It's like watching carefully rationed food stores dwindling. It's loss of memory, loss of ritual and its meaning, loss of magic. It's one of thousands of extinctions and endangerments of this planet."

"And we're the cause." Carlo sobered as he settled next to her. "Humans are the worst. I thought you were talking about a different kind of race. You mean species, don't you? Their whole species is going extinct."

"We can cross-breed, so I'm not positive they're a completely different species so much as a distant variation, like dogs and wolves. Then again, we can mate with humans in spite of our radically different origins, so who knows?" She shrugged. "The Bearskins struggled against fur trade and frontier encroachment for years, but it wasn't until your kind really started clearing land, killing everything in the way if it threatened anything on that stolen land, trophy-hunting, that extinction became imminent. I never had a problem helping them with that. I was raised with the understanding that I would sacrifice for the greater good. Just because I won't be doing it for the ring doesn't mean I can't still help. And if he makes it well worth my while, why wouldn't I help save a race?"

"It still seems like a lot to ask of one person, especially if the fae marry for their whole long life."

"Until one of us dies...probably him." Sera finished off her second corndog and tossed what was left in the trash.

"Silver lining?"

"I don't make up the statistics." Sera held her hand out for Carlo to take, and he swung from her grip down to the ground. He rarely let anyone help him up or down from anywhere. The Horned God had his antlers. Carlo had his autonomy. Both were honors gifted to her, and Sera did not accept them lightly.

"I hope I don't offend, but would you be interested in an actual bed tonight? Don't get me wrong. The outdoors thing has been hot as hell. Really touches on that exhibitionist streak we learn early in Arcanium. But the grass gets kind of itchy."

"Oh, you mean *now*?" Sera was glad she hadn't been eating or drinking when he'd asked, because she choked on her own swallow. "You did bleed for me, though. I could taste it in the air."

"I didn't know faeries were vampires. That's new."

"Blood is life, darling. The fae feed on life."

She knelt in the middle of the food court, with guests still milling around, to bring her face close to his. She breathed in the scent of his skin where the blood had been. He'd thoroughly cleaned it all away, but she remembered the blood well enough to almost smell it again. And it still rushed underneath. His quickening heartbeat deepened and darkened his scent.

The stubble of his facial hair roughed against her nose and lips, and the sound of his breathing close to her ear drove her mad. She closed her fist in his hair to jerk his head back just a little. Carlo liked everything both ways, one of the most flexible people she'd ever met, as comfortable with control as yielding it—a gourmand of pleasure in a very different way than immortals. He groaned just as much at her pulling his hair as he did pulling hers.

"The circus isn't closed yet," Carlo murmured against her lips.

"Where's that exhibitionist streak you were talking about?" Sera drifted her fingertips down the harness to the front of his briefs. Then she sent him what the taste of his blood in the air was like, gave him the image of her tongue over his blood-dripped skin—a fantasy rather than a memory. He swelled fast and hard against the binding of the leather, struggling to fill her hand.

"I usually save it for the Funhouse, just to avoid the lawsuits." He cupped her breast, bothering the nipple through the silk until she finally gasped then kissed him hard, fast. Carlo met her for each beat, and the only memories she sensed from him were good—of Misha, of Maya, of women and men from well before Locke's Arcanium.

He held her close to him, as tightly against his body as he could. It helped balance him on the stumps of his legs, but it had the added benefit of letting her feel his torso against hers, his cock low on her abdomen.

Sera singlehandedly unbuckled the harness. She didn't want anything blocking her from him, nothing to interrupt the course of her palm over his back. She tossed it to the side, not caring where it went, not caring who saw her dig her fingers into his ass as she moved her hips against his. After what he'd done, she'd wanted him while he was still bloody, but memory and fantasy were good enough for her, and she'd been resisting since the relief after the confrontation.

That resistance had been complicated by her heightened awareness of other people's arousal near her, perhaps stimulated by Carlo's question to the crowd that had forced the matter to the front of their minds every time she passed them, but there was also arousal for each other that had nothing to do with her. Bell winning the challenge against him had resulted in more relief-desire than what had surfaced in her. A few cast members had taken brief moments in tents or behind booths, or they'd joined patrons in cars, if that was their preference. There had been little bursts of magic, like little fires with smoke she could see from anywhere in the circus.

But she and Carlo had resisted, and the Horned God had again been impossible to find, although she'd wanted to make sure he was okay after what he'd broken to protect her, to protect Carlo.

He'd had no reason to protect him, to be the one who would step forward for him over any of the other monsters and demons Carlo would had known better or longer. He could have done it solely for her loyalty to him, but he'd also offered Carlo the gift of his broken antler—blood and bone, a gift of absolute vulnerability, even for someone who didn't know the first thing about how the body could be used in magic. It wasn't the kind of gift given on behalf of another.

"Bed, Sera." He pinched her nipple hard, bit her lip after she cried out. "I'll come right here if we don't leave now. I've wanted you all afternoon, and you've been looking at me like you've wanted to jump my bones the whole time, teasing me mercilessly. After Okeyo dancing against me, I'm about ready to blow."

"What if I want you to?" Sera kissed the sensitive places on his neck leading up to his ear, sucked the lobe, kissed right behind it. "It won't be your last."

Carlo panted, idly rolling her nipple between his fingers and moving his chin over her shoulder as he looked around them, perhaps to gauge whether they'd been seen and whether he cared who saw them.

He slipped his hand underneath the deep V of the halter top to take her whole breast in his hand. No one would be able to see her, but they'd know what he was doing, and she rewarded him with the pulse of her tongue against his flesh, in mimicry of what she could do elsewhere and to trigger the same places in his body and mind that would react to it.

"Okay, quickly," he said breathlessly. "Then bed. I want... I'll fuck you tonight, if that's what you want from me."

Sera paused, breath shuddering out of her. She withdrew just enough to meet his eyes. "Are you sure?"

"I can't stop thinking about it. I can't stop dreaming about it. And after today...yeah, I'm ready. I've haven't wanted to fuck anyone this much since before, and I don't think I could hold back even if I wanted to once you take this thing off." He tugged on the halter strap on her shoulder with his teeth. "Turns out fighting for a lady's honor really does interesting things to the libido, love. I guess this is why all the thick-necked lunkheads used to do it all the time. Of course, being a punching bag does other things to that libido, but hell, this is Arcanium, and it's much harder for the libido not to win in a fight—"

She forced her hand under the tight band of the briefs to wrap her hand around his cock, guiding it up to stroke it more easily, the firmness of her grip on one side and the leather on the other. She didn't bother with saliva or magic to slick the way. She wouldn't need to stroke him long enough for chafing to matter, because she sent him her fantasy of him fucking her, the shift and play of the muscles in his back and ass through each thrust, the way she felt when being taken, informed now by the innumerable times that the Horned God had entered her. She sent him her near-climax arousal, the urge to quicken, to pull him in harder, the sounds they made when they were close, when they came…

"Oh God, Sera." He shuddered, tensed under her fingers on his back, heated and came over her fingers in his briefs. "Yes, just like that. Slow and hard, love. Buried deep inside you, *fuck*… It's been so fucking long."

"I know exactly how long it's been." She stroked him through his orgasm, magic pulsing around her, turning the yellow court lights red as she dissuaded any wanderers from the area, made the two of them insignificant. She wanted Carlo's vulnerability all to herself. "I know what you'll do to me, and I know how it will feel. I want it. I want you, want to ride you until *you* scream."

"Fuck, yeah, sweetheart." He slumped against her, trusting her deceptive strength. "Power to the people."

She giggled then cleaned him and her hand before withdrawing, releasing the magic that discouraged people from noticing them. "I expect you to make me scream first."

"Yes, please."

Even if he had no skill, of which he had plenty, his sheer enthusiasm would have been more than enough for her.

"You feed off of me, love?" Carlo asked as they left the food court. He carried his harness over his shoulder.

"You're delicious."

"You bet your sweet ass I am. You're much kinder than a succubus with your feeding, though."

"I could be less kind, but I have no desire to be."

"That's hot."

She smoothed her hands up her costume, shifting the silk over her breasts without touching them directly. She wanted his mouth on them, wanted the silk off her skin, because it was coarse in comparison to her. Since that afternoon, she was so hypersensitive, desiring freedom.

She'd open the window in Carlo's RV—the fact that everyone could hear them wasn't what had bothered him about fucking outdoors.

Almost past the big top, the Horned God came around the tent and stood white and still, a lantern in the darkness. The performances had ended and most of the crowd, even the last lingering members of the audience, were almost to the gate, which meant that the Horned God had no need to thicken the fur over his cock. He made what he wanted plain without words, his magic curling and embracing hers, sinking within it and within her to entice and arouse her further.

Sera's knees buckled, but she managed to stay standing.

Carlo stopped with her, staring. Maybe he'd never been this close to the god when he was this hard, or maybe he just appreciated what he saw. But he backed away. "It's okay, Sera. You go ahead. We can do this another time, possibly under the big top bleachers like teenagers tomorrow if you tease me like you did today."

Even if he knew how to dominate, the man clearly didn't have an alpha bone in his body. As a woman of the monarchy, she'd been surrounded by masters and servants all her life, those who commanded and those who obeyed. Carlo was neither. It had opened her to a world of thought she hadn't been able to consider until he'd touched her skin, given her the gift of his contact, his memories, his desire, his imagination.

"Carlo…"

"Really, I'm not going to get in the way of such a magnificent beast. I don't even want to compete with that, because it's honestly impressive on a grand, mind-blowing scale. We have time, Sera. All the time we need. Juggling multiple partners is all about knowing what your partner needs more at any given time, and I… Oh. *Oh.*" He dropped to the ground, doubling over. "Oh God, that *is* big. Is he always that big in your head? It's like hitting a gong in there, except it's thought and feeling and… Holy fuck, he's really good at sharing an image, isn't he? So…fucking…good."

Sera glanced up at the Horned God, sensing his mirth in spite of the lack of a smile. On a hunch, she started undoing the laces on Carlo's briefs.

Carlo fumbled to help after they were half undone, pushed the leather down over his renewed, thickened erection, flushed and as hard as he could become. He swiftly peeled his briefs off entirely, uncaring that any guest looking back at the circus would get the full view of a backside far more impressive than one would expect from someone who didn't have the rest of his legs to help in strengthening his flanks.

Sera sidled up beside the Horned God and wrapped her arm around the small of his back, considering Carlo's reaction with slower, more heated lust, because as delightful as it was to be the cause, she finally understood why Carlo would be content with watching her taken by someone else. It fascinated her to be on the outside looking in, although the pheromones both men emanated included her in whatever was going on between them.

"I didn't know you could do that with everyone," she said.

"You would be astonished at what I can do."

If a single 'no' was the most Carlo had ever heard him say, the Horned God had just surpassed his previous record. Each word took effort, but he also managed a slight smile as he turned his head toward her.

"Shall we?" This time, he rang in her head, but the quality of sound was such that his voice couldn't only be in her own.

Carlo managed to straighten, although pre-cum dripped from his cock in a thin line to the ground, catching in the moonlight. "We? That's all right, really. I don't need to interrupt whatever you do with… Oh, sweet Jesus, I don't think I can survive another one of those, man. I really don't." Carlo grabbed the base of his cock, squeezed hard enough that it had to be uncomfortable rather than the pleasant side of pain. But then he stroked up the shaft, caught the pre-cum on the way back down. "Fuck. You really want me there? Why would you want me if you have her?"

"Springtime calls me to my Maiden, but Arcanium makes spring of all seasons. A season of fertility, yes, but a season of virility as well." He crooked his fingers to Carlo to join

him the way that Sera joined him, with the benefit of contact. *"Come with us. I have a bed."*

"Of moss and flowers, but it will itch less than the grass. Come with us, Carlo. I want to know what he showed you, and you have a vow to keep."

"I do, don't I?" Carlo came closer, tentative but still tightly aroused, his gaze flitting from the prominent erection arisen in the thatch of white fur above eye level for him, then the god's face, then Sera's, then the press of her hard nipples against the thin silk.

Sera pulled on the tie of the halter and let the top half fall.

"Yes," he hissed, almost a moan on its own. Then, more firmly, "Yes."

Sera parted her legs to let the silk fall.

She and Carlo walked with the Horned God as naked as he through the darkened courtyard and Oddity Row. Carlo vaulted up onto the platform in the Horned God's oddity tent, and Sera stepped up on her own this time.

"This is new. This is very new." Carlo stared at the sliver of forest, sliver of moon in the sky. "It's the clearing in your memories, isn't it? Re-created."

"Yes." The Horned God preceded them into the clearing to recline back on his natural bed, his hooves on either side in unabashed invitation. Nailed to the trees around him were the broken antlers that he hadn't gifted to her or Carlo, giant branches still bloodstained where they had pierced Salem. They overlapped the bed like a strange canopy. "Wine, Maiden."

Sera poured three glasses of the oblivion, but she didn't bring them to the bed.

"It will affect you differently," she said to Carlo. "It can render men mad, desperate for pleasure and pain and all manner of sensation. The fae use it against those who enter our rings uninvited to make them last longer before exhaustion sets in. You don't have to have it if you don't want it. You might taste enough from our lips."

Carlo drank in the sight of the Horned God reclined but not resting, his erection dark and straining and tight. "No. Not tonight. I don't think I need the help." Not even apprehension flagged his own erection, the second of the night.

Sera left the third glass on the cabinet in case Carlo changed his mind or the Horned God decided to deepen his oblivion.

"Just reminding you two crazy kids while I'm still coherent and somewhat responsible that we have work in the morning," Carlo said.

"Then you're going to need coffee." Sera drained her glass. Oblivion warmed her, tingled all over her scalp and her folds, inside her cunt. "We're going to coax more than three climaxes from you tonight, Carlo."

"Fucking hell, woman. You brought me here to kill me, didn't you? This is where I die." But he couldn't tear his gaze away as a line of oblivion dripped from the corner of her mouth. It hit her chest, stained a curve around her breast.

"Sweetly." Sera lowered herself between the Horned God's spread legs, resting back against the moss and rubbing her cheek against his coarse fur. As Carlo came closer, licking his lips, the Horned God lifted himself up to see them better.

Carlo caught the droplet of oblivion with his tongue before it passed her navel. At the thin sample, he gripped her arms bruisingly hard and moaned as he traveled up the wine to her mouth, delving into her to taste it on her tongue. She shared what was left inside her, tasted oblivion on him as well, tangier when it reacted to the flesh of a human man.

"That's wicked strong, Sera. What would I do if I had the whole glass?" He didn't let her answer, taking her mouth again and slotting himself between her legs, his cock spreading her folds as he rocked his hips against her. The shaft brushed against her clit, but it wasn't the right kind of touch, more maddening than satisfying.

She purred as she moved against his instinct-driven body. His mind wasn't quite obliterated, but just that little taste would be as good as a few shots of tequila and a good night's lust spell. He might even be able to keep up with them.

"The question is, what wouldn't you do?" she murmured before she pushed him away, hard enough for him to tumble onto his back.

"Maybe one day I'll take you up on that glass... when we know each other a little better," he added to the Horned God, in his wonderfully egalitarian way that had so bewildered Vinia.

"Your vow, sir." Sera ran her hands down the Horned God's legs as she parted hers. "Make me scream."

Carlo flipped over onto his belly then crawled forward between her legs with unnatural speed, eagerness in the wet cast of his lips, gleaming with the oblivion from her mouth.

When he reached her, he didn't dive in. He kissed her thighs, up one then up the other, smiling when she twitched, when she tried to close her thighs on either side of his head to draw him in. He curled his arms around them to hold them away, to control her as he kissed and licked closer where the influence of the wine and the musky scent of the men had settled warm, thick, soft and wet.

He blew cold air over her clit, laughing when she twitched again. She didn't know why that would heighten her arousal, but it did and she squirmed, biting her tongue against commanding him to do the one thing he wasn't doing, just put his damn tongue on her clit and make her come, in the name of all things wild and beautiful.

The Horned God tangled his fingers in her hair, massaging her scalp and holding her in place for Carlo to torment just short of where she wanted him. When he sliced his tongue through her folds, she planted her feet on the forest floor and arched into his mouth, but he pulled back, taunting, with only the tip of his tongue flicking over her.

"Goddammit!" Her desperation grated through her throat, not quite the scream he had promised.

He laughed. "Everything tastes different with the wine on my tongue. You still taste like you, but fuck, inside your cunt? I don't even have a word for it. Hold her steady, big guy. I'm going in."

With his arms locked around her legs, he brought his thumbs around to her mound, pulling the flesh around her clit taut, retracting the hood. That, in itself, stimulated, but he didn't lower his mouth to her clit. He brought his tongue back to her cunt and slithered it in, drinking her arousal while he rubbed and pulled against the flesh near her clit, keeping her hot, keeping her hard, keeping her wet for him to taste. She moaned, tried to writhe, but both the Horned God and Carlo held her down, not sparing their strength just because she was small, because they knew better.

Her arousal didn't fall off, didn't fade, didn't plateau, just kept getting higher and higher and higher without going over the edge, because he wasn't doing enough in the right place to bring her over. Finally, when tears streaked one side of her face because she wanted to come so bad, Carlo surfaced, gasping for breath. The whole bottom half of his face gleamed wet.

"God, that's good. You never hear me complain about eating anyone out, but that was special, love. That was sublime. Makes a man wonder, big guy, how would you taste under the influence?"

Sera grabbed him by the hair and pushed him down. "Stop talking and take to your task."

Carlo laughed. "You're not much for edging, are you, love?"

"I don't know what that means, but no. Stop talking."

He continued to laugh as he licked his lips then closed his mouth over her clit, with broad, wet, fire-hot licks over the flesh. His hums vibrated through, an extra layer of sensation that stole her own words as well.

This time he drank her reactions rather than her arousal, feeding on how close she came before he switched his pattern or rhythm to keep her from coming, sometimes a second before the climax would have peaked. She clenched her eye shut, spasmed, but the Horned God and Carlo continued to hold her down.

She saw through the Horned God's eyes, through his amusement and the texture of his own desire at the sight of Carlo's mouth buried between her thighs. He relished the sight of another man giving her pleasure, the sight of her in the throes of it, relished her magical mist passing through him and bringing his erection up tight against his abdomen with what they shared, what he saw.

She cried, shouted, moaned. Sounds came from her throat that had no word, no descriptor, except that they were feral and frustrated, practically pain.

Carlo curled two fingers into her cunt, slick from her juices and from his saliva. He searched and quickly found what made her arch again, *pushing* down against and around him. He doubled down on her clit as he rubbed over that spot inside her. Without that arm around her, he couldn't stop her from tightening her thighs on either side of his head, but if he'd been content to smother himself in her cunt, he seemed just as willing to smother himself in the sharp, harsh orgasm that assaulted her, throttled his fingers, moved like fire inside her, too hot, too hard, too strong. He came through on his promise, bringing her to a scream, deer fur in her mouth from trying to muffle it in the Horned God's leg.

As Carlo licked his way back up her still-twitching body, the Horned God conjured the third glass of oblivion and turned it over her open mouth. She drank from it and shuddered again, the seconds-old memory of her orgasm almost as strong as the orgasm itself as she drank more deeply.

Carlo caught what dripped again from her lips. He groaned, bringing himself back tight against her, his cock blunt against her folds. She shared with him what she could then shifted out from under him. He clutched desperately at her body to draw her back under, but she used her own strength now, coupled with her magic, to extricate herself and hold him back.

"Is that your magic I feel?" Carlo swallowed hard, struggling for composure that oblivion ensured would be tenuous at best. "Are you wrapped around my cock already, sweetheart? Are you inside me?"

"You said you wanted to taste him."

Sera didn't force Carlo forward, but she gently guided his head from her to the thick, taut cock just behind her, where the Horned God had shifted forward. His own moonbeam magic came out of his nostrils with each exhale, like breath in winter, to join hers around Carlo's cock, overlapping with hers inside him. It wasn't compulsive magic, merely suggestion—suggestion to which Carlo's own desires were already extremely amenable. But he hesitated, every muscle visibly tightening in a mixture of tenuously suppressed lust and fear.

"What are you afraid of?" Sera whispered in his ear, a repetition of what he had done to her.

"More men than women came to Locke's circus. I want it. God, I want it. I'm salivating. Maybe it's the wine, maybe it's me. I'm just—"

"Only do what you want to do, Carlo. I can take over if you can't. You can watch me take him in like you taught me, sink slowly over him while you sink into me, both of you inside me at the same time..."

Sera squeaked a little as he kissed her hard, using more teeth than she was used to from him. She closed her hand around his erection even as she wrapped her magic more tightly around it, keeping it hard and keeping his second climax at bay. He gathered more courage from her mouth, whatever he hadn't managed to plunder the first time, then turned back to the bed, where the Horned God waited far more patiently than he should have been able to do with a cock smearing pre-cum over his abdomen and fur and dripping down the length of him.

"Show me what you want again," Carlo said, almost shy as he looked up into the mad god's eyes. "Remind me."

He winced, doubled over again, and this time he grabbed his own cock to keep from coming, pulling down on his balls and squeezing the base of the shaft so hard it left brief white marks when he released himself again.

Sera climbed into the bed next to the Horned God, sucking lightly on her fingertips as Carlo struggled to control himself. She bit the pad when Carlo straightened, fresh pre-cum of his own dripping down his cock again. He determinedly removed his hands from his erection, grasped the moss of the bed, less determinedly slid his fingers up into the thick elk fur of the god's legs.

The Horned God cupped the back of Carlo's head, reassured him with the tenderness of his touch as he drew Carlo not to his cock but to his mouth.

Bell had kissed the corner of the Horned God's lips, which had been suggestive enough at the time, because Bell didn't seem particularly European in his mannerisms. But this was without ambiguity. The Horned God had no checks on his lust beyond the ones that he gave himself, and in his own tent, there was no reason to use them. He was thorough, patient but undeniably forceful. In spite of that force, Sera sensed care, his own kinder calculation—calibrating the tension in Carlo's neck, measuring the sounds he made, the eagerness with which he kissed back, searching for any sign that what the Horned God did without words was unwanted.

But Carlo responded immediately, stroking over the fur, digging his fingers into the thick, strong thighs with such enthusiasm that Sera wondered if he'd ever actually had sex with any of the demons or monsters of Arcanium before. He'd never spoken of one of them as a lover, even in the pre-Locke past. Of all the people he had admitted to fucking, she thought an Arcanium demon would have been a badge of honor, but none of the demons seemed to show him particular favor, even those who worked with him in an acrobatic capacity. If so, she valued his bravery and flexibility even more as he used his hands to study a body different from one he would have known before.

Carlo withdrew first. The Horned God chased him with a groan but didn't protest as Carlo lowered his mouth over the head of the god's cock instead. Unlike his play with Sera, Carlo bobbed over the erection without preamble. The Horned God groaned again, an unrestrained, animal sound with which Sera was now intimately familiar. He let his head fall back, his antlers heavy and magnificent but not straining his strength.

Carlo sucked hard with each upstroke, his hand supplementing the sensation over the shaft whenever he brought his mouth to the head. No play, all business, and business was good, because the Horned God's hips jerked, his abdomen twitching.

Semen filled Carlo's mouth, but he swallowed as hard and fast as he'd sucked. On the downstroke, Sera caught a gleam of seed dripping down the Horned God's cock, but Carlo bobbed down to take it all in. He wouldn't know what it was he consumed, wouldn't know why his hair would seem thicker in the morning, his skin healthier and glowing. He might not even notice, any more than he noticed the iridescence of the god's magic enfolding him, although the Horned God held himself away through the climax, until he could come no more.

Then the god leaned back in over Carlo, running his hands over the curved expanse of back, the beautiful play of muscle and spine, the pearls of scars. Carlo eased from the Horned God's cock, his only clue to stop that there was no more fluid to lick away. The god stayed just as hard.

"So that's the way it is, then." Carlo licked the blue vein up the underside to the edge of the foreskin. "You're one of *those* people around here, huh?"

Carlo wouldn't see the smile—always slight, because it took so much muscle work for the Horned God to do it at all—but he let himself be led back up into a kiss, let himself be lifted into the bed. The Horned God turned onto his side, lingering for a while on the taste of a kiss flavored with his own pleasure. Then he raised himself up on his hands and knees in the bed and beckoned Sera underneath, withdrew completely as Sera ducked under his arm.

Carlo yanked her down against him. She lifted her wings up and closed so that he could touch her everywhere he could reach, his need in no way diminished from the Horned God's distraction.

She spread her wings again and pulled him over her. "Are you sure?"

"Sweetheart, I'm breaking barriers all over tonight. I'm pretty sure I'm not going to last very long, so I'm depending on you to keep me honest for you."

"Is that what they call it these days?"

"How else can we swear that we're honest men?"

She smiled more broadly than the Horned God could and spread her legs wider as he took himself in hand to position his cock against her cunt.

"Honestly, it's a good thing this isn't your first time, because I don't know how good I can make this for you. I'm usually all about pleasing my partner, love, but..." He choked on his words as he thrust forward and into her, where she was still ridiculously wet from the first orgasm he'd given her.

She cried out, pulling him in by his ass until he couldn't go any deeper.

"If I wanted you to go slow and sweet, I would have made you come again before this," she whispered, urging him in again, again, harder, harder.

He obliged every time, didn't need her permission anymore to do what his body already needed.

As he took her, between them rocked every dirty thing she wanted him to do to her—none of the romantic things that he had done and that she loved, but the kinds of things she could never say out loud, because even all her fae memories couldn't suppress the blush.

"I'll let you pick any one of those you like tonight if you fuck me. Just fuck me. Come on." Her growl mingled with his helpless groan, and although he had been so careful with her from the beginning, the way she had been careful with him in her own way, neither of them showed any care now. They didn't have to ask or check if the other was enjoying it, because they'd never been inclined to hold back how good something felt. Here in the Horned God's forest, they discovered how much more they were willing to share when no one but the god himself could hear them.

There was still mental hesitation—comparison to what had been done to him, as though entering her was violence in and of itself. He remembered what would happen the few times a demon would let him inside them.

But once sheathed inside her, his body functioned on a different level, taking what it needed, what it desired so powerfully that it overrode memory. The hesitation slowed his ascent to his climax, but it didn't stall him completely. The more he took her and the more she wanted him to, her cries clearly ones of pleasure rather than any trace of pain, the more easily he was able to let go of the cords that had held him down, held him back, bound him like chains still left in his scars. The memories juddered out of focus and into the black. He lost himself inside her, buried his face in her neck and shouted as he came.

She shuddered through her own orgasm—not from anything he'd done but from the seed that entered her, from the wide-open mind so close to hers. She drank and drank her fill of him from either end. It wasn't cruel or dangerous, because he couldn't feel it, and he had such deep reservoirs from which to drain. Arcanium gave them such capacity for pleasure, as long as neither she nor the Horned God tried to take too much. She didn't think that would be easy—the bottom was still so very deep and out of her reach, and she could always give him something in return.

Sera held on to the core of his desire—the place that made him feel her inside of him where nothing should have reached—and kept him as hard as the Horned God, kept him awake and alert and alive, as though he hadn't come at all.

"Holy fuck on a Ferris wheel." Carlo remained in her cunt, flexing his hips to keep stroking himself with the wet, clasping walls within. He lifted himself up to look at her while he fucked her, at her face, down where they met, the way her breasts quivered with each thrust. "It's like being in your mouth. You're almost cool in comparison to what I'm used to, but instead of cold-showering me, I don't want to leave. I can still jerk off in a cold swimming pool in July, love, and that's what you are. You make me feel so hot. It's like I'm burning."

"Everyone burns to me." Sera brought her legs closer together, her thighs against Carlo's hips, as the Horned God climbed back onto the bed over them, a massive shadow in comparison.

He traced the edge of the damage on her face down to her mouth, where he slid two fingers inside, pressing against her tongue then twisting them around to curl against her palate. She sucked his fingers like a cock, slathered them with her hunger until they dripped when he drew them out again. She caught the droplets with her tongue, laughed as Carlo stopped pumping into her to watch better.

Then Carlo stiffened, because the Horned God slid his spit-slicked hand down Carlo's spine to his ass.

"No. I'm not ready for that. That's… I'm sorry. That's still something I can't…"

The Horned God slid his hand back up and kissed along Carlo's shoulder. "I won't," he managed to say. *"But I can make you feel it. No pain. Nothing to stretch, nothing to burn. Nothing inside. But as though I were. Safe."* He brought his wet fingers to Carlo's mouth instead, leaving marks where he kissed up Carlo's shoulder and neck.

In spite of the abrupt return of Carlo's fear—and with it, the memories Sera tried not to see, tried not to feel with him, tried to replace with the fantasies they shared to keep him hard, keep him happy—he turned his head to take in the Horned God's fingers. Moving within her meant moving against the Horned God, who kept his hips away but pressed his chest to Carlo's back as he fucked Carlo's mouth again.

The god waited until Carlo's tension had somewhat dissipated. Then he whispered, as much as a god like him could whisper in their heads, *"Do you want to feel it? Do you want to feel me, safe?"*

The image of the Horned God fucking Carlo alone in the forest on this very bed was so strong that Sera initially thought it had come from the god, but it shifted without enough focus or power to Sera in a bed, to Okeyo in front of everyone in the big top tent, to Lazarus and Magda, to the Horned God again—things Carlo wanted but hadn't had or couldn't have the way he imagined them.

Sera caught the silver bar at Carlo's nipple with her tongue then in her mouth, tugging at it and worrying the piercing until Carlo thrust harder into her.

He pulled his mouth off of the Horned God's fingers and nodded, holding Sera's mouth to his chest. "Yes. Yes, I can try that tonight."

The Horned God brought his hips up against Carlo's, aligning their bodies. He didn't enter, just rested his cock against the small of Carlo's back, the base slotted between his cheeks. *"I will take you both."*

When he thrust forward, Carlo nearly collapsed. All three of them moaned, discordant bliss caught in the close space between them. He did it again, just sliding his cock over Carlo's skin. Two distinct cocks moved inside her. Although they occupied the same space, they struck different places, stimulated different nerves. Only one of them felt substantial, spatial, physical. The other took her as though it wasn't there at all, only the effects.

"It doesn't feel... I don't feel... But God, I do feel..." Once again, Carlo had lost his words.

The Horned God kissed his neck again, grabbing hold with his teeth. He met Sera's eyes and thrust his hips again and again, building a rhythm, building shared sensation, building the magic within himself and in her, building what was inside Carlo that could feed their magic and into which they could pour their own.

Sera opened her hands for the Horned God to take. Their fingers intertwined as he pressed her back against the moss. His antlers grew from his head, from his back, curving like a cage on every side, but the shadows of the branches were warm rather than cold as they extended over the bed. He did not cage them so much as promise that he would keep everything within the lovely, arching points safe from anything that would try to cross them, as he had walled the fae from Carlo when he'd fallen.

The antlers stabbed into tree trunks, into forest floor, into the soft bed, grounding them where they were until only his body moved, his head steady, his arms strong. They were skin to skin, body to body, their pleasure ebbing and flowing at the same pace, their magic overlapping each other and Carlo between them. Carlo couldn't speak, couldn't rub two pieces of flint together for the spark of a word, but he kissed Sera and the Horned God in turns, because kissing one was like kissing the other. They made their three bodies one.

When they came, the antlers holding them in place creaked like branches in a haunted forest. Sera kissed Carlo's cries, gave him plenty of her own as the Horned God's feral grunts filled their ears. He spent into the valley of Carlo's back, smearing his belly as he continued to thrust, kept going until Carlo shook his head, his face twisted as though in pain, although Sera sensed none of the past in his overstimulation.

The Horned God slowed, tendered, his kisses over the sometimes-bloody marks on Carlo's shoulders soft and lingering rather than rough. Carlo settled, stilled, his cock finally softening. They'd hardly finished with him tonight, but the day had been long, and he would require rest.

Sera stroked his sandpaper cheeks, his messy hair, the tears and her arousal and saliva dry on his skin. He couldn't smile, but he fell to the side next to her in the bed with a resounding sigh, all the tension of now and then releasing.

The Horned God stayed above them, nothing about him human to her, in spite of the top half of his body. The antlers continued to creak as he loomed over his lovers, the harvesters of his springtime—a cup that always flowed over, vines that always produced fruit, full wheat without chaff, an endless night with a bright moon. He drew her up to drink the wine of her magic, and she tasted the moonlight on his lips.

The Horned God broke away from his own antlers, this time with deliberate care, each broken end smoothing and sharpening over as he lowered himself over her.

"Let them try to take you. Let him try to make you less than what you are. I will protect you…both of you."

Sera grasped for Carlo's hand as the Horned God entered her and they began again.

Want to see more from this author? Here's a taster for you to enjoy!

Arcanium: Illusion

Aurelia T. Evans

Excerpt

Bell closed his eyes in the golden lantern light backstage.

When Bell let go, spread himself wide over the web of Arcanium, he was its omnipresent god and omnipotent voyeur, from the thoughts of his cast backstage with him to the audience anticipating the performances, the guests putting in their last efforts in the midway and the Skeletons settling in for their evening meal. He could see what they'd done yesterday and what they would do tomorrow. Even when he didn't try, he had a finger on every pulse within the borders of Arcanium.

There had been nothing since Locke that had come close to taking Arcanium again. The fae hadn't even constituted a threat. They would have left with far more chagrin if they had known how distant they had been from taking Arcanium by force. And Locke was now a red diamond on Neve's finger, waiting for the day she was ready to kill him slowly.

Bell's opiate of choice had always been pleasure, but his taste for violence went in and out with the seasons. He hadn't the heart anymore for the punishment of man. He had enough of that to contend with in his cast's memories and nightmares—but he'd rediscovered the old joy in punishing the immortals who had exploited his Arcanium, even if he had to experience the act of punishment secondhand.

Man swallowed against the apple every second they breathed, and Bell burned with the same sadistic sickness as his fireborn brethren. He kept the Ringmaster in Arcanium as much to remind himself of the line he couldn't cross as to do the things he shouldn't.

No one had ever told him what he could and couldn't do. He was neither angel nor demon nor creation from dust. He had determined his own lines, chiseled his own moral code into his skin before Hammurabi had commissioned his scribes. He was free will incarnate, an agent of chaos to cast awry best-laid plans. He was his own, and so he made his world in his own image, populated it with free wills of all shapes and sizes to shape to his liking—which was often to theirs, because it pleased him to manipulate but not necessarily to control. Manipulation meant nothing without will. If he'd wanted slaves, he would have filled the circus with more convincing golems—like a flea circus of mechanical illusion but with zombies.

But where would be the fun in that?

Bell opened his eyes again, returning himself to the moment, although a blink could send him back out into the circus, forward or backward. All Arcanium and beyond was as accessible to him as the palace of his memories, but although grasping the world in his hands became easy when he made himself more of the god he was, he didn't see much fun in that either. He made things *easier* for his cast and for himself, imparting skills that they hadn't or couldn't have learned before, gifting talent, but even the demons preferred to work for their performances. Without effort, there could be no achievement, and without achievement, no satisfaction. Pleasure, as with pain, had to be earned.

Selena wrapped her arms around his shoulders from behind, her sharp smile against his cheek. She kissed him lightly. "Ready, darling?"

As a demon, Selena could twist her body into shapes that Valorie couldn't have hoped to create. In Valorie's case, Bell had wanted a contortionist human enough to be both awe-inspiring and credible. When Selena had offered her services as a demon, he no longer had to keep the contortions credible. He didn't need her to inspire awe. She preferred to inspire fear.

With her black eyes, dead blue skin and blood-stained hair, she was beautiful, but she was still a demon and plied most of her contortionist trade in the Haunted Funhouse rather than in the big top. For the big top performances, she'd taken over Maya's role as his magician's assistant and damsel in distress—at least, Arcanium's version of a damsel in distress, which rarely followed a traditional plot.

Selena retrieved one of the steel knives, gleaming silver as new for every performance, from the bandolier around his torso and brought it to his throat. He lifted his chin, threaded his fingers through her locked hair, breathed in her craving for impure blood. When she shifted her kiss to his mouth, he met that craving with his tongue, hissing as her sharp teeth caught him and she slid the blade over his chin. Then she kissed down to the trickle of blood and drank from the wound until he healed it under her mouth.

She fed from his corruption instead of feeding from his people or too many of his guests, and in return, she made him numb. She could render men into oblivion, but the best she could do for Bell was take both the pleasure and the pain away for a time.

Most of the human cast believed he was sleeping with Selena. Kitty knew better. Neve and Elizabeth had guessed otherwise. And, to his annoyance, Vivian suspected, although because she didn't know, she hadn't shared that information with Dom or Delilah. The demons and the faerie could tell just by looking at him, but they wouldn't share that information one way or the other. A jinni's business, like that of a demon's, was his own.

Selena kept his secret, liked keeping secrets in general, because secrets so easily corrupted, improving the flavor of that which she fed upon. It was only apt that she'd chosen an actual lover among his humans who was as ingenuous as they came. The fact that she regularly drained Victor of corruption that he had done nothing to earn satisfied Bell.

Selena licked the smear of blood from the edge of the blade before returning it to the bandolier. Then she jumped onto his back, wrapping her legs and arms around him. She was taller than him by half a head without heels, over a head with the ones she wore for the performance, but although taking a human form limited him in many ways, it didn't impede his strength. He caught her legs and tucked her against him as he carried her to the curtains. Chelsine would finish her fire dance any minute, which would cue the lights for Sera's aerial act. After Sera, Bell and Selena would enter. Though Selena should have been getting into place, Sasha and Mikhail had worked their magic, as they always did, and both Bell and Selena were reluctant to part.

Bell had never been so frustrated for so long.

Selena would find her own satisfaction after the performance, as most of his cast did. Some didn't even wait until they were out from backstage.

To be surrounded by the lust and love of his people, to feel it against his skin, against his teeth, to drink it like milk and honey, hum with the vibrations of their moans and screams, watch them dance around each other, caress, kiss, their pupils dilated and their cheeks flushed, the touch of their tongue to their lips… It was the torture of his own dungeon, to be surrounded by everything he wanted but not to partake himself, even when he was tempted.

Instead, he rested his head back against Selena's chest as her hair draped on either side of his face.

Selena slid from his back and kissed his shoulder. "Hard out there for a demon with a soul. You, of all people, should know better than to resist. God, Bell, there are so many willing victims. Why do you do this to yourself?"

He didn't have a word she would understand. Demons punished with ease, but they had little concept of self-punishment. The closest any of them came was limited self-denial.

"I'll see you in the ring." Bell would seem casual to anyone without an extra sense or two to detect the deception.

"Sure, handsome." Selena broke away, scurrying up the ladder to the heavens, where the trapeze swings, spotlights and aerial silks lived.

Neve was his crown jewel—the Spider, a black diamond he would keep in a vault if he could, but Kitty, who reclined on the chaise longue, was the life's blood, the very beating heart of his circus. Locke had understood that she was valuable but hadn't understood how much, or else he would never have allowed the Ringmaster to take her for himself.

Without an ounce of magic in her blood, Kitty sensed his attention, opened her eyes and met Bell's gaze across backstage. Though she couldn't see it, the Ringmaster's darkness seeped from under the curtains as he introduced Sera, but when it reached Kitty, it dissipated. She was a pink, floral oasis in a sea of smoke.

Bell sent her what love he could spare from a distance. She received it like a blanket warmed in sunlight, because she was his Kitty Cat and he could rest his head on her shoulder and hold her until the sun rose and set again. Even if she blamed him like the rest, she'd lost none of her love for him. If a human being could become family to jinn, they had bound themselves with something thicker than blood.

She was the only other one who truly loved the circus. The others, demon and human, dwelled within it, sheltered in its shade for a time, but they could all find shelter elsewhere. He had a number of voluntaries but none with so much to lose if they left. That she would lose it broke his heart for her. He cradled her heart as much as he could without making his hands a cage.

Sera's sweeping cinematic score faded. Bell closed his eyes again, gathering himself into the persona who people recognized and believed was him. Since Locke, never had he so wished to be the man people assumed he was. Not a good man, not harmless, but one who could be measured and fitted, warm and enticing as melting butter and honey, burnt cinnamon incense in a small world of cedar, silk and sawdust—the mysterious stranger who could manipulate emotions like clay on a wheel to make people feel flattered, comfortable, content, to lower their guard and put themselves in his hands.

"Here in Arcanium, we hope that you have survived your foray into the fantastic, into the dream and the nightmare, indistinguishable—deadly, dangerous, a glimpse into beautiful darkness for a short time. What has been real, what fantasy? We offer no answers." The Ringmaster's deep, resonant voice richened each word in his script, imparted emotional significance he was incapable of meaning. In some ways, the Ringmaster himself was the greatest illusion of Arcanium, but it was the only one that the audience never questioned.

"In this dream within a dream, let this be the finale of seem. During the day, he is a teller of fortunes, both good and bad, but with the setting of the sun, he weaves reality from the stuff of imagination. What is real and what is illusion? Let us blur the lines further."

The light on the other side of the red velvet curtains dimmed to near darkness. Bell let in the barest of lantern light as he entered, nothing but a shadow in the silence. As the curtains closed again, the darkness was absolute, but like the Ringmaster, Bell didn't need the light. He knew the big top like he knew his own mind, because it was his creation.

The lights flashed up in a splash of jewel colors, with the spotlight on him in the center of the ring, just as the music switched on, not the symphonic metal or sweeping cinematic pop of the other performances, but a bleacher-vibrating blast of Fall Out Boys' *My Songs Know What You Did in the Dark*. Because Bell, like most immortals, had an unhealthy appetite for irony. The only song that made an audience reel faster was when he used Britney Spears' *Circus* with unrepentant aplomb.

Selena descended from the heavens, untethered to rope or rigging. As with Sera, the audience strained to see whatever transparent cord held her hovering in the air. They could strain until their eyes popped out. Creating the illusion that there was illusion at all was one of his greatest joys that had nothing to do with lust, and he had precious little joy these days. Within the big top and fortune teller tent, the best he could hope for was glimmers, so he took what he could get.

Selena could do her portion of the illusionist danger act under her own power, but there was no need for her to exert herself when making magic look like tricks was effortless to him. What magicians did to make their illusions seem like magic took far more work than he needed to make magic look like illusion.

They also used his magic instead of hers to establish their dynamic from the beginning. Sometimes Selena even tried—and failed—to wrest control from him. It helped her maintain character and convinced the audience of his dominance over the scene, over magic and illusion, over his magician's assistant, over the audience itself.

There was benefit to submission for beings such as him. The demons in his care actually seemed to thrive, living under the consummate control of someone like him, someone who kept them leashed and collared and relieved them of the usual expectations. They liked having restrictions to push and pull against.

Selena could take or leave D/s games the rest of the time, but in a circus like Arcanium—a circus of leather, latex and enough innuendo to power a mid-size city—she was more than willing to play the part of the unwilling prisoner, with her left leg straight in the air by her ear, her arm wrapped around her thigh and bound to the collar around her neck to trap her leg there and keep her from being able to run.

Like Valorie, she was thin, her narrower curves setting off her flexible limbs and the purple latex she wore to unique advantage. She didn't reach the level of his Skellies—no one healthy and living could—but she made him seem strapping in comparison.

He conjured her down to the center of the ring with him. She struggled in vain against the leather bonds holding her, wriggling her beautiful body against his until she reached the ground. His chest to her back, he smoothed his hand up the length of her thigh to the delicate ankle then hooked his arm around her waist to bring her closer against him. He had much more license for lascivious intent during the big top performances, where children under thirteen were not permitted—at well-documented risk of life and limb, not that anyone believed the warnings.

He went through the motions of lust within their dance, Latin style mingled with his magic and demonstrations of Selena's flexibility and ferocity through her resistance, struggling against but never managing to shake either the leather bindings or the effect of his touch on her. The incubus and succubus had already planted seeds in the audience's heads. It didn't take much for Bell and Selena together to make them grow.

Until his magic flung Selena from the center of the ring to the wooden target that had appeared in front of the curtains. She slammed face-forward against the wood with real force that no sound effect could replicate.

"Mmm, harder, darling." She writhed against the target, grasped the edge of the pallet with her free

hand, but she couldn't budge from where Bell had put her.

He drew two knives from the bandolier that crossed his otherwise-bare chest. He paused only for the audience to blink against the shine on the silver before flinging both toward the decidedly squirmy demon twenty feet in front of him.

They hit right on either side of her waist. The audience winced for her. She only became more agitated.

Bell flourished his hand like a flower. Another leather shackle appeared in his palm, with no sleeve from which he could have retrieved it, not even the usual leather bag on his belt.

He pitched the shackle straight at her. The right leg and arm that had been free jerked to the side, so that her legs were arranged at twelve and three on the clock. The wrist that wasn't bound to the collar was now shackled to her leg just short of her knee. Selena could slip from each of these bindings if she chose—with work, given that leather and latex didn't lend themselves to slipping anywhere, especially on each other—but the audience wouldn't know quite how flexible or determined she could be.

And Selena wasn't actually trying to get free so much as challenge him by attempting to shake his magic off—like a goat trying to shake off a reticulated python. No mean feat, as his snake charmer could attest. Impossible, really.

This time without hesitation, Bell flung two more knives. They hit outside each of her elbows.

He flipped her around on the target to face him and the audience, proving that she wasn't bound to anything but herself. The chorus of *oohs* and *aahs* from the crowd barely made it through the music.

Rather than one of the knives in his bandolier, he went for the etched Bowie knife in the sheath on his belt and held it up for the audience to admire. Selena's eyes widened without guile—not the easiest thing for a demon to manage, but Selena had been passing for human for longer than her lover of choice had been alive, and before that, she'd possessed enough humans to learn how to pull it off.

The song determined the pace, and everyone loved a fast-paced danger show. He threw the Bowie knife directly at Selena's pretty face, square between her black eyes.

The tip of the blade dented the skin, but it drew no blood.

Bell called the five knives out of the wooden target, one by one, until they hovered in front of Selena's body. He quickly but casually removed the rest from their bandolier sheath and tossed them in front of him to hover in a staggered formation.

With a push to the air, the knives flew once again at Selena—face, neck, heart, gut, all potentially fatal blows alone, undeniably so together.

Selena fell back through the wooden target as though it weren't there, although it caught each of the blades with a series of *thunks*. She sank into the ground with a burst of sawdust and a high-pitched cry.

The music abruptly stopped.

In the midst of such a quick-beat act, Bell took his time turning around, his bare feet quieter than the brush of his cotton pants in the sawdust.

Hold the pause. The audience looked around wildly then back to him, because he was pleasant to look at and he held attention without having to hold on to souls to do it.

Then he pointed into the bleachers. Music burst through the big top once more as the spotlight found Selena in the middle of the audience, twisted into full demon-possessed, spider-like contortion, her mouth a dark, crooked cavern as black behind the snaggle teeth as her eyes.

Her deafening shriek blended with the music and the startled screams and laughter of the audience as she scurried down the bleachers, still in her contorted state—nimbler than anyone had any right to be with their limbs in all the wrong places and angles, going down headfirst and backward. She leaped from the bottom bleacher over the ring partition, unraveling herself and stretching out her limbs to strike him with her claws like a lion.

The magical web of his circus trembled.

Bell almost didn't catch Selena. If he hadn't, she would have landed on all fours like a cat, but she would have reamed him after the performance. But he saw her hitting the ground and blinked himself back to the present, back to the ring and snatched her from the air in a *Dirty Dancing* lift. She launched from his shoulders in a double flip to land on her heels—not quite stilettos but still not the best shoes for uneven earth. Little could make Selena fall when she didn't want to.

The web still shivered, the movement of someone with uncertain motives, certainly not the usual thought patterns of those who entered Arcanium—to enjoy a circus, to leer at the sun-glistening bodies of the more revealing of his cast, to terrify themselves in the unprepossessing funhouse. And from his cast, their efforts to entertain themselves and others, to serve the guests, to keep them politely distant or unprofessionally close. To make it through another day.

This wasn't that.

This was *nothing*.

And nothing was not good. It was a void, a gap in his sight as prominent as a dark cloud in his eye, like watching someone walk across the edge of a forest at night. The average person would never see anything, but demon and jinn made no distinction between a new-moon night and a high-noon day, and Bell was attuned to anomaly.

While he and Selena sparred in a dance fight that showed off the full extent of her gymnastic contortion and his speed, style and timing to the musical transition of Beyond the Black's *Hysteria,* Bell followed the invisible void moving through his circus.

The only reason he didn't stop or send one or more of his demons or monsters to meet the shadow was that it didn't seem malicious. It was at peace, calm, serene, its movement measured rather than furtive.

Locke had been more effective at concealing himself when he'd entered. Bell had only ever been able to feel the trail that his presence had left behind, never where he had been at any given moment. He'd cloaked himself in innocuous motives, predictable thoughts. Only the Spider's and Neve's memories had made his motivations better known, because he'd hidden himself less from them.

This was something that only cloaked itself from being recognized. Bell sensed curiosity, amusement, intrigue and trepidation like music from a staticky radio station. Multiple voices. A crowd where there should not have been one, because most of the guests still in Arcanium after eight came to the big top performances.

Bell conjured playing cards from his palms in a bird-flock rush. The ruby-backed cards fluttered around

Selena, herding her to the sawing table and transparent coffin, where the playing cards forced her in.

He called the decks back to his hands for a number of shuffling tricks that impressed audiences as much as any magic he offered, which was why he appreciated real skills within his circus more than the non-illusions that he peddled. He loved card tricks, juggling, tumbling and knife-throwing, and he had little patience for the usual mentalist game—not when the truth was more interesting to him than the trick.

The shadow came closer, toward the big top, an inverted storm eye.

A shrieking power saw descended from the heavens toward the coffin, set for a classic woman-sawn-in-half stunt. His version was far bloodier and pushed the limits of the illusion of error, but it was no less than what fans expected from Arcanium.

From there, he let the saw do its trick, which wasn't a trick at all, because Selena couldn't die from being cut in half. Buckets of blood splattered the sides of the transparent glass. Selena's guts quivered in place when the two parts of the coffin pulled apart.

Bell rolled the halves of the coffin around the ring with his magic. People would rave about how secretly high-tech Arcanium must be or praise the quality of their prosthetics team, when all a good demonic circus needed was a jinni with an occasionally gory sense of humor.

The saw would do as well as the knives and playing cards if what approached was worse than it seemed. For now, his curiosity met the shadow's own, although he was wary enough from the events of the last two years that, beneath his calm, controlled exterior, the core of his power was rigid and cold as steel.

Selena's body came together in the blood-strewn glass coffin on the other side of the ring, her blood replenished, the latex reconstituted. Selena, whole and unstained by the blood she'd lost, burst through the lid of the coffin to the cheers of the crowd, especially when she flipped from the coffin with a graceful scissoring of her legs and, popping joints the whole way, approached the cruel magician who had trapped her.

The shadow entered the big top.

Bell was capable of fear. He kept it within reach these days, like a bottle of bourbon in a nightstand. With fear came rare anticipation—not from within the shadow but within himself. Suspense only worked if one didn't know the outcome, and most outcomes weren't so necessary to him that they hid themselves from his sight. Of course, there were consequences to keeping himself ignorant, too—like Vivian trying to kill everybody. He hadn't hidden the future from himself since.

This outcome was genuinely hidden, which meant only that the outcome was significant, not that it was bad. And because the impression he received from the shadow wasn't angry or baleful, he strongly suspected that this was *not* another Locke or even a small faerie army come to take Arcanium away.

Hence, anticipation—anxiety and thrill all mixed into one heady emotion, headier because of how infrequently he contended with the effects.

"Your heart's not really in this tonight," Selena spoke in his head. *"What's up, doc? Do I need to show some skin, pull out a heart, bulge a few eyeballs to get some attention around here?"*

Bell didn't answer. He committed to the dance fighting that they'd resumed, this time with Selena performing more and more impossible acts until he'd tangled her in her own limbs and conjured steel chains from the heavens to hold her hostage.

He could never have done that with the older cast. Even some of the demons were cagey about being chained. Many of them could still stand the leather, because they had fonder memories of Sasha's artistry, but although demons could recover from torture, being chained was another issue altogether.

Bell held out his hand in front of Selena's chomping mouth and flexed his fingers outward.

The shackles pulled away in every direction, but there were no blood and guts, no need for repair or holding back pain. Selena tightened into herself like a knot on a string, deep into her torso, then kept tightening until she disappeared, all in a matter of seconds.

Selena would reappear backstage to take her leave from the big top tent, which left Bell alone in the ring.

He spun around with a master flourish and bowed to the usual thunderous applause. He liked an audience, but applause had never been his favored response—too predictable, too socially required, too strange an action for people to have agreed upon as a signal of appreciation. He took in the wonder lighting up their minds with color and sound instead, bowed until the applause subsided.

Except it didn't.

A single slow clap, loud and steady, pierced through the parting shadow.

TOTALLY
BOUND
Home of Erotic Romance

About the Author

Aurelia T. Evans is an up-and-coming erotica author with a penchant for horror and the supernatural.

She's the twisted mind behind the werewolf/shifter Sanctuary trilogy, demonic circus series Arcanium, and vampire serial Bloodbound. She's also had short stories featured in various erotic anthologies.

Aurelia presently lives in Dallas, Texas (although she doesn't ride horses or wear hats). She loves cats and enjoys baking as much as she dislikes cooking. She's a walker, not a runner, and she writes outside as often as possible.

Aurelia loves to hear from readers. You can find her contact information, website details and author profile page at https://www.totallybound.com

www.ingramcontent.com/pod-product-compliance
Lightning Source LLC
Chambersburg PA
CBHW020219260626
47156CB00002B/451
9781839439520